Dear Bartleby

Dear Bartleby

A Queer Fantasy Romance

By

Sarah Wallace

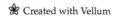 Created with Vellum

For those still learning to find peace in the quiet,
this book is for you.

CONTENTS

CONTENT WARNING

M<small>Y</small> <small>BOOKS WILL ALWAYS BE</small> about the power of kindness and hope and will always have a HEA, but please note that this book includes the following:

• References to past bullying, particularly in the form of verbal and sexual abuse
• References to a side character having been a sex trafficking victim
• On page verbal sexual assault

PROPERTY OF:

Sebastian Hartford

25 December 1816

I DARESAY Father thought it a great joke, giving me a journal for Christmas. As if I should want such a thing.

He said, "I think a little introspection is what's wanted for you, Sebastian."

I suppose I ought not to be surprised by it, receiving a gift at Christmas that is meant to improve me. Seems inevitable really.

John said I ought to enjoy writing in a journal as I always like hearing myself talk. The beast. Besides, he has it wrong. I don't enjoy hearing myself talk; I enjoy hearing myself talk to other people. It is an entirely different thing! Writing in a journal is highly unsatisfying.

Couldn't stand John having the last word, so I cast a spell on all his kerchiefs so they left streaks of green whenever he wiped his skin. Hilarious!

Thought it might be good to jot all this down so I remember what this journal is later. Also, must remember to pack it when I leave. Otherwise Father might find it and get angry with me. Not that it takes much these days.

28 February 1817

NOTE:

Essay on Henry VIII due 3 Mar.

27 March 1817

NOTE:

window 20 paces from fountain. Illusion spell poss.? Must put focus out of view of dean office.

29 April 1817

NOTE:

chestnut mare too big to fit through dorm. door. Try grey mare?

1 May 1817

NOTE:

Grey mare weakness for oats, not carrots. Ha. Parks can stop joking I'll be sufficient bait.

6 May 1817

HAVE BEEN SENT DOWN.

The dean told Father about the horse in the dormitory hallway. Odious man. Not particularly enjoyable to return home "in disgrace" as John put it. Father was seething. Read me a fine scold. Quite frightening, really. I will keep forgetting just how terrifying a person he is. That is one nice thing about being at school—I am spared his disapproving looks.

It was the usual rubbish about what a disappointment I am. How I never try to improve. He even brought up this journal.

"Have you been attempting some amount of introspection as I asked?" he said.

"Well," I said. "It is hardly the done thing, you know. Writing in a journal. Least of all at school. What if one of my friends found it? I'd never live it down. I am using it, though," I added hastily. "It's come in handy for keeping notes and things."

Father frowned at this and was quiet for a long time. "I suppose quiet reflection is a skill one must develop," he said at last. "I should like for you to start learning, Sebastian."

"Learning what?" I ventured.

"Learning who you are and what sort of a person you have become," he said. "You can start by spending time alone. From here on out, I would like you to devote some time each day to contemplation. Use the journal to track your progress, if you please. There will be no one around that you should fear finding it."

I did not point out that John would most certainly not quibble about reading my journal.

He sighed. "I don't know what I shall do with you, Sebastian. You will be confined to your room until I have come to a satisfactory decision. I do not believe I need to tell you I am very disappointed in your behavior."

It was all so predictable, really. Problems afoot. Writing in the journal because there's nothing else to do.

7 May 1817

REALIZED THAT IF I'M TO TRACK MY PROGRESS—WHATEVER THAT means—I may need this journal as evidence. I'm not at all sure what I'm to write in it each day but needs must, I suppose.

I've been thinking about the matter and I must admit I'm very put out about Father declaring I never try to improve myself. I mean to say, what does he expect? My marks are just about as good as any of my friends'. And just because I'm the only one who gets caught playing pranks does not mean I'm the only one who does them. Besides, if I didn't have pranks, I wouldn't have any friends. Not that I can explain that to Father. I daresay he'd tell me that having no friends is a noble sacrifice. Or some such rot.

8 May 1817

I AM QUITE BORED TO TEARS.

Being at home now is even worse than it was before I

went to Oxford. At least back then I had Gerry and Gavin around sometimes. Of course, they were usually off doing something or other—riding across the estate, swimming in the lake, or whatever else older siblings do when they're chummy. I suppose they did invite me to join when they remembered to do so. But I do hate pity invitations.

I am already well sick of this ridiculous journal. Doesn't help that I feel as though my future rests in its pages. That is, even if I can't be the person Father seems to think I should be, I'd like to have something to show for myself when all is said and done. Can't help thinking it is a useless effort, though.

9 May 1817

FATHER SAT ME DOWN IN HIS STUDY AND TOLD ME I NEED TO learn to be a proper gentleman. Ominous start. He listed out all manner of qualities I appear to be lacking: responsibility, gravity, good judgment. Frankly, I forget the rest of them. Said he was sending me to Bedfordshire to stay with Gavin and his husband. Pretty sure I dodged a much nastier solution. Could have been John, who was, by the way, furious—highly insulted that Father does not consider him a proper role model. So I am to go to a tiny village in the middle of nowhere in order to see how Gavin and his Mr. Kentworthy behave, apparently. Also, Father insisted I take the journal with me. Reiterated his desire for me to learn introspection.

12 May 1817

HAVE ARRIVED.

Tutting-on-Cress is so small as to be idyllic. Hate it already. It is abominably peaceful and quiet and everyone keeps to themselves. I'm not thrilled with the notion of rattling around in this place with no one to talk to.

Gavin somberly told me that he was instructed to ensure I

spend at least two hours every day in quiet contemplation with this journal or a book or something. God help me! As if I need more quiet in my life.

Since I appear to be stuck with the infernal thing, I have decided to name it. It will feel a great deal less pathetic if I feel as though I am writing to someone. So, future entries shall be addressed to Bartleby. Quite like the name. Feels good in the mouth. I do so love things that feel good in the mouth.

Lord, Gerry has arrived. I sense more lectures to come.

13 May 1817

DEAR BARTLEBY,

Allow me to introduce myself. The name is Sebastian Hartford. I am twenty years old and the youngest of four siblings.

My oldest brother, John, is beastly and married to an equally beastly woman named Veronica. They have a child who is also named John and is too small to have any personality yet but will likely take after his parents, so I am predisposed to dislike him.

After John is Gavin, who is solemn, quiet, and mad for poetry. He is married to a Mr. Charles Kentworthy, *Esquire*, if you please.

Then comes my sister, Geraldine. The only people who actually call her that are Mama and Father and other adult-types. Oh, and John, but he only does it to be irritating. Everyone else calls her Gerry. It suits her far better. She sort of inherited a spell shop from some old spellmaster she'd met and so she has settled down to work in trade. It was quite the upset, really. I believe she may be a bit of a social pariah to some of her old acquaintances. But my parents do not seem to mind.

Gavin and Gerry are easily the nicest of my siblings.

Although nowadays they lecture me as much as everyone else does. Well, Gavin does it a little less, I fancy. At any rate, they are closer in age to each other than to me. So I've never quite achieved that level of friendship they seem to share.

Then there's me, Sebastian, or Seb as I prefer to be called. I am handsome and charming, which are two things nobody in my family seems to appreciate, and is probably why I am now stuck being watched over by two of my siblings. It is a damned nuisance.

Do you care to know what we all look like? I can't imagine you do, but for the sake of posterity, let me describe us. Besides, it will give me something to write as I am expected to sit here for two bloody hours. So: we all look very related, with pale skin that comes over all blotchy when we're embarrassed. Gerry blushes the most becomingly, which is hardly surprising. She is the most perfect of us all. Gavin and I have always been horrid blushers. John probably is too; that is, he would if he were ever ashamed of anything. As it is, he always thinks he is in the right, so he only blushes when he is angry. Now that I think about it, I guess he does blush often in that case. Anyway, we all have dark brown eyes, narrow noses, small mouths, and high cheekbones. We also all have red hair, to some degree. Much to my annoyance, my hair is practically orange in color, which I'm not at all fond of. Gerry's hair is more coppery than mine, which makes her look all romantic and whatnot. John's hair is more of an auburn color. Gavin really got the best part of the situation with dark brown hair that only looks red when he's in the sun or standing by a candle. I used to wish my hair would get darker as I got older and change to a shade more like his. What am I saying? I still wish that would happen.

My mama is sweet and solicitous. She's the one who gave us all of our red hair. Her hair is like mine, only on her it looks becoming. She's often busy taking care of baby John. Mama has strong opinions about leaving children to be brought up solely by nannies. Veronica believes children should be seen and not heard and therefore nannies are the perfect solution. So Mama is doing most of the rearing of their child. I suppose, given that, he may actually grow up to be somewhat tolerable. But Mama had the raising of John, and he is the most toffee-nosed nincompoop to ever grace the earth. I suppose we will have to wait and see.

Father is very austere, very distant, and very, very frightening. Gavin looks most like him, really, with his dark-colored hair. That and the fact that Gavin is also rather solemn. Father never smiles either. At least not to me. I must confess I'm a little relieved he didn't want to oversee my redemption himself. I'm not sure I'd have survived it.

If you were a real person and not a silly journal, you might tell me a bit of your own family, Bartleby.

14 May 1817

Dear Bartleby,

As this is meant to be a time of contemplation, allow me to contemplate the following things: Tutting-on-Cress is small, pastoral, and quiet. The house is quite nice, all things considered. A little bigger than our own. Gerry also lives here, as does her shop assistant, a pretty fellow named Mr. Standish.

Not sure if I'm still grateful I was sent to live with Gavin as he seems to be taking this whole situation far too seriously. Mind, Gavin is always serious about everything. But I think he's a trifle nervous to be in charge of me. I have a notion that Gavin gets grumpy when he's uncomfortable and he has been exceedingly grumpy since I arrived. So it's either me or married life making him uncomfortable. Hard to imagine it's the latter. He's living in the lap of luxury here and his husband clearly adores him, despite his crankiness. I do think he has to shoulder the burden of running the house, so that might have something to do with it; Gavin never did strike me as the domestic type. I'm sure I should hate it. If I ever manage to snag a husband like Charles Kentworthy, I'll be sure to hire someone to run the house for me.

15 May 1817

DEAR BARTLEBY,

Allow me to indulge in a few contemplations of the inhabitants of the house.

Gavin: Far too solemn as per usual. You'd think he'd have learned to smile a bit after marrying someone so absurdly rich and handsome. Far better than John, don't misunderstand me. But I don't know how Gerry and I managed to be born of the same stock as the other two. Gavin is, at least, a decent person, and less inclined to scold. He also generally keeps to himself. It is a shame he is taking his role of guardian this seriously. We used to get on so well, but he's so easily upset these days. He was not amused when I told him about the time I made the soup tureens levitate during the evening meals at Oxford. No one caught me at it for weeks! One of my best pranks yet! But he was proper shocked about it. Not even a little bit impressed. He did always have a weakness for soup, I suppose.

Charles Kentworthy: Honestly have no idea how Gavin nabbed him as a husband. The man is far too tall for him and outrageously handsome. He has large dark eyes that are angular and twinkly. He has black hair and tan skin. Broad shoulders and quite muscular, which I am a bit envious of. No one would ever mistake me for muscular. He has a wide, pretty mouth. Very inclined to smile. Did not, however, smile when I asked why on earth he married Gavin of all people. Very generous. Gave me liberty of the house and the stables. My outings, I have been warned, are to be restricted to the estate. Such a nuisance.

Gerry: Perfect as always. She actually seemed pleased to

see me, which was nice of her. The only person who was pleased to see me, now that I think on it. I'd be more appreciative of that if it weren't for the fact that Gerry always manages to do everything right. I can't help but feel as though I'm forever being compared to her and found wanting. So I tend to avoid her company. I'm sure none of us could have gotten away with going into trade and still maintain our parents' respect. Don't know how she does it. Wants me to see her little shop. I don't know how I'm supposed to manage that when I'm tied to the house. I daresay someone will accompany me. It is too insufferable, really.

Mr. Standish: Bartleby, I have saved the best for last. The one person who will likely save me from absolutely abhorring this place. Mr. Standish is, in a word, adorable. Dark curly hair, long eyelashes, fawn-colored skin, slender, shorter than me. Thick London accent. Has the most devastating smile, but barely shows it. Also, he is outrageously shy, a particular weakness of mine. Always poses such a delicious challenge, don't you know? Everyone calls him Pip, but I'm not on good enough terms with the man for first names. Gavin has informed me that flirting with Mr. Standish is strictly forbidden, which makes no sense whatsoever. He is a single gentleman, after all. I've never known any single gentleman to be truly unavailable. How else would you explain my managing to get Reggie Warrow into my bed? Warrow is one of the most attractive fellows at school and I met him by vomiting onto his shoes. Hardly an auspicious start. So you see, Bartleby? No such thing as forbidden single gentlemen! Even after I've retched on them. I have taken Mr. Standish as a personal challenge. Why is he forbidden and how is the gorgeous thing still single? I shall keep you abreast of my findings.

16 May 1817

DEAR BARTLEBY,

I have noticed Kentworthy addresses everyone with terms of endearment. Except me. To Gavin, it is all "darling" and "dearest." To Gerry and Mr. Standish, it is "my dear," and "my friend." I am "Sebastian." I'm not sure he approves of me. Perhaps it is my presence that is making Gavin so grumpy after all. I'm sure I don't care if Kentworthy approves of me, but I don't particularly enjoy being singled out like that. I suppose if I really am to stay here long-term (God help me), I shall have to ingratiate myself. Hopefully he'll be easier than Father. Not sure I'll ever manage to get on Father's good side. Don't mistake me, Bartleby, I don't give a fig for Kentworthy's good opinion. But I'm sure it will make my stay here less horrid if he doesn't despise me the way Father does.

17 May 1817

DEAR BARTLEBY,

We had dinner guests last night. I rather expected to meet some country bumpkin friends, but was shocked that one of the guests was Viscount Finlington. Gavin really did move up in society when he married Kentworthy. God knows none of us would ever have entered Finlington's sphere on our own. I've heard the man is an intimate friend of the Prince Regent. What on earth he's doing living in Bedfordshire, I can't imagine. It seems as though he and Kentworthy are very friendly, but I don't think any friendship would induce me to purchase a house in a place as small and unexceptional as Tutting-on-Cress.

Lord Finlington is portly, pale, and a little taller than, well, all of us Hartfords. We're such an annoyingly short bunch of people. The adorable Mr. Standish is the only one shorter. It would be nice to kiss someone shorter than me, for a change.

Anyway, Finlington is very good-looking and very good-humored. Also, a tremendous flirt. Greeted me with enthusiasm, saying I was the "mischievous Hartford" he'd heard so much about. Proclaimed me to be as adorably attractive as the rest of my siblings. Which is a trifle unfair. I am, clearly, the handsomest of my brothers, orange hair color notwithstanding. Nevertheless, it is nice to be complimented. Especially when one is living out a punishment. He did not have the same reticence as Kentworthy in addressing me with terms of endearment. Is this a trend in the upper echelons of society, I wonder? Or are they just like each other in that way? At any rate, very pleasant chap. But altogether too comfortable with talking about my being tied down here, which I did not appreciate.

Our cousin Rose and her wife, Julia, were also there. I haven't seen Rose since I was a baby, so I can't pretend I had any strong feelings about the reunion. She is practically a stranger to me. There is no doubt that we are cousins though. She looks as though she could be our sister. Same cheekbones and narrow nose and whatnot. Rose talks in arch tones and she seems to take issue with Gerry's single status. Nice enough person, though, I suppose. Julia has light brown skin and honey-colored hair and is a round sort of individual. She was of a very different temperament. Soft-spoken and sweet. I rather think she pitied me for being sent down. Not at all fond of pity. But I suppose it's better than disappointment.

Food was excellent, which was not surprising. Kentworthy employs a superb cook. Although there was far too little concern about proper seating arrangements, in my opinion. Mr. Standish was seated next to Finlington, for God's sakes, and he's only a shop assistant. Of course, I'm not entirely sure how seating arrangements ought to be conducted. Still, I'm a little disappointed there wasn't more pomp. I was seated between Gerry and Gavin. I suppose they were considered the best suited to keep an eye on me.

Although I can't imagine what anyone thinks I shall accomplish at dinner. I didn't even levitate the soup tureen. Abominable lack of trust, truly.

All right, so I did perform a discreet Motion spell to swap out my water with Gerry's wine because the blasted girl would insist I should not drink more than one glass. God, it felt good to do that. Just like old times at Oxford.

She never even noticed, I'll have you know. No one noticed. In fact, I'm quite sure no one noticed me at all for most of the meal. They were all talking animatedly to each other in the way of close friends, and often discussing people and events that were unknown to me. I fancy Julia and Finlington attempted to pull me into the conversation occasionally, but it felt too much like I was a child sitting at a table of adults. It made me wish I had at least one of my mates from Oxford there, just so I could have someone to talk to. Then again, I'm not sure I've ever shared that sort of enthusiastic discourse with anybody. At any rate, it was not a particularly enjoyable evening, but it was nice to have other people around for once.

18 May 1817

Dear Bartleby,

Kentworthy and Gavin took me to see Gerry's shop today. It is very well kept. Everything is tidy and organized, the prices are reasonable, and everyone seems to adore her. I've said it once and I'll say it again, Bartleby: my sister is annoyingly perfect. Only she can step down the social ladder with so much grace.

While she was helping a customer, I wandered around and looked through the spells. There was one that caught my eye: a quieting spell. Never heard of anything like that before, so I was looking at it and trying to figure out what it was supposed to quiet when Mr. Standish came to stand next to me.

"Should I be surprised at your interest in this one, Mr. Hartford?" he said in his soft voice. "Or concerned?"

I grinned at him. "Oh, a bit of both, I think. What exactly is it supposed to quiet?"

"Not other people, lest you think of using it for a prank."

"I never!"

He raised an eyebrow. God, his eyes are gorgeous. "I believe Gerry intended to drink much more of her wine last night," he said.

I laughed. "I didn't think anyone had noticed."

"Oh, I think everybody noticed," he replied, reaching past me to pluck the spell bag off the hook. "They just didn't want to give you the satisfaction. As for the spell," he went on, opening the bag, "it includes a bit of chalk for the sigil and the circle, a scrap of wool, and a cut of reed, as you see here. The spellcaster would be expected to include their own pocket watch or timepiece." He pulled each item out and I confess, Bartleby, I was a mite distracted by his slender fingers. "It creates a quiet atmosphere for the caster, temporary, rather like a small bubble, within the confines of the chalk circle. The larger the circle, however, the weaker the spell will be. It is intended for small spaces."

"Good God, why on earth would that be desirable?"

Mr. Standish flashed one of those sweet, brief smiles of his. "A little quiet, Mr. Hartford, can be very restful sometimes."

"Hardly," I said. "If you ask me, this place is already too quiet by half."

He said nothing as he closed up the bag and replaced it on the hook. He was very close to my space, which I always consider something of an invitation, so I leaned forward a bit and said, "Is it possible, Mr. Standish, you commented on the wine because you wish to see me satisfied?"

I had really hoped to see him blush and stutter or something equally adorable. But damn me, the man regarded me in a manner more thoughtful than anything else.

"You're not very much like your siblings, are you, Mr. Hartford?" he said at last.

"God, I hope not."

"A pity, that," he said, and walked away.

He left me alone and the rest of the visit was dull as tombs. Gerry has done a fine job of herself, of course, but I could have told you that without the visit because it's Gerry and that's what she does.

One last item of note: saw a gentleman walk into the shop as we were leaving it. He was shorter than I am, with medium brown skin and dark brown eyes and he gave me the most charmingly open smile I've ever seen in my life. Almost tried to go back inside for an introduction to the fellow, but that seems like a silly thing to do in my sister's shop. Besides, Standish was in there and it wouldn't do to pursue two people at once.

19 May 1817

Dear Bartleby,

Have been here for over a week and it has been the longest damn week of my life. Shall have to find something to occupy my time. There is nothing to do here. I feel cooped up. I feel stuck. I am sick to death of all of the quiet. Gerry is chatty enough, but she works most days so the house is abominably still until she and Standish get home. The two of them are tired from working all day, so after dinner it's more of the same dull silence. Don't know why Standish said quiet is restful. I may have to ask him. Quiet makes my ears prickle. It makes me come over all twitchy. Hate it. Tired of sitting still. Going to pace around the garden, simply for a lack of anything better to do. Kentworthy keeps a good gardener.

Gavin mentioned that in a letter once. They're well-kept, but I've never been one for florals. So it is all wasted on me.

20 May 1817

DEAR BARTLEBY,

I am coming to the realization that slow-moving seduction plots are significantly more difficult when the other person is never around. Standish is at the shop every day with Gerry. He does not even spend dinner with us every night, although I do not know where he goes. Perhaps he eats in the village. And this is every day, excepting Sundays. The shop is apparently closed on Sundays. Shall have to see if I can work out a plan. Not a Sunday shall be wasted!

21 May 1817

DEAR BARTLEBY,

This house is a tomb. Every day, it is just me, Gavin, and Kentworthy. And they keep to themselves most of the time. They each have their own study. Gavin spends a great deal of his time in the library or the garden. So it is mostly just me rattling about the place. Not overly fond of it, I can tell you.

On the bright side, I think I have come up with a good plan for making use of Sunday. I shall ask Standish if he would care for a walk in the gardens with me. Bit of fresh air and all that. There's a lovely little spot around a curl of hedge that is completely hidden from the house. I won't force myself upon him. Don't be crass. But I can lean in and whisper something, or brush my hand against his. It's all in the little moments, Bartleby.

22 May 1817

DEAR BARTLEBY,

The old prank master is back.

Went into the henhouse today and set up a long-term levitation spell in the corner. Now the nests are about a foot above the shelves. Chickens were all squawking and carrying on. Positively hilarious! I wish some of my friends could have seen it. Wrote to Parks and told him about it. Cannot wait to hear what he says.

23 May 1817

DEAR BARTLEBY,

The chicken nests are already back to normal. More's the pity. Shall have to find something else. There are far too few people here, so it is a good deal less satisfying. Nevertheless, I really must find something to do.

24 May 1817

DEAR BARTLEBY,

Did the chicken roost spell again. Mostly because it really was humorous to see them all squawking about. I know it shall probably be taken down tomorrow. But as no one seems intent on talking to me about my pranks, I might as well keep on doing them.

25 May 1817

DEAR BARTLEBY,

The first Sunday did not go as planned. In fact, it might have put paid to the plans I had for every Sunday after. I asked Standish, quite innocently I'll have you know, if he would like to wander about the garden with me. He said he would be delighted, so I thought it would all fall pat. He asked me to wait for him outside, so I did. Next, he comes strolling out with Gavin and Gerry! Insufferable. They said they wished to wander through the gardens, too. Well, of course, I couldn't try a damned thing. It was all pleasantries and banalities and how is the shop and what am I doing every day. What a lot of rot.

Afterwards, Gavin cornered me and reminded me in a low voice that Mr. Standish was not to be trifled with. So I daresay I shall have to bide my time even more. Bother.

26 May 1817

D EAR B ARTLEBY,

I believe I have found a better prank than the chicken house, if you can believe it! I wandered up to the servants' quarters and found a lovely little empty corner by a window, visible from the stairs but no doors around it, just empty space. Perfection! I have ideas churning. I shall have more details later.

27 May 1817

D EAR B ARTLEBY,

Have set up a hilarious little trap spell in that corner of the house. It is an illusion spell that, to be brutally frank, I'm not supposed to know. I'm not really supposed to know any illusion spells, considering how advanced they are and how dangerous they can be. But hang it all, half of my pranks are built on illusions. What is a chap to do except learn what he can? I set up a trap that when someone hits a particular part of the third stair from the top, there's a little flutter of light by the window. Quite ghost-like! I am, I daresay, a genius.

28 May 1817

DEAR BARTLEBY,

No word yet on how the spell is going, but a couple of the maids seem a little on edge. I believe a few of them saw it. I shall keep you informed.

29 May 1817

DEAR BARTLEBY,

There is definitely alarm spreading around the house. Brilliant! All I have to do is sit somewhere centrally located and I hear all sorts of prattle about the ghost. It even came up at breakfast. I pretended all shock and surprise, I can tell you. Such a great joke! The beauty of it is no one will catch me at it. Perhaps this place is not quite so boring after all. Wrote about it to Parks. What a laugh he will get out of it! Oh, and apparently Finlington is coming to dine tonight. At least the conversation will be somewhat varied, for once.

30 May 1817

DEAR BARTLEBY,

I don't know how they did it, but they found my trap spell. How the bloody hell did they do it so fast? I hid the blasted thing. The spell itself was set up well out of the way from the stair and quite out of view. Finlington, Gerry, and Standish all went up to the servants' quarters and poked around, apparently. Gerry announced at breakfast that they had exorcized it. Who knew my own perfect older sister could be so good at fibbing? Not a soul looked at me the whole time. It was very irritating. Not a bit of credit from a single one of them. I almost announced it had all been my invention. I declare a lecture would have been more satisfying than being completely ignored.

Cannot decide if pining for the gorgeous Mr. Standish is making my stay here more bearable or less. I can tell you, Bartleby, I know what would make it more bearable. Having the gorgeous man in...well, anywhere. I'd take him in a closet at this point. God, it's been simply ages. The last time was Freddie Harencourt and that was...I can't even think when that was. April? March? Time no longer has meaning, Bartleby. That is what it means to be locked up in an absurdly boring estate with absurdly boring relations. Sadly, shall have to take the whole Standish matter slowly and gently. Like with a spooked horse. Especially when I've been warned off the gentleman. Twice.

Just occurred to me Gavin is meant to check on my progress on this whole contemplation game. What a nuisance that is. I hope he doesn't actually intend to read my journal. Perhaps I'd better ask. Might be better to tear out incriminating pages and be scolded for missing dates than to be scolded for flagrantly ignoring Gavin's warnings.

WENT AND ASKED ABOUT IT. GAVIN GAVE ME THE MOST BAFFLED look I have ever seen on his face.

"Why the devil would I want to actually read the blasted thing?" he asked.

I told him I was worried he'd be sending word back to Father.

Gavin frowned in his usual way and said, "Seb, a journal is for personal thoughts. I would never betray your privacy in such a way. But this does give me a great deal of concern for what your personal thoughts actually are."

This line of thought was a bit alarming, so I said, "I don't see why he's so bent on having me use a journal in the first place."

He folded his hands on his desk and said, "Well, as you know, he is keen to see you mature a bit."

"And a journal is supposed to do that, is it?" I said, a little irritably.

"Oh, I don't think anyone expects a journal to provide any sort of magical change in you. But if you ask me…" He gave me a questioning look and I nodded for him to proceed. "If you ask me, Father is worried that you are too in your own head. It's a family trait, you know. I have a tendency to withdraw, and I'm sure John does too. So it isn't the least bit surprising that you have shown a similar inclination. I know when I've written letters, it helps me to write out what I'm thinking. It allows me to analyze my thoughts a bit more, come to understand myself. If I had a guess, I'd say he wants you to analyze your thoughts and understand yourself in much the same way. I'm sure he doesn't much care how you do it, but since you haven't been talking to any of us, the journal was the best solution he could come up with."

"I talk to you," I protested. "I talk to everybody."

He raised an eyebrow. "Chatter is not the same as confiding, Seb, and you know it. Do you have anyone to confide to?"

I kicked at the rug a bit. "Not much to confide."

He sighed. "Then I daresay you're stuck with his instructions. As to your concerns about my reading it, don't worry about that. He has asked that I ensure you're spending some quiet time alone and that I encourage you to use the journal. I have promised to do so but beyond a quick leaf through, I assure you, I will read nothing."

I can tell you, Bartleby, I was very relieved. Do you know, I really am terribly grateful to have been sent here instead of being put under the watchful eye of John and Veronica. For you know as well as I do (well, perhaps not since you are not sentient), that John would have no such scruples.

31 May 1817

Dᴇᴀʀ Bᴀʀᴛʟᴇʙʏ,

Have discovered a rather handsome footman among the staff. A bit of a pug nose, I fancy. But the Standish situation will be a very slow process. So I shall take a pug-nosed footman in the meantime. Must determine his schedule and duties first.

1 June 1817

Dᴇᴀʀ Bᴀʀᴛʟᴇʙʏ,

Had a lark keeping an eye out for the footman. I think he's on to me, but I don't think he seems to mind it. He's courteous and solicitous, and not in the cold way of servants who don't approve of you. I might get some satisfaction as soon as tomorrow.

2 June 1817

Dᴇᴀʀ Bᴀʀᴛʟᴇʙʏ,

What started out as a very promising afternoon has turned out to be not so promising. In fact, it was a bit of a disaster. Found the footman and was in the process of encouraging the man into a closet for a quick nip, as it were, when the door was flung open and Kentworthy was staring down at me in a most disapproving manner. The footman was very embarrassed and I daresay Kentworthy was a damn sight more civil to him than he was to me. He assured the footman he was not in any trouble and sent the man scurrying off to his duties. Then he gave me a grim look and asked if I might join him in his study. Of course I jolly well couldn't say no.

I'm quite sure Gavin has no interest in having children and it's almost a shame, really, because Kentworthy has the makings of a very firm father. He reminded me of my own with the disapproving look he gave me. I'm an expert on disapproving looks at this point. Would you believe, Bartleby, that he had me sit down in a chair while he leaned up against the desk? As if the blasted man should need any more height than he already has. Terribly uncalled for.

"I do not know what you have been taught at Oxford, Sebastian," he said. "But while you are in my house, you will not harass the servants."

"Harassment was not exactly what I had in mind," I joked, but then wished I hadn't; he did not look amused. "Well, he didn't seem bothered by the idea," I protested.

"He is not at liberty to be honest," Kentworthy said. "It is inappropriate to conduct such things with servants. Has no one ever told you this?"

"I would never have taken you for a classist," I retorted.

"Far from it," he said. "It is not inappropriate because they are of a lower class than you. It is inappropriate because you are a guest in the home in which they are working. Many would not feel comfortable refusing advances, even if they did not want them."

"I'll have you know I've never forced myself on anyone. I resent the implication."

"I'm very glad to hear it," he replied in a mild tone that sounded anything but *very glad*.

I sighed and leaned my head back to look at the ceiling. "God's teeth. There's nothing to do here. How can you people live like this? What do you do all day?"

Bartleby, I wish I hadn't said anything. Because Kentworthy then looked amused, which I believe may be a more frightening expression than his disapproval.

"Well, if you're bored, Sebastian, then I daresay we can find something for you to do."

Damn my blasted ruddy mouth.

3 June 1817

D*EAR* B*ARTLEBY*,

Kentworthy made me wait until this morning to discuss the matter. I don't know that I've ever been so nervous. Not even when the dean learned I was the one who had stolen the gargoyle off the top of the library. With the dean, I had an idea of what my punishments might be. And I could usually charm him down from anything too extreme. But Kentworthy is a mysterious entity and I haven't figured him out yet. Curses that he should take it into his head to cure me of my boredom before I've had a chance to learn his weak spots.

He brought it up at breakfast—in front of everyone, I'll have you know—Well, everyone being Gavin, Gerry, and Standish. I strolled in last and they greeted me cheerfully, which was my first ominous hint.

No sooner had I filled up my plate and sat down, Kentworthy said, "I've been giving the matter a great deal of thought, Sebastian. I fear I have neglected my duties as host since you arrived. I did not consider proper entertainment for you."

"You really needn't trouble yourself," I said hastily.

He smiled. "Oh, but I do. It would appear that you are lacking in things to do, given your recent pranks and attempted seductions."

It was the first time anyone has mentioned my pranks, other than Standish saying something in the shop. It was a good deal less satisfying than I would have liked. It was so casually mentioned, as if it were unimportant, a mere detail, a practically forgotten incident. I'll have you know I worked hard on those! Well, I worked hard on the ghost spell. That one took planning. The chicken coop was just for a laugh.

Kentworthy continued, "So we have put our heads together and compiled a list."

I groaned.

His smile widened. Curse him. He picked up a paper and I could see a schedule had been written on it. "Every morning, your valet shall wake you up early so you might go riding before breakfast."

"What?"

"I shall accompany you," he said.

This did not make me feel better, Bartleby.

"I might join as well," Gavin put in. "If I wake up early enough."

This made me feel a little better.

"Then," Kentworthy went on, "we shall come inside for breakfast. After which, you shall have the morning for studies. After all, you would normally be in school at this time of year and we do not want your education to be neglected. Gerry, Gavin, and I are working on a curriculum for you to follow for the duration of your stay. You shall study in the library until lunch. I will take responsibility for seeing your work is done and we shall divide your work amongst the three of us to see it is done properly. After lunch, you shall have a couple of hours of leisure time. I have drawn up a list of activities that might interest you for that period. Please note: footmen are not on the list."

I cringed and sank in my chair.

"Then, you will be expected to join Gavin and myself for tea in the sitting room, along with some etiquette lessons."

"You must be joking."

"I assure you I am not."

I groaned again.

"After tea, you shall have your customary two hours of time for contemplation, per your father's request. Then, I should like you to spend more time outside, weather permitting. You may go riding, walk in the garden, walk anywhere in the estate you like. After that, you will join the rest of us for dinner and after-dinner-socialization." He put the paper aside. "Any questions?"

"Yes," I said. "Why are you punishing me like this? I promise I won't do...what I was going to do."

"Well," he said. "I admit I had forgotten you were supposed to be in school at this time. It did not occur to me until you mentioned your boredom—"

"Damn it—"

"—we discovered we ought to rectify it." He paused. "Currently, I have planned for you to study alone, but if you would prefer to have a tutor—"

"Lord, no. Please."

"Very well. But know that I am trusting you to study as you ought. If you shirk your studies, I shall consider that a breach of trust and hire a tutor for you. Is that clear?"

Nobody saved me from this indignity. So of course I had no choice in the matter.

Gavin walked me to the library after breakfast to explain what they had set up for me. When I sat down, he pulled a chair out and sat next to me.

"Seb," he said in a low voice. "What happened when you went to Oxford?"

"What are you talking about?"

He sighed. "You were never like this before you went there. Yes, you were an idiot occasionally, but I've never known you to be cruel."

"Cruel?"

He gave me a steady look. "The horse in the dormitory hall? Do you know they had to sedate the poor thing to get it out safely? And the soup tureens? Do you have any idea how much those servants were likely punished before they figured out it was you?"

I shifted in my chair. "God's teeth, Gavin. I didn't intend for anything like that."

"And then you come here and do the same nonsense. I had to talk down three maids from quitting out of fright. And the chickens are still traumatized from their nests being moved. It is one thing to play a joke on someone who can retaliate or defend themselves. But servants and animals can do no such thing. It is shockingly bad form."

"Just trying for a laugh," I said. I was annoyed by how plaintive I sounded.

"I rather suspect there's more to it than that. I hope you'll tell me when you're ready."

This whole conversation made me very uncomfortable. Cruelty was never my object, Bartleby, I hope you know that. I hated to have Gavin thinking of me as some sort of bully. I decided a change of subject was in order.

"Would you tell your husband to stop haranguing me? The only good thing about coming here was I didn't have to be in school."

He tilted his head. "Really? The only good thing?"

"Well, and I'm glad I wasn't made to live with John," I admitted.

"Praise indeed," he remarked drily. "I am glad as well. He would have made the situation worse, I daresay. Not to mention the fact that I do actually enjoy your company, when you aren't being a callous sod." He stood to go. "And no," he said, turning to look at me. "I will not tell Charles any such thing. Frankly, I'm glad he's here to help me. I'm worried about you, Seb. I don't mind telling you."

Which, of course, put me in an even fouler mood, I don't mind telling *you*, Bartleby.

4 June 1817

DEAR BARTLEBY,

I already hate getting up early and I've only done it once now. Kentworthy kept up a punishing pace and I was extremely out of sorts when we finally reached the house again. What have I done to deserve such treatment? Never mind. Don't tell me.

Not at all inclined to study. But I shudder to think what sort of tutor Kentworthy would saddle me to. So, must press on. I take back all of my complaints about being bored. I would to God I was bored now.

The curriculum that was seen fit to give me is unique to everyone's tastes. It is positively absurd. Gerry is having me study Magical Theory. I'm to write reports on Norton and Pechard and Sandellini and all their tiresome theories and findings. She is even making me memorize the entire bloody list of common Constitutional Properties. Why the devil should I need to know all of them? Besides, there's almost always a written-out version of the spell. It is a damned nuisance. Who would have thought my sister would be so hard-hearted?

Gavin is in charge of literature, God help me, so there's simply loads of poetry and essays and all sorts of nonsense. In class, I could just shirk out of such assignments, but I can't very well do it when Gavin has no other students to distract him.

Kentworthy has taken over history, which is bad enough, but he has also gotten it into his head that I should learn about a whole mess of things: how to manage finances, property laws, marriage laws, and the British government. It is all exceedingly dull and, quite frankly, I don't understand most of it. No one at Oxford ever had to study such matters. I imagine parents are expected to teach their firstborns. I expect Father taught John. I'm the youngest child, so why the devil do I have to learn such rot?

I have come to the dreadful conclusion, Bartleby, that I quite despise Mr. Charles Kentworthy. And I don't mind saying it. Although I am glad that Gavin isn't really reading these, for I wouldn't want him to know.

Far too tired to write out anything more. I'm going to spend the rest of my contemplation time reading instead.

5 June 1817,

DEAR BARTLEBY,

Not sure when Gerry expects me to fit all of this in. I'll be memorizing this ridiculous list until Christmas. It's five pages long! On top of that, I have to read the poetry and literature that Gavin picked out for me and write an essay about them, and write about the fall of the Roman Empire for Kentworthy, not to mention his governmental nonsense. It is, quite simply, too much. I hate them all.

6 June 1817

DEAR BARTLEBY,

Hate to admit it, but learning Magical Theory is actually rather interesting. I am finally realizing why tarragon never worked so well in my healing tinctures. Turns out I should have used mint instead. More appropriate Constitutional Property when it comes to healing apparently. Still angry about this list though.

Have completed my essay for Gavin, finally. I'm sure it's terrible, but I should like to see him try for a better essay.

Not quite sure what to do as one of the passages Kentworthy assigned me is utterly confusing. I have no idea what I'm supposed to be getting from it. It's incredibly long and all about marriage laws and I can't make sense of any of it. He has told me he wishes for me to write a report on the damn subject. Under normal circumstances, I'd find Adelaide Forrester or some other brainy classmate to explain it or even write it for me. But I have no one to explain it here, and I have no desire whatsoever to ask Kenworthy. He doesn't deserve the satisfaction. So I made something up when I wrote the report. I daresay I'll get some sort of lecture about it. But he can't exactly fail me in a nonexistent class, after all. Can he?

My hand is cramping from writing too much. I daresay I

didn't do this amount of work at Oxford. My friends don't know how good they have it.

7 June 1817

DEAR BARTLEBY,

The wrathful god does show mercy at times, it seems. I have been given a day off from my studies. Kentworthy told me, himself, that I shall not be expected to study on Saturdays. Although he does seem intent on me continuing my studies on Sundays, which seems a trifle atheistic of him. I'd complain except then I'd probably be made to sit in church and I'm not quite sure that's an agreeable alternative.

I'm still expected to have my time of contemplation as usual, as that is Father's particular request. But Kentworthy didn't even make me get up early to go riding this morning. I woke up anyway because I'm getting accustomed to it, confound the man. I saw him and Gavin from my bedroom window, riding off across the estate. I went back to bed, simply because I had the option.

8 June 1817

DEAR BARTLEBY,

I have not spoken to you of the travesty that is etiquette lessons, have I?

Well, allow me to do so now.

Despite the fact that I have already learned a great deal of this sort of thing already, I apparently require a review of the subject. Etiquette lessons are a dreadful bore and I wish them to perdition. More aptly, I wish Kentworthy to perdition, for I'm sure they're all his idea.

Every afternoon, we convene in the sitting room. I am served tea and must answer trivial questions about my day and what I'm reading or whatnot. I am also expected to ask trivial questions. Gavin and Kentworthy (but, really, Bartleby, it is mostly Kentworthy) will make little comments about my posture or suggest that a particular topic might not be suitable for a nextborn like myself, but might be appropriate after I'm married. That sort of nonsense. So very tiresome.

Today, Gerry and Standish joined us as it is their day off from the shop. I was a little surprised that Standish joined. I wouldn't have expected him to be interested in witnessing my personal torture. But he was there, politely accepting his tea from Gerry. He drinks his tea black, Bartleby, which strikes me as a rather odd thing to do. He even joined the conversation a little. Asked me what Oxford is like. I gave him an enthusiastic description of the place, told him about the food and the campus and the fun we all have. He acted as though he didn't know anything about university, which intrigued me a little. Although I suppose a shop assistant doesn't need a university education.

At any rate, Standish made the tea less abhorrent. Gerry added some pleasant conversation, but she also had critiques on the way I held my cup and sat in my chair. I'm only five years her junior, but you'd think I was ten with the way she bosses me about. Then again, she talks to Gavin in exactly the same tone. I suppose that's just how she is to everybody.

9 June 1817

DEAR BARTLEBY,

Kentworthy read over my report on British marriage laws and handed it back to me with a grim expression and the words, "Do it over, if you please."

I do not please. I do not please at all. Curse the man. I put it off and did everything else first and then I had simply no time to do the report over. He shall have to wait. Particularly since I still have no idea what he expects me to write.

10 June 1817

D*EAR* B*ARTLEBY*,

Once again, did not have time to do the report over. Not sure how long I shall be able to keep this up before Kentworthy reads me a lecture. But, frankly, I don't care. I'm working far more on my studies here than I ever did at Oxford and that's the truth.

I quite detest the man.

11 June 1817

D*EAR* B*ARTLEBY*,

Kentworthy noticed and adjusted my workload so that I might have time to do the report over today. Let me amend that: so that I *will* have time to do the report today. He made it quite clear that it was to be a priority.

Well, I sat with the blasted book for an hour, trying to figure out what he wanted me to understand. I finally gave up and decided to find Gavin and have him explain it to me. Only I couldn't find him. I looked everywhere. Finally ran into Kentworthy as he was going into his study and asked where Gavin was. He informed me that Gavin had gone out for a walk.

I asked when he might be expected to return and Kentworthy looked at me in that insufferably amused way of his, glanced at the book in my hand, and said, "I'm not at all sure. Can I be of assistance?"

I told him I would wait for Gavin and turned to return to the library.

"Sebastian."

I sighed and turned back around to him.

"Are you having difficulties with that report?"

I glowered at him and said nothing.

"Because, if you are," he continued. "You know you need only ask. I'd be happy to provide any explanations for you."

"I'd prefer to wait for Gavin," I said.

"Very well. I'll tell him you were looking for him."

"Thank you."

"And Sebastian? I expect that report today. If it is not completed during your usual study period, you may use some of your personal leisure time for the task."

Damn the man. I stomped back to the library and worked through the rest of my assignments until Gavin found me.

"Charles said you were looking for me?"

"Finally," I said. "Here." I pulled out the book in question. "He wants me to write a report on marriage law and I have no idea what he wants me to explain. I tried writing it already and he is making me do it over."

Gavin did not take the book or the paper. "Why the blazes did you not ask him?"

I huffed. "And give him the satisfaction? No, thank you. The man hates me enough. I don't need to give him more ammunition."

"Don't be ridiculous. He doesn't hate you."

"Then I suppose he's putting me through all of this out of a deep fondness?"

"Well, yes," Gavin replied simply. "He believes—we all believe you're better than this," he waved his hand vaguely at me, "whatever phase you seem to be going through. We're trying to help you. Frankly," he added, picking up the book at last and glancing over the page, "I don't understand why these things aren't taught at school. They're terribly important." He put the book back down and gave me a steady look. "Talk to him." And then he left.

I procrastinated the conversation until after lunch and I was in my leisure time. It was not a pleasant experience, going cap in hand to a man who is essentially my jailer. I suppose Gavin can get some of the blame on that part, but

Kentworthy is the one who seems determined to make me miserable here. I found him in his study. The door was wide open, as if he was waiting for me. Although I think his door is often open. Frankly, I try to avoid his study so I can't say that I've noticed one way or the other.

"Yes, Sebastian?" he said when I came in.

"I don't know what it is you want from me," I said.

He frowned a little, confused.

"What am I to write?"

"Was the assignment not clear enough?"

I sighed. "The assignment was clear, but this damned book is far too confusing. Nothing is written plainly. I don't understand any of it."

He gave a small smile. "I'd have to agree with you. Legal writing is always outrageously fustian."

"Then why do you make me suffer through it?" I said. "Why do you insist on punishing me this way?"

He leaned back in his chair. "Well, unless I'm much mistaken, you intend to be married someday."

"Well, yes, eventually."

"So, it will be in your best interest to understand marriage laws. It can be quite confusing. I would hate for you to be married and find yourself unprepared for the responsibilities expected of you."

"Is that what happened to you?" I ventured.

He chuckled. "No, not at all. I was very aware of what to expect. But Gavin was not entirely aware of what was expected of him until we were already engaged. I would like to see you more prepared. If you are not careful, you may find yourself in a predicament if you wed yourself to someone who takes advantage of your ignorance. Although," he added, "I would certainly do my best to prevent such a thing."

"Is that liable to happen?"

"It happens to many people," he said. "For the most part,

if a nextborn marries a firstborn, the expectations are rather straightforward. But if you were to marry another nextborn, it can be decidedly confusing. It would be to your benefit to know exactly what you're getting into regardless of the birth order of the gentleman you marry. You may need to discuss with him the division of responsibilities and expectations. Decide whose name shall be taken. The laws can be very complex and messy. That is why I assigned that essay to you."

I looked at the book in my hands. "Oh."

"Now," he continued. "If you would like my assistance, I would be happy to supply it. Do you need my help, Sebastian?"

Curse the man for making me say it.

"Yes. I'm afraid I do."

"Very good. I shall be delighted to help you. I will join you in the library tomorrow after breakfast to talk you through the passages in question. You may take the rest of your leisure time as you will."

That did surprise me. "Oh," I said. "Er. Thank you."

He smiled. "You're quite welcome. I shall see you at tea. Unless, of course, there is anything else you wish to discuss?"

I told him there wasn't and walked out.

12 June 1817

Dear Bartleby,

Today, Kentworthy sat down next to me in the library and explained marriage laws. It is odiously complicated but also, I do so hate to say it, quite fascinating. When a firstborn and a nextborn marry, you see, the firstborn is responsible for the finances and any property they might own. The nextborn is in charge of running the household, hiring and managing the household staff, hosting whenever there is company, that sort of thing.

But if two nextborns marry, it all gets rather muddled.

Who controls the finances or finds an occupation? Who takes precedence? There's even an added step to the whole marriage process where one person signs a form that they shall be assuming those responsibilities. Kentworthy explained that this means fortune hunters will try to coerce spouses into signing over all of their fortune to them. It is dreadful. I have no property, of course, so that shan't be a problem for me. The person who has control of property is also the one in charge of finances and securing a house and that sort of thing. There is a division of labors or responsibilities and those have to be ironed out in advance, as do details like who takes the other's name. In Gavin's case, since he married a firstborn, he took Kentworthy's name and, according to the law, he's now Kentworthy's dependent. Kentworthy is sort of the head of the house, as it were.

It's all very particular and strange. I don't see why it should be so very complicated. Kentworthy went on to say that this is all strictly in terms of legality and property and has nothing to do with the actual relationship dynamic. He advised that when I do get married, I take into account my own temperament, personality, strengths, and interests, as well as that of my husband. And, of course, consider such things as inheritance and property and all that.

I had dreaded the conversation all night and all morning. But Kentworthy was, surprisingly, not smug like I feared he'd be. He was very patient and explained everything very clearly. He even helped me to write the essay, which seemed like a strange thing to do since he would have to read it later. Well, he got me started on it; I wrote the rest of it myself. I'm annoyed that I cannot detest him as much as I wish to now. For I was rather glad to learn it all. I have much to think about. What a bother it is to be wrong.

13 June 1817

DEAR BARTLEBY,

Who knew all it took for Kentworthy to not hate me was for me to ask him for help? The man is a complete mystery to me. Nothing has changed exactly, but I fancy he is not so cold in his manner of talking to me. I wonder if the mood is only temporary and he shall remember he dislikes me later.

14 June 1817

DEAR BARTLEBY,

Typically during the evenings I walk to the lake and back. Kentworthy wants me to do something outside before dinner, you may recall. Anyway, last night I walked around the house before dinner instead and strode past the chicken coop. It was my first time passing the chicken coop since the last time I pranked it. And do you know, Bartleby, I was struck with guilt for the whole thing. I have never felt guilty for a prank before. I've been thinking about it all day and about how the servants here probably all hate me for the whole ghost thing.

I almost brought it up to Kentworthy, but didn't quite have the nerve.

I suppose I may owe him an apology for frightening his servants. And perhaps Gavin as well. Curses.

15 June 1817

DEAR BARTLEBY,

Worked up the nerve to apologize to Gavin. He was easier. He came into the library while I was working on memorizing Gerry's list—yes, I'm still working through the blasted thing —and went to grab a book from the shelves. I cleared my throat to get his attention, for I had myself all worked up.

He turned and looked at me. "Something the matter?"

I stared down at my pen as I rolled it around in my hand. "I…er…I'm sorry about the pranks earlier. The coop and the ghost trap," I added, glancing up at him, lest he think I had done more. "I didn't intend to be cruel."

"Oh," Gavin said. "Thank you. I'm glad to hear it." He looked at the book in his hand for a moment and then said, "How did you get into all those pranks, anyway?"

I shrugged. "Something to do, I suppose."

He hummed in a noncommittal way that suggested it was not the answer he was hoping for, but he didn't push. That is one thing I like about Gavin. He isn't one to push.

I suppose I ought to say the same thing to Kentworthy tomorrow. After all, it is his house and everything.

16 June 1817

Dear Bartleby,

I worked up the nerve to apologize to Kentworthy. I did it on our ride this morning. Typically, we don't talk much on our rides. It's a quick canter around the estate. But I thought it was the best time to talk to him. If he spurned the apology, I'd have the whole ride back to get over it. When we got to the glen where we usually turn left and start making our way back, I reined in and looked across at the morning mist, hoping he'd slow down too.

Fortunately, he did, and guided his horse back to where I was.

"Everything all right?" he asked.

I felt nervous to look him in the face while I said it, just as when I talked to Gavin, so I kept my eyes ahead on the mist and said, "I'm afraid I owe you an apology."

"Oh?" he said.

I sighed. "I'm sorry about the whole mess with the chicken coop and the ghost trap."

"Ah," he said.

"You see, I never really considered it from their point of view. The chickens, I mean. And the servants. I didn't mean to be cruel. I was just..."

I glanced at him and he was looking at me with an unreadable expression.

"I don't know," I said. "I guess I've just made a habit of doing it and I never stopped to think. I'm truly not a cruel person, or a bully or anything, whatever you may think."

"I don't think of you as cruel, Sebastian."

"I suppose your servants do," I said. "I daresay they all quite despise me."

"No, dear boy," he said. "They don't. They weren't pleased, of course, when it was explained to them. But Gavin assured them that we would keep you from doing anything too terrible in the future."

I was so startled by the term of endearment that I stared at him, dumbfounded.

He raised his eyebrows.

"I...er...rather thought you despised me, too," I said.

"Of course I don't," he said. "I believe you still have a great deal to learn. But I never consider anyone a lost cause, least of all someone related to Gavin."

"Then you haven't met John, I suppose."

He chuckled. "I actually have."

"You mean you don't think he's a lost cause?"

He laughed louder and some birds flew up in alarm. "I think John means well but is clumsy about it."

I didn't quite agree with that, but I didn't say anything.

We sat in silence for a few moments while I digested the fact that my brother-in-law did not entirely hate me and was realizing I didn't entirely hate him.

"Now, the chickens," he said. "They might not be so fond of you now. Dashed difficult to talk sense to, chickens, you know."

I laughed. "Well, I suppose I can steer clear of the coop then."

"Thank you, darling. Very wise. Are you ready to go back?"

I nodded and we returned home.

And now I'm digesting the fact that Kentworthy made a joke about chickens.

17 June 1817

DEAR BARTLEBY,

At breakfast, Gerry asked me how I was getting on with the list of Constitutional Properties and I explained to her that it was far too long and damn near impossible to memorize. She told me not to be a twit and that if I really needed help, all I had to do was ask. She has even, apparently, taken a leaf out of Kentworthy's book and told me that I must have the list memorized by Friday. Not sure I shall have any time for leisure at all now. Drat the girl.

Stole a glance at Kentworthy who was, dash it all, looking at me with amusement. I refuse to ask for help two weeks in a row, Bartleby. Absolutely refuse.

18 June 1817

DEAR BARTLEBY,

Finlington came over for dinner last night. Asked me how I was getting on with my studies and everything. I realized partway through dinner that the viscount is quite an eligible bachelor. And from the way he flirts, it's easy to guess his persuasion. Ordinarily, I'd use that to my advantage. But he's considerably older than I am, about Kentworthy's age. It's funny because when Gavin first met Kentworthy, I had it in my head that I might be able to fall in love with him. But he's at least ten years older than I am. That seems a bit much, don't you think? I'm sure I should much prefer someone who sees me as his equal, rather than a child or something. As much as Finlington does flirt, I cannot help but think he sees me as a schoolboy, or at best, Gavin's baby brother. I'm well aware that I am, but I don't think that's a good dynamic for a relationship.

I'm blaming this entire entry on Kentworthy's blasted marriage laws lesson. I declare I've never thought this carefully about marriage before. Not sure I enjoy it.

19 June 1817

DEAR BARTLEBY,

I don't know how I'm going to get Gerry's list down by memory by tomorrow. I suppose I shall have to go to her for help. That seems to be the *modus operandi* lately (You see, Bartleby? I did learn things in Oxford). What a bother it all is.

20 June 1817

DEAR BARTLEBY,

Asked Gerry for help with the list and she looked so absurdly pleased by it. Why does everyone enjoy being asked for help? So very bizarre. She extended the deadline for the assignment and evenings after dinner will be spent working through the list together. I'm not sure I am pleased with this solution, but at least I can move on from this blasted assignment at last.

21 June 1817

DEAR BARTLEBY,

First in-person lesson with Gerry went fairly well. She mentioned that memorizing the list is something I ought to have been told to do ages ago and she seemed rather unimpressed with my education at Oxford. Frankly, Bartleby, it is a little unsettling that I am learning more living with my brother in the country than I learned at university. I imagine it is because I am the only student here.

Received a letter from Father today. He told me that Gavin has assured him I am showing some marked improvement. However, he is using this as an argument for my staying here indefinitely. It is a bit of a wrench, for it seems as though I won't go back to Oxford at all now. But I'm not sure I hate it here quite as much as I did before. Except that it's a little isolating.

Speaking of which, this letter is the first one I have received since arriving. Can you countenance it, Bartleby? I should think my friends would have learned of my change of address by now. Parks definitely has my new direction as I have sent him two letters. Father would at least forward the letters on if they were sent home. At least I'd hope he would. I rather hate to ask Gavin about it because if there are no letters to forward, he will look at me with pity. About the only thing worse than a stern older brother is a sympathetic one.

22 June 1817

DEAR BARTLEBY,

Aunt Lily and Uncle Gregory came to tea today. Aunt Lily fusses just as much as Mama does. Quite glad I'm living here and not there. At one point, Charles critiqued my posture, which Aunt Lily took as permission to also interject with her opinion. They just returned from taking one of my cousins to London for the Season, so she was full of talk about the latest fashions and seemed to feel she was an expert on society in general. Uncle Gregory was pleasant enough, although his resemblance to Father is uncanny and, frankly, unnerving. I'm sure I shouldn't be surprised since he is his younger brother. Still, it was strange because he looks and sounds a great deal like Father, but he's softer in tone and more inclined to smile and make jokes about things. Aunt Lily told me to be sure I come and visit now that they were at home. I must confess, I was pleased for once that I am restricted to Kentworthy's property. Thank heavens I managed to dodge that obligation. I have no desire to have another set of adults tell me what I'm doing wrong, particularly when one of them looks like my father.

Decided to swallow some of my pride and wrote a few letters today. I feel that it is very low of my friends to make me write to them first when I am the one who was sent away. Nevertheless, here we are. Since it seems unlikely that I shall be returning, at least anytime soon, I suppose I had better take some responsibility in maintaining the friendships I made at Oxford. Wrote to Warrow and Forrester, sent another letter to Parks, and told them all where they might find me should they care to write. Gave each an account of how I'm getting on and said that I'm unlikely to return. Asked how things are going with them and if there is any gossip I've missed since I've been away.

God, my hand is cramping something awful now.

23 June 1817

DEAR BARTLEBY,

Working through the list with Gerry still. You know, she's actually very smart. She had some marvelous suggestions for memorizing things. We're clipping along at a decent pace now. When I asked her why memorizing the list was so frightfully important, she said that strong magical abilities seem to run in our family and it would be a good idea for me to get the best grounding possible. It is, honestly, the closest thing I've had to a compliment in quite some time. So then I didn't mind the prospect as much.

I was not best pleased when she turned the conversation to a more personal one.

"Are you missing your friends?" she asked.

"Of course," I said, shrugging. "I wrote them all letters yesterday."

"Yes, I saw them on the stack to go out."

Then she looked so blasted contemplative that I had to ask what she was thinking.

"Well," she said at last. "I'm sorry you miss them, but I can't help but be glad you're not around people who talk to you the way your friends and lovers do."

I sighed. Gerry has said this sort of thing every time I wrote to her about my friends or my time at Oxford. "I don't know how many times I have to tell you that this is how friends talk. My friends are always teasing me. It's perfectly normal. And calling Warrow my lover makes the whole thing sound decidedly more serious than it really was. It was all a lark, you know."

She gave me a dubious look.

"Oh, do stop looking at me that way. You only think I'm wrong because you always have to be perfect about everything."

"I rather think you should talk to Gavin then," she said primly. "Or Charles. I'm sure they would agree with my assessment."

"Very well," I said. "I will. Just to prove to you that I'm right."

I might bring it up to Gavin if I happen to think of it.

24 June 1817

DEAR BARTLEBY,

By my reckoning, my letters should arrive at Oxford either today or tomorrow. Which means that I should receive letters within the next, oh, four to five days. I'm strangely eager about it. I daresay I didn't realize I missed everyone quite so much. I'm sure there will be a lot of teasing about my being stuck in the country. But perhaps one or two of them could be persuaded to visit. I'm sure Kentworthy would approve of it. That is, I'd hope he would.

Finlington came to dinner again last night. He mentioned putting in an advertisement for an assistant. Said he's been at a loss since someone named Nell left his employ last year.

Gerry kept giving me long, considering looks when we worked on the list afterward. I finally asked her what had her thinking so hard. But she pretended not to know what I was talking about.

25 June 1817

DEAR BARTLEBY,

Bumped into Standish when I was wandering through the gardens before dinner last night. Do you know I'd almost forgotten I planned to seduce him? Remembered as soon as I saw him because he was breathtaking in the evening light. He joined me in my stroll and asked how my studies were getting along. He commiserated with me on Magical Theory and said he finds theory easier to understand when he knows the practical side of it first.

He asked me if I was enjoying my stay and, frankly, I didn't know what to tell him. Am I enjoying myself now? It is surprisingly hard to say. I'm certainly not having as much fun as I had at Oxford. I feel as though I'm left alone a lot of the time, which is trying since I am not used to it. And it smarts a bit to be doing so much out of punishment.

I don't know how to explain it, but I can tell Gavin and Kentworthy and Gerry are pleased with whatever progress or whatnot they are seeing in me. I can't tell that I'm changing so very much, but there are fewer tense looks when I'm in the room than there were when I first arrived.

I was so wrapped up in where my thoughts went with his question that I completely forgot to try to whisper something sweet in his ear.

I was thinking about that all last night when I went to bed. I'm quite sure Gavin and Kentworthy would be very displeased if I did try to seduce him, and I'm not sure I want that. It has been surprisingly pleasant to not be disapproved of for once.

26 June 1817

DEAR BARTLEBY,

Have finally completed Gerry's list and we're moving on to theories and diagrams. I have learned these things in school, but no one has made me actually take notes and learn it all properly. I feel as though I am learning it for the first time all over again.

Gerry has told me that next month she will start putting me through more practical magical exercises. I do know how to do all of that—I can cast spells very well and I've even mastered quite a few Motion spells—but I'm rather thrilled to finally move on to something other than books and reports and essays.

She asked me if I managed to talk to Gavin or Kentworthy about our discussion on friendships. I hadn't, so I had to immediately go find Gavin to keep Gerry from pestering.

It was a decidedly trickier conversation to initiate than I anticipated. I found Gavin and Kentworthy coming in from an evening stroll in the garden. I hadn't really planned to ask them both, so I was suddenly very nervous and it must have shown on my face because they both immediately reacted with concern.

"Everything all right?" Kentworthy said.

"Oh, yes," I said. "Just hoping you could settle a debate for me."

"Debate between you and who else?" Gavin said.

"Gerry, of course. You don't think I'd be debating with Mr. Standish, do you?"

Kentworthy smirked and led us both to a sitting room. "All right then, Sebastian," he said as soon as he and Gavin were settled. "Tell us."

It's all well and good to brag about my exploits to Gerry via letter, Bartleby, but trying to explain that in conversation was very awkward. I cleared my throat several times, trying to come up with the right way to start.

"Oh, for heaven's sake," Gavin said. "What on earth are you talking to Gerry about that you can't bring up to us?"

I huffed. "Well, you see, it's like this. I was describing some…er…intimate experiences I've had at Oxford to her…"

Gavin rolled his eyes and Kentworthy looked like he was trying not to laugh.

"Highly inappropriate, of course," Gavin said. "But go on."

"And I was telling her about this fellow, Warrow. Friend of mine. Devilishly good looking, you know. He was always a marvelously good bedmate, and I was telling Gerry about how he would always…erm…tease me, you know?"

Gavin's brow furrowed. "Tease you?"

"Yes, you know. How friends tease each other. Joked about my knobby knees or would make a cutting remark about my performance or something."

"He did this in bed?" Gavin said, looking mildly horrified.

"Yes," I said, a little exasperated by his reaction. "And Gerry said that friends don't do that sort of thing but, hang it all, everyone I know talks like that. At least to some extent. So I know it isn't all that peculiar. I've been explaining to Gerry that it's just how blokes talk to each other. And she said she didn't believe me."

I looked at them expectantly.

Gavin let out a long breath. "I suppose I can't give you

much by way of comparison, Seb," he said at last. "I didn't experience any intimacy before marriage. And I did not have a great many friends at university. However, I can tell you that of the few I did have, none of them were particularly cutting."

"Never?" I said incredulously.

He shrugged. "Not really. Although, I kept to myself mostly. So it's possible I'm not the right person to ask. Charles?"

Kentworthy gave me a measured look. Finally, he said, "Did you enjoy the way he spoke to you?"

I shifted in my seat. "What do you mean?"

"Did it make the experience more pleasurable to you?"

"Er...no, but I always assumed that was just his way."

"Well, like you, Sebastian, I did experience a great deal of intimacy while at university. I confess I had multiple partners before meeting your brother. But never," he went on, "have I had someone insult me while I was in bed with them. Regardless of gender, that is something none of my partners did. And if a friend were to do so, I wouldn't count them as such."

"Oh," I said. "Not even just...you know...good-natured teasing?"

"Never," he said in a gentle tone. "There are, of course, particular tastes to that type of thing. So under different circumstances, it wouldn't be an issue. But if you did not enjoy it and if you did not agree to being treated in such a way, his behavior was grossly inappropriate."

"Were all of your friends like that?" Gavin said.

"No, not all of them," I said in as airy a tone as I could muster. I felt incredibly foolish because they kept looking at me with these pitying and studious expressions. I couldn't stand it, so I got up and said, "Well, thank you for settling the debate. I'll go tell Gerry, shall I?"

"Seb," Gavin said.

"Oh, do stop looking at me like that," I said as I backed

out of the room. "My friends have a different sense of humor than yours do, clearly. That's all. I'm just irritated that Gerry was right. How is she always so infuriatingly perfect all the time?" I could tell Gavin was going to say something else, so I hurried out before he could.

I must admit, Bartleby, I did not tell Gerry that she was right. Which is cowardly, I know. But I simply cannot stand having yet another person looking at me in that sad way.

27 June 1817

Dear Bartleby,

Went to the village with Kentworthy today. He said I was wearing out my green coat and the elbows were looking thin. So he took me to a tailor to get fitted for a new one. I did not have high hopes for the venture since Tutting-on-Cress is so very small. But Kentworthy assured me he has found the quality to be very satisfactory.

I was rather surprised that he should put forth the expense. After all, I'm still Father's responsibility, technically. I said as much to him when we were walking back home and he said he didn't have any younger siblings of his own and that he adores spoiling people.

"Oh, really?" I said, "And you consider a rigorous schooling regimen to be spoiling a person?"

"Not all that rigorous, I think," he said. "You don't have a tutor, after all."

I huffed rather than say anything that would encourage him along that line of thought.

He smiled as if he knew exactly what I was thinking. "How are you getting on, Sebastian? Truly?"

I shrugged. "Well, enough, I suppose."

"Not bored anymore, I hope?"

"God, no," I said hurriedly.

He smirked. "Glad to hear it." He paused. "Do you want

to talk about our conversation last night?"

"Decidedly not," I said. "I'm just glad Gerry will stop harping on about it now."

"Well, if you change your mind, do let me know. As Gavin said last night, he has less experience than you do, even. If you would like advice on anything you cannot go to Gavin or Gerry for, please know you can always come to me."

I stuffed my hands in my pockets and kicked at a pebble. "Thank you." We walked in silence for a few minutes. "For what it's worth," I said. "No one calls me Sebastian except my parents and John."

"Noted," he said. "And I do not expect family to call me Kentworthy."

I was startled into looking up at him.

"Don't look so surprised," he said, chuckling. "I've always wanted a younger brother and I quite like your company when you aren't being a rascal."

I grinned. "No one ever believes me when I tell them I'm charming."

He laughed outright at that.

So I probably ought to refer to him as Charles here rather than Kentworthy, or else I'll get it wrong when I talk to him. I suppose I have three older brothers now. Is that a good thing, I wonder?

28 June 1817

DEAR BARTLEBY,

Lord Finlington came by again today and, to my complete shock, was here to see me.

He met me in the sitting room and was very polite and chattery, as per usual. He must have seen the confusion on my face because he cut right to the point.

"You may have heard, darling," he said, "that I am in need of an assistant."

I nodded. "I believe you said you were putting in an advertisement."

"Excellent," he said. "You do pay attention. How marvelous. As it happens, I did not put in an advertisement after all. I have been discussing the matter with your family, you see, and Gerry suggested you might be a good solution, at least for the time being."

"Me? As a gentleman's assistant?"

He smiled. "Well, m'dear, it is really more along the lines of a spellcaster's assistant."

"Oh," I said. I had no idea Finlington was the sort of spellcaster who required an assistant. It was a remarkable revelation for I found I was rather curious about the position.

He continued, "I know you are not staying here permanently, so it will only be until you leave. Assuming you wish to do it, that is. Last year, I employed a young woman named Nell Birks while I was still living in London. I had never had an assistant before and I found her to be invaluable. The work is not too difficult. You will primarily be helping me prepare my workspace and clean it up when I'm done. You have different education and experience than Nell did, so I might change some of the tasks accordingly. Does it sound like something that would appeal to you?"

"It does, but I'm not sure I'd be allowed to," I ventured. "I am meant to stay at the house, you know."

He laughed. "Yes, m'dear. I am aware. However, Charlie and Gavin are supportive of this idea."

"Really?" I said, sitting a little straighter.

"There will be some rules, of course," he went on. "You would be expected to travel straight between your house and mine, and there may be some alterations to your daily schedule to accommodate it. As I understand it, you are here so that you might learn responsibility. Working for me would provide that. And," he added, "there would of course be some compensation for your work. I shall pay you wages.

Gerry and I are considering the possibility of splitting your magic lessons between the two of us, should you accept."

"You want to teach me magic?"

"Well," he replied with a smile. "Between you and me, m'dear, that little trap spell you placed in the servants' quarters was quite the clever invention. I should like to see you put your talents to better use, of course, than frightening the poor maids. How else to ensure that than to teach you m'self?"

I was a little stunned. "Oh," I said. "Well, if it really is all right. I think I should like that."

"Excellent," he said, clapping his hands. "You will start tomorrow. Charlie will work out your new schedule. I'm sure we shall get along famously, darling."

Then he left to go talk to Charles.

It would appear I am now a man of employment, Bartleby.

29 June 1817

DEAR BARTLEBY,

My new schedule is as follows:

I wake up early to ride with Charles—that is still on.

Then, breakfast, my studies, lunch.

After lunch, I walk to Finlington's house, work with him through tea, and walk home.

Then I have my contemplation time followed by dinner.

My leisure time has now been moved to after dinner and I am no longer required to socialize with everyone unless I wish to.

30 June 1817

DEAR BARTLEBY,

Working for Finlington is a unique experience. First off, he insists I call him Bertie. I suppose I am addressing everyone by their first names now, except for Standish. My work with him is mostly mundane, moving furniture when he has to do particularly large spells and that kind of thing. He asked me how comfortable I was with taking notes and I assured him I was very comfortable. I prepare the space for him, he sets up the spell, performs the casting, he makes observations as I take down the notes, and then I clean it all up for him.

It shouldn't be fun, Bartleby. I daresay I shall hate it eventually, but it is fascinating stuff. The man can do magic I've never even seen before. Most remarkable. I am now definitely looking forward to the prospect of having him teach me. Although no one has explained how that will work out yet.

1 July 1817

DEAR BARTLEBY,

Am exhausted. Riding early in the morning and walking to and from Bertie's house every day is far more activity than I am accustomed to. Not to mention the fact that my work as his assistant is often fairly physical in terms of moving and cleaning things. I am on my feet quite a bit now.

Wrote simply gobs of notes for Bertie today. Hand cramping up. Cannot write anymore.

2 July 1817

DEAR BARTLEBY,

Bertie saw me flicking my hand today to ease the cramping I was still getting when I wrote—don't forget, I still have to study and write reports and all sorts of things in the mornings—and he showed me how to make a balm to soak my hand in. Worked a treat, I can tell you.

Also learned that he is apparently being considered for the position of Royal Spellcaster to the Crown. Or maybe he's considering the position. Mighty lofty stuff. I asked him if it meant he would go back to London, and he smiled and said, "I daresay I shall have to go there occasionally. I rather like the idea of spending some amount of time here and there, for I do enjoy both places exceedingly. As I'm sure you understand, darling, nearly all the people I love most are here now, so I'm not sure London holds quite the same appeal as it used to."

I did not know what to say to that. I should also note that he did not promise to take me with him if he went to London, which is a shame, for I dearly want to go.

3 July 1817

Dear Bartleby,

I have been wondering whether Gavin is really checking to see if I'm writing in this thing. But, I have discovered, he truly is. I walked into the library this evening for my contemplation period and he was flipping through the pages to see that they were all written in. He was going far too fast to actually read any of it so I'm glad to know he really did mean it when he said he wasn't reading my entries. He didn't seem embarrassed at being caught at it. He simply said, "You're doing very well, Seb. I'm proud of you." Then he walked out.

I can't stop thinking about it, really. I'm not sure Gavin's ever said he's proud of me. I'm not sure anyone has ever been proud of me.

4 July 1817

Dear Bartleby,

Not in a particularly fine mood today, I'm afraid. Finally got a response to one of the letters I sent over a fortnight ago. I received it while I was in the library doing my studies. It was from Parks. All he really had to say was that I must have simply oodles of coin now since I'm sitting around cooling my heels in the country. So could I possibly spot him for a bit of a gaming debt he ran up? I was so angry he had taken this long to respond and didn't even ask how I was that I balled up the letter, tossed it on the floor, and left the library at once.

I paced around the garden, fuming for a good while. Is it really too much to ask for my friends to ask after my health? To miss me in the slightest? It was all perfectly galling.

What made it worse was that Gavin came and found me while I was pacing about.

"Are you all right?" he asked.

I waved my hand to halt his incoming worries. "Just getting a bit of air, that's all."

He frowned and said, "Does it have anything to do with the letter in the library?"

I turned and looked at him. "You read it?"

He huffed. "Don't be an idiot. You know I'd never do that. But it was balled up and on the floor, so it must have irritated you. Do you want to talk about it?"

"'Course not," I said. "It was just a letter from my friend, Parks. He was being a prat, as usual. Got me in a miff."

He was looking unconvinced and, what is worse, very concerned. This put me in an even fouler mood, so I stepped past him and started back to the house. "I'll go back to my studies then."

Thankfully, he did not follow me inside.

5 July 1817

Dear Bartleby,

I was thinking about it all last night and all day today. I have come to the horrifying conclusion that my friends are quite dreadful. It is a sobering thought. Some evidence, should you doubt my assessment:

Forrester did help me with assignments when I asked, but she was an absolute pig about it. She would always tell me I was an idiot for not understanding things properly. While she did help me write several essays, she never did it for free. I had to pay her to do it one time, another time I had to play cupid for her to win Vincent Abernathy's heart (little though she deserves him), and then there was the time she made me give up my favorite book in exchange. I don't know why I gave the beastly woman so much respect. I daresay she didn't deserve it.

I'd always thought Warrow was rather sporting about the whole vomiting thing, but then I started thinking about how unkind he was afterward. He was awfully good in bed, but I still think he was the one who started that one rumor last year. I know he denied it, but truly. Making everyone believe I was in love with Professor Shelley is exactly the sort of rumor Warrow would start. I suppose I always accepted his ridiculing because he's attractive enough to get any fellow he wants. It always seemed like such an honor to be in bed with him. Perhaps I was giving him more credit than he deserved, if Charles was telling the truth.

And then Parks is the blasted person who talked me into all those pranks in the first place. I'm sure he wouldn't have thought twice about the cruelty of it all, as I have. Do you know, even when it was his suggestion, I was always the one who was blamed. He was always abusing my character, which at the time seemed normal and simply what friends do. But since coming here, I've realized that nobody has spoken to me in the way any of my friends did, least of all the way Parks or Warrow did. I'm not sure why I put up with it.

God, I'm the biggest clodpole that ever lived, aren't I, Bartleby? No, don't answer that.

The worst of it is that Gavin has been saying for simply ages that my friends are terrible. I hate that he was right about it. Maybe it isn't an entirely bad thing that I was sent here after all. Of course I can never tell any of this to Gavin or Gerry. Or Charles. They'd all tell me I was utterly daft. And I daresay they'd be right. What a humbling revelation it is. I'm not at all pleased about it, I need hardly tell you.

6 July 1817

Dear Bartleby,

I regret to inform you that the plan to seduce Standish is most decidedly and unequivocally put to rest. He is not exactly a single gentleman after all. I walked to Bertie's house today for my usual work and found him having tea with Standish. They were sitting on the same sofa and—well, I don't know how to describe it, really. For they weren't even touching. But they were looking at each other with such obvious affection that I felt a pang at the sight.

Bertie noticed me standing in the doorway, looking like a prize idiot, and greeted me. I was so embarrassed for having caught them in what was likely an intimate moment that I begged off for the afternoon, claiming I did not feel quite the thing.

Bertie was all solicitous and they both looked worried, which made me feel like a complete rotter. But I managed to talk Bertie out of sending for his carriage and I walked home.

So, not only was I completely idiotic about my friends, I was also completely idiotic about this. Thank God I never actually put forth much of an effort to seduce Standish. I shudder to think what a cake I'd make of myself. Now I can see why Gavin tried warning me off. I'm so bloody foolish.

The worst part of all of this, Bartleby, is that I've come to the realization that I haven't a single friend, really. Now I'm in the middle of nowhere and, even though I'm living with a number of people...well, I'm left a great deal to my own devices. Not that this is anything new, really. I mean to say, before I went to school, I was often left to my own devices too. Not that Gavin and Gerry didn't try, of course. But it isn't quite so fun being invited along out of pity rather than actual preference. I mean, I really don't think I've ever had anyone prefer my company to anyone else's. Certainly no one in my family does. Even in school, I was still tagging along with people, only instead of my siblings, it was Parks and everyone. At least then I had a purpose, you know? Granted, my purpose was to provide entertainment with pranks, but still there was a purpose to my being there.

And what's more, it would appear that Gerry is the only other person in the entire house who is unattached. She at least has friends, simply loads of them. God, I don't think I've felt this alone since my first term at Oxford. No one would talk to me then either, except to tease me. It wasn't until Parks dared me to pull a prank that anyone noticed me at all.

Not sure how I shall face Standish at dinner. No one has noticed I'm home yet, but I daresay they'll wonder why I left Bertie's so quickly. Perhaps I shall complain of the headache. Gerry will probably fuss. What a nuisance it all is.

7 July 1817

Dᴇᴀʀ Bᴀʀᴛʟᴇʙʏ,

Well, I was right and there was a great deal of fussing. Gerry suggested I've been too much in the sun, and Charles was worried he had pushed me into too busy a schedule, and Gavin kept pestering me about Parks's damn letter and asked if that was why I've been so off lately. In the end, Gerry sent me to bed with a remedy for the headache and said it would help me to sleep. I didn't have the headache, of course, but I took the remedy anyway and slept until this morning. I got up earlier than my usual time and rang for my valet, got dressed, and went out riding before Charles had made it to the stables.

And yes, I know it was perfectly rude to do such a thing,

but I really needed time to think. The horse seemed a bit jumpy, probably because I'd taken her out so early, so I went back before I'd barely ridden a mile away from the house.

Charles was waiting for me, as was Gavin, to my shock and embarrassment. Gavin was in his banyan as if he'd come down in a hurry, so I suspect Charles went and fetched him as soon as he realized I'd gone off alone. I was sure I was in for a great lecture, but when I dismounted I could see that neither of them was angry. They didn't say a word as they led me to the library and closed the door. I was sat down on a settee, Gavin sat next to me, and Charles pulled up a chair across from me.

Then Gavin said, "I don't know what has you in such a fit of pique, Seb, but it has lasted for days now. For heaven's sake, what is the matter?"

"I don't wish to talk about it."

"Is it the letter?"

I sighed. "I do wish you would stop harping on about that."

"Bertie said you looked stricken when you showed up at his house," Charles said. "Did something happen along the way?"

"No," I said. "It's truly nothing. Do stop fussing."

"Seb," Gavin said, his voice sounding unusually harsh. "You know perfectly well that stubbornness runs in our family. I assure you I can keep this up just as long as you can. Stop trying to put us off. It won't work."

I said nothing.

Gavin sighed. He put a hand on my back and said in a softer tone, "Then does it have something to do with Bartleby?"

I looked up in shock. "I thought you didn't read my entries."

"I don't," he said. "But I could hardly help but notice that every single entry is addressed to him. Who is he?"

Now, I felt very silly indeed. "It's no one."

"Darling," Charles said, "You can tell us any—"

"No," I said, cutting him off. "I mean it really is no one. It's just...a way I write in my journal." They both looked completely baffled, so I sighed and continued, "It felt silly to just be writing to myself all the time. I wanted to have someone to write to, even if it was nobody at all. So I invented Bartleby. And yes, I know it is utterly foolish and ridiculous."

"Oh," Gavin said after a moment. "I see. I thought it might have been a friend from school."

"I have no friends at school," I said, before I could stop myself.

"You have loads of friends. You talk about them all the time. You sent all those letters," Gavin said. "I thought—"

"They didn't write back to me," I responded. "Well, Parks did, but only to ask me for money." I scrubbed through my hair. "I've come to the ghastly conclusion that I'm a completely terrible judge of character. So, go ahead and get the scolding over with, if you please."

"Oh, Seb," Gavin said softly. "How awful for you."

It was not what I was expecting to hear. I glanced up in surprise.

"Why didn't you tell us you were so lonely, darling?" Charles said. "We could have done something about it."

"Lonely?" I said. "Don't be ridiculous, Charles."

"Perhaps we ought to sit in here during his studies so he's not by himself all the time," Charles said to Gavin.

"I beg you to not," I said.

"I daresay it might help," Gavin said, completely ignoring me. He began rubbing circles across my back as if to soothe me. "Besides, he's shown marked improvement when he has someone working with him."

"Are you even listening to me?"

"I'll talk to Gerry," Charles added. "She mentioned that

Bertie might help with the magic lessons. Perhaps he should take over for the time being. He can teach Seb when he goes to his house every day."

"It's like I'm not even in the room," I said.

Charles chuckled and reached forward to clasp my hand. "I'm so sorry, Seb. It would seem we have been neglecting you."

"I don't like the sound of that," I said. "The last time you said something like that, I got saddled with schoolwork and an absurdly busy schedule."

Charles smiled. "My dear, I think we all know by now that you like being busy."

"Don't need to be so smug about it," I grumbled.

"I know," Gavin said. He dropped his hand from my back and leaned his arm against the back of the settee. "He is so insufferable when he's right, isn't he? I'm always telling him this."

"Well, if you Hartfords weren't so stubborn all the time, you might realize sooner when I'm right about things."

Gavin rolled his eyes. "Impossible man," he said with obvious affection.

I was, I confess, a little at a loss with this exchange.

Charles seemed to notice my confusion for he laughed, stood, framed my head with his hands, and kissed me on the top of my head as though I were a small child. "Thank you for telling us, Seb. I'm glad we were able to get it sorted out."

Gavin stood next to his husband. "Just tell us sooner next time, all right? Much easier for everyone."

Charles nodded in agreement and they both turned to leave the room.

"Don't you want breakfast?" Charles said over his shoulder.

I have to say, Bartleby, my family is the most confounded nuisance.

8 July 1817

DEAR BARTLEBY,

Have been here over two months and it strangely feels as though I've been here forever and also for no time at all. Bertie told me today that he and Gerry are discussing how best to split up my magic lessons between the two of them. They haven't decided the best method yet, considering their schedules and mine. But he said he expects to start teaching me next month. Although that does mean I will have more studies to do on top of everything else. Needs must, I suppose.

9 July 1817

DEAR BARTLEBY,

Charles was not joking about changing my study period. I am now always with someone, except during my contemplation time and my leisure time—well, for the latter, it's optional, as I can always join everyone in the sitting room. Which, now that I think about it, I almost always do. I suppose I'm alone when I'm walking to and from Bertie's house, but otherwise, someone is always at my side. It makes me feel a bit odd, to be perfectly frank. To have admitted to being lonely and have it listened to so earnestly. Although, I don't think I actually did admit to anything. But you know what I mean. They both inferred it and now they're both striving to correct it.

Part of me feels as if I am being watched over, but another part of me...well, really, Bartleby, it is rather nice to have someone to talk to more often. It is usually Gavin or Charles sitting in the library with me, so it is nice not having to hunt around for someone when I have questions. When it's Charles, he'll interrupt my studies every half hour or so to ask me how it's going. When it's Gavin, studies are broken up about once an hour with a quick walk in the garden or a pot of tea being brought in.

I don't know that I've ever had so much company in my entire life, and that's the truth. I suppose in Oxford I was usually around people, but it was not always quite so companionable. I did not know how much I should like to have company until I did. It is a little irksome that they should know me better than I know myself. What a trial it is to be a younger sibling.

10 July 1817

DEAR BARTLEBY,

Had managed to avoid talking to Standish for a couple of days, but he approached me last night before dinner and asked if I might take a stroll in the garden with him. I very nearly turned him down, for I am still very embarrassed about my behavior on Sunday and I'm sure he recognizes that I had hoped to pursue him. Rejecting his invitation would have made it all the worse so I reluctantly agreed to join him.

We walked through the shrubbery in silence for a few minutes and I had begun to believe that he really just wanted some quiet company when he said at last, "I believe I owe you an apology, Mr. Hartford."

I looked at him in surprise. "I can't imagine what for," I said.

"I said something to you shortly after your arrival that was a bit unfair."

I frowned, trying to think back on our past conversations.

"When you flirted with me in Gerry's shop—" (God, Bartleby, I'm sure I was absolutely bright red when he said this.) "—I said that you were very unlike your siblings." He stopped and turned to look at me, a small crease between his eyebrows. "I was wrong. I hope you will forgive me."

I had no idea what to say to this. Finally, I managed, "I confess I was confused by your meaning then. I still am."

He smiled a little. "I'm not particularly comfortable with flirtations," he said. "Your family, and Bertie, have been very…considerate of that discomfort. I was so surprised by your interest that I was unkind about it."

I looked down and kicked at the gravel with my shoe. "I wish you wouldn't apologize, Mr. Standish," I said. "You had every right to react that way. Gavin warned me not to flirt with you and I did it anyway."

"To be honest, I thought you had given up after I blocked your attempt to get me alone in the garden."

I looked up at him. "You knew about that?"

He chuckled. "Why do you think I came out with chaperones?"

"Oh, God." I said, covering my face with my hands.

He gently took my wrists and pulled them down. "However," he said softly, "you never tried again. I was sure you had lost interest. Until you walked in when Bertie and I were having tea. I saw the expression on your face and—" He sighed. "I am sorry I didn't have the courage to talk to you about it sooner."

I'm sure I was still blushing furiously. "You don't owe me an explanation, Mr. Standish. I'm sorry I was such a cad."

He smiled and let go of my wrists. "You're not, actually. A cad, I mean. You are much more like Gerry and Gavin than you give yourself credit for. I daresay you will make another man very happy someday."

I looked down and kicked at the gravel again. "Not very likely to find another man when I'm stuck here all the time though, am I?"

"Oh, I don't know," he said, turning to lead us both back to the house. "You might be surprised. Tutting-on-Cress is small, but it has a funny way of giving a person what they need, even if they don't know yet what that may be."

"Is that what happened to you?" I said.

"Yes," he said. "It is."

"May I ask what it was?"

He turned and smiled at me and God, Bartleby, the man has the most beautiful dimples. "Myself," he said simply.

We said nothing more until we were at the door to the house. Then he paused and said, "I hope we can be friends, Mr. Hartford."

"I think I should like that," I said. "Although I'm very embarrassed that you knew all the time."

"Don't be," he said with a laugh. "Believe me, I've suffered far worse attention than yours. Friends?" he said, holding out his hand.

I shook it.

"I've never liked to be called Mr. Standish. Would you be so kind as to call me Pip?"

I smiled and squeezed his hand. "My friends—that is, I prefer to be called Seb."

So, Bartleby, it would appear I do have friends now. Or I should say, I have a friend. And that is something.

11 July 1817

Dear Bartleby,

Walked into Bertie's study today to find the man in a flurry of writing. He had piles of papers stacked on his desk.

He looked up when I came in and said, "Wonderful. You are so delightfully punctual, darling. Do you know?"

"Blame Charles," I said.

He laughed. "I have a great deal of work for you today. But it shall be a bit different."

"Does it have to do with all of this?" I said, gesturing at the stacks of papers.

"Yes. Do take a seat, dear." He propped his elbows on the desk and folded his hands together in front of them. "I believe you are aware that I have been offered the position of Royal Spellcaster, yes?"

I nodded.

He paused and then said, "A little while ago, I submitted my refusal for the post."

"What?" I said. "Why? You would be perfect for that position."

He smiled. "How kind, darling. I daresay it could be a very interesting experience. Nevertheless, I have given it a great deal of thought. I have come to the conclusion that I don't need the appointment. I have money, title, and property. I don't need a royal appointment on top of it all. I'm certainly never bored, having you sweet things as neighbors. So I have offered the crown a different service instead."

"What's that?"

"I have offered to find someone else. I hope you won't think me conceited when I say that I am one of the country's leading experts in determining a person's magical talents. I felt I would be more useful in finding the right person for the position. I have offered to bring three spellcasters to London. The crown will have final say in who is selected, but I will provide my own recommendation."

"You're going to find someone to take the job you were offered?"

"It is no great sacrifice, m'dear. I'll have a great deal more fun determining finalists than I would trotting back and forth to London all the time."

"Is that what you're doing right now?"

"In a manner of speaking. You see, I put forth an advertisement a fortnight ago, requesting spellcasters who were interested in the position to apply to me. These are the replies."

"Good Lord," I said.

"I am going through each one now and determining whether or not the applicant fits my requirements. Most do not, sadly. So I am putting those in a stack. You will be helping me respond to each letter, notifying the applicant that they are not to be considered."

"You're going to narrow it down to three from this?" I said, looking at a particularly large stack.

"No, darling. I'm going to narrow it down to about fifty. It will take some time. But I hope between the two of us we can work through it."

"This will take ages, Bertie. Isn't there a spell we could use?"

"None to my knowledge," he replied. "But if you come up with something in your free time, please don't hesitate to bring it forward. You know I love to experiment. Now, will you take this stack, dearest? The one on top is already written out so you can just copy what I've written down."

I hauled the stack over to his worktable and got started. We wrote in silence for about two hours before Bertie made us stop for tea. He whipped up a balm for us to soak our hands while we rested.

"What are you going to do with the fifty?" I asked.

"I'm so glad you asked, darling," he said, beaming at me. Bertie has a way of making every question seem brilliant. I rather like it. "I'm going to interview every applicant and narrow it down to a handful of people. Then I will have those people come here."

"Here? Whatever for?"

"So I can put them through their paces. Won't it be fun?"

"Does Gerry know about this?"

He smiled. "She does. She isn't interested, I'm afraid. It's a pity, really, for she would do an excellent job." He shrugged. "Ah well. Pip turned it down too."

"Pip? Is he a good spellcaster?"

"My darling, he is one of the most powerful spellcasters I've ever had the privilege to meet."

"Why did they turn it down?"

"You might ask them, dearest."

I privately resolved to do so.

All right. I've written far too much for one day. I'm going to soak my hand again.

12 July 1817

DEAR BARTLEBY,

Asked Gerry and Pip why they turned down the prospect of being Royal Spellcaster. Gerry said the position is technically for firstborns only. "I know Bertie would have fought for me," she added. "But I have no desire to fight for something that I'm not sure I'm interested in doing when I have a job I like perfectly well."

"But it's a royal appointment!"

"Yes," she said. "But even if I were to get it, how seriously will they take my advice? How much will they actually listen to me? I have no wish to be talked down to by a bunch of royal idiots. I have a shop of my own, my customers respect me, they like me. I have plenty of time to experiment in making new spells, which is what I really love best. I'm perfectly satisfied."

I did not understand her at all. Pip surprised me as well.

"I don't like London," he said simply.

"How can you not like London?" I asked, incredulous.

He smiled. "I lived there most of my life and I was perfectly miserable. I have never been happier than when I've lived here."

I am utterly shocked by how unambitious my family and friend are. Truly outrageous.

I wrote a great deal today as well, as you can ruddy imagine. Off to soak my hand.

13 July 1817

DEAR BARTLEBY,

My hand aches, my shoulders ache, my back aches. Going to see if I can have a bath instead of contemplation time.

14 July 1817

DEAR BARTLEBY,

Bertie has sorted through about half of the letters. I'm about halfway through the ones he's already sorted. Very slow going. Not much fun.

15 July 1817

DEAR BARTLEBY,

Determined to put an end to this madness. Used my leisure time last night to look up spells that might make this all go a bit faster. Found some illusion spells that might do the job, as well as a drawing spell. Going to ask Gerry when she gets home if any of them might work.

16 July 1817

DEAR BARTLEBY,

Gerry was intrigued by my idea, so we stayed up late looking over the spells I'd found. She thinks the drawing spell shows the most promise. The trick is to make it draw exactly what we need and also have recastability. I should like to make it work on multiple pens at once, but Gerry isn't entirely confident that this is a feasible goal. But I'll take what I can get. She promised to work on it while she was at the shop this week and see what she can come up with.

17 July 1817

DEAR BARTLEBY,

Nothing from Gerry yet. She said experiments take time. We may very well be done before she figures it out. But I suppose it would still be a useful spell to invent. Is it selfish of me to be annoyed that I might have helped invent a spell that won't even help me? How irritating.

18 July 1817

DEAR BARTLEBY,

Bertie has compiled a stack of fifty applicants. He said he wishes to interview the fifty and narrow it down from there. Glad to know there is an end in sight. We still have piles of rejections to go through, though.

19 July 1817

DEAR BARTLEBY,

Gerry says that she managed to get the drawing spell to write a legible and clear letter. But she added that it is so slow-going, it will not actually be very much help yet. She promised to keep working on it.

20 July 1817

DEAR BARTLEBY,

Bertie finished writing to his fifty applicants today. Now he is helping me work through the remaining rejections. We're going at a faster clip now that we're both doing it.

21 July 1817

DEAR BARTLEBY,

Gerry completed the spell! She sent Pip to tell us she was coming after she closed the shop and to make sure I stayed behind. It was incredible to watch. The spell is still not very fast, but Bertie was impressed. Gerry gave me a great deal of credit for the idea and for finding the initial spells to work with. It was quite gratifying. Bertie said once we finish the letters he's going to work on my magic lessons. He also said he was pleased to know I had such a good handle on the basics. It felt...well, it felt downright wonderful, Bartleby. They all seemed so impressed. Not just impressed. I daresay they were proud of me. And that was a singular experience. I'm not accustomed to it. I'm still floating on the sensation.

22 July 1817

DEAR BARTLEBY,

We have finished the letters! Gerry's spell definitely helped. We divided the remaining letters into three stacks: one for me, one for Bertie, and one for the spell. Bertie had me check back over all of the bespelled letters to make sure they turned out all right.

Now we wait for the fifty applicants to arrive for their interviews. Bertie informed me that he wants me there for notetaking. Must confess, it makes me feel a little grand and important to be a part of the whole process. I know I shall only be taking notes, but I will have contributed in finding the next Royal Spellcaster. I daresay even Father might be a little pleased to hear of it.

23 July 1817

DEAR BARTLEBY,

Bertie says the first interviews will take place in a few days. In the meantime, he is taking over my magic lessons. Which are, in a word, wonderful.

They *are* challenging, but it is exactly the sort of challenge I like. Even better, Bertie isn't training me like the professors at Oxford. That is, he isn't taking one spell and going through all of the theories behind it and explaining the history of it and then slowly making me put it together. No, he's assigning me problems to solve with magic. It is the most fun I've ever had.

He'll say things like, "I want you to move this book from the table to the shelf and I want you to do so without touching it and without damaging it." When I've done it, he'll put the book back and say, "Very good, darling. Now do it again and use a different spell." He doesn't rush me. Sometimes I have to go through and look up spells that will fit what he's asking me. I'm not allowed to use Motion spells yet as he wants me to master traditional casting first. I get it wrong quite often. But, Lord, it's a lark!

24 July 1817

DEAR BARTLEBY,

Talked about nothing but my magic lessons all through dinner. I don't know that I've talked so much since I came here. Gerry was fascinated with the way Bertie was teaching me.

"I'd never have thought to do it that way," she said.

"Bertie has a knack for knowing how to teach people magic in a way that works for them," Pip said. "He and Gerry taught me, you see," he added.

"Did he teach you the same way?"

"No," he said, laughing. "And I'm sure I would have hated learning your way. I was learning completely from scratch, so it was a little different. But he and Gerry would show me the spell before explaining the theory."

"You learned from scratch?" I asked.

He nodded. "I've only been doing magic for a year or so."

Gerry beamed at him. "I can't believe it has been such a short time. You're so very good at it. I forget you haven't known it all your life."

He ducked his head. Lord, the man is adorable.

"Nell learned a different way, too," Gerry said. "Bertie made her learn the theories completely before he even introduced her to practical spells. But that worked for her. She liked to know the 'why' of things."

I thought about it all night and I have no idea how he came upon the notion to teach me this way. I shall have to ask him.

25 July 1817

DEAR BARTLEBY,

Asked Bertie today how he came up with his method for teaching me.

"Your pranks, dearest," he said. "You go about magic from a problem-solving standpoint. It is quite brilliant. I'm merely working to explore that strength a bit. You see an end result and use magic to get to what you're imagining: a floating hen nest, a ghost in the window, a shortcut for letter-writing."

"Isn't that what magic is for?"

He shrugged. "Well, yes. But not everyone approaches it that way. Some people, like Gerry, take magic into pieces first and see how many ways they can assemble it. She sees a warming spell or a drying spell and experiments with it, changes it, expands it."

"And Pip?"

"He goes by intuition. He can feel magic, you see. It's a very rare thing. Not many people come by that without a great deal of training. It's a gift, really. His approach is all instinct, the theory is more of an afterthought."

"What about you?"

He smiled and chucked me under the chin. "I'll let you sort that one out, my sweet."

It was a rather baffling thing to say. Bertie really is quite mysterious when I think about it.

The first interview is tomorrow. I am to arrive at Bertie's house early. He even invited me to join him for lunch. So, as soon as my studies are over, I'm walking to his house to prepare. I shall be sitting behind him and taking notes. He wants the name of the applicant, where they come from, their age, and then he gave me a list of questions he plans to ask. He asked that I include a small description so he can keep track of which applicant is which. He wants to know how long they've been doing magic and if they can master common spells, advanced spells, and Motion spells. He is also going to make them do one of Gerry's spells—as no one else has cast them outside of Tutting-on-Cress—as he wants to see how the applicant handles a brand-new spell. He assures me he'll tell me what to write, but explained he doesn't want to have to pause in the interview to write it all down himself.

I'm a trifle nervous, actually. This seems so very important. What if I write down the wrong thing?

26 July 1817

DEAR BARTLEBY,

First interview went fairly smoothly. The applicant was a thin, reedy sort of fellow. Very nervous. Can't exactly blame him. Bertie was very kind, as usual, and tried to put the man at ease. He was also very good at telling me what to write. So I'm glad that's all right. The man had to do a few spells a couple of times over as he was so nervous. Felt a bit sorry for him, actually.

27 July 1817

DEAR BARTLEBY,

Pip walked with me to Bertie's house today so that he might join us for tea.

It's funny how different I expected our relationship to be when I first entered the house. But I'm finding I don't mind as much. I mean, he really is the most attractive person I've ever met. But I rather like having him to talk to. He always listens to what I have to say. He's very soft spoken, but as we're coming to know one another better, he's showing that he has a good sense of humor and a very, I don't know, tender sort of spirit. He never ever insults me. I've never known anyone like him before.

And before you suggest it, Bartleby. I'm not falling in love. It's just—I've never had a friend quite like him. I find I don't have to be anything other than who I am around him. He isn't expecting me to be funny or bold or charming. And I don't have to worry about misjudging his character as I met him through everyone else. If Gavin, Gerry, Charles, and Bertie all like the gentleman, then he is clearly a decent sort of person. It's a new experience, this friendship.

At tea, Bertie and Pip acted more like two friends than anything else. It is strange for I'm sure they have feelings for each other. But they aren't in the least bit affectionate and nobody talks about them as if they are a couple. I don't understand it at all. They both seem so very happy to be in each other's company, so I suppose it doesn't much matter.

Pip asked how my magic lessons were getting along and Bertie invited him to stay and watch. Pip asked if I minded. To be honest, I was nervous about the prospect. Bertie did say that Pip is one of the strongest spellcasters he's ever met. I didn't exactly fancy him observing my spellcasting. But it seemed rude to protest, so I pretended I didn't mind.

Bertie balanced a book on top of his globe and told me to spin the globe without making the book fall off. It took me several tries to get it right, which was quite embarrassing with Pip watching. But he didn't say anything cutting. Bertie is always encouraging, even when I make mistakes. So I didn't even have to ignore them both standing there, as they were both nice about it. I finally got it by casting two spells simultaneously. I had to find spells that didn't require incantations and only used hand signals for activation. It took quite a while to find what I needed. They were both breeze spells, but I had one circling the globe to get it to spin and one under the book to keep it from falling. It was very fiddly and I wasn't able to keep it up for very long, but Bertie pronounced himself satisfied.

Pip, I'm pleased to say, was very impressed. "You have a lot of control," he said while I was cleaning the spell up.

"Yes," Bertie agreed. "He does. When it comes to magic, our Seb is a master of restraint."

"Won't Father be surprised to hear that?" I said.

Bertie threw back his head and laughed and Pip smiled so broadly, his dimples showed.

It occurs to me, Bartleby, that I haven't written to Father once since I've been here.

28 July 1817

DEAR BARTLEBY,

Wrote to Father today. Told him about my studies—went into far too much detail about my magic lessons, I'm afraid—assured him I'm writing in my journal every day, and wrote about my job with Bertie. I feel a little guilty that I haven't written to him in the months I've been here. I didn't even respond to his letter to me. I apologized for all of that. Added a postscript that I was enjoying myself.

It occurred to me he might think I'm so improved I can go back to Oxford and that thought troubled me exceedingly. Isn't that strange? It was not that long ago that I was wanting to go back. Now I can't think of anything worse. I should hate to leave my magic lessons and miss out on helping Bertie while he picks out the finalists. And I would miss having Gavin, Gerry, Charles, Pip, and Bertie to talk to. Do you think Father might send for me? I'd better ask Gavin.

29 July 1817

DEAR BARTLEBY,

Talked to Gavin and he assured me Father will not send me back to Oxford as long as I continue to do well here.

"Is it possible you're enjoying yourself, Seb?" he asked. He looked solemn as ever, but there was a corner of his mouth twitching.

I shrugged in what I hoped was a casual way. "It's not so bad after all," I said.

"Admit it, you goose," he said, smirking. "You like living here."

I huffed. "You're as bad as Charles sometimes. Do you know that?"

He laughed and ruffled my hair in a very irritating way.

I'm sure I shall be teased about that now. But I am relieved that I won't have to leave any time soon. Don't tell anyone Bartleby, but I think I love it here.

30 July 1817

DEAR BARTLEBY,

We conducted another three interviews today. One was a

very severe sort of woman. To be perfectly honest, I was a little afraid of her. But she was very thorough and did all of her spellwork without any errors. Bertie was impressed.

He has warned me that the interviews will be daily now, as most of the people have replied with when they can come see him.

31 July 1817

DEAR BARTLEBY,

Two interviews today. They were a married couple, which was interesting.

1 August 1817

DEAR BARTLEBY,

Another four interviews today. None of them particularly noteworthy, except that one was a gentleman who had tied a phenomenal cravat. I almost asked him how he did it.

2 August 1817

DEAR BARTLEBY,

Five more interviews today. One of them sneezed all through the interview. She even sneezed during her casting. Quite frankly, it was a little impressive. I mean, her sneeze didn't disrupt her magic at all!

3 August 1817

DEAR BARTLEBY,

Three interviews today. Bertie escorted me home in his carriage and then stayed for dinner. We talked of nothing but the current interview process. My studies are to halt temporarily so that I might assist Bertie all day until they are done.

4 August 1817

DEAR BARTLEBY,

First day coming straight to Bertie's after breakfast. We had eight interviews today. One of them was a man who, I swear, was mentally undressing me the entire time. Couldn't decide if I liked it or not. He did have very lovely eyes and a rather fine mouth. Ordinarily, I would be quite enthused by such attention, but he had a look in his eyes that I didn't quite like, even if they were lovely.

Oh, and Father responded to my letter. Did not suggest I go back to Oxford, thank heavens.

5 August 1817

DEAR BARTLEBY,

Seven interviews today. Notable applicants include a major with gleaming Hessian boots, a lady who brought her dog with her, and the tallest man I've ever met in my life. He was even taller than Charles.

6 August 1817

DEAR BARTLEBY,

Another eight today. One of the applicants was a local from Tutting-on-Cress. Walked here, if you can believe it. Bertie seemed impressed with him. He's quite handsome actually, had a very nice smile. Looked familiar, but as I don't really know anyone here I imagine he just reminds me of someone I know or I saw him in passing. Although I like to think I usually have a better memory about faces. At any rate,

Bertie had to give him a different spell to try as the applicant had already done most of Gerry's spells. There was also a very shy young lady who wore glasses. I rather expected her to be like the first bloke and get so nervous she flubbed her spells. But she didn't, so I guess she wasn't nervous, only quiet by nature.

7 August 1817

DEAR BARTLEBY,

Last eight interviews done. One man tried to get me to fetch him tea today. I was not fond of that.

Another was a very sweet old lady who brought us a tea cake. I quite liked her. But she didn't have the Motion spells mastered. Pity. She made wonderful tea cake.

8 August 1817

DEAR BARTLEBY,

Bertie told me to take the day off. He said he has to go through my notes and make up his mind. Also said I've been working very hard and that I deserve to relax.

Of course, it is very hard to relax when all I want is to know who Bertie plans to pick. I am not good at being patient, Bartleby. You probably know this by now.

9 August 1817

DEAR BARTLEBY,

Went back today and Bertie gave me a rejection letter to copy. I used the spell Gerry made and got all forty-four letters written today. The remaining six are going to come for about a month while he gets to know them and determines their talent, their work ethic, and their personality. He also said something about having a ball at the end to announce the three finalists, and my God, Bartleby, I'm practically giddy at the thought. I adore dancing and it has been ever so long!

He had stacked all of my notes into the piles of the people who were rejected and the people who are coming to stay. The six are: the severe woman from the beginning who intimidated me, the military man, the shy and quiet woman with the glasses, the man with the lovely eyes, the man who asked me to fetch him tea, and the man who lives here in town. I wonder if the local one will stay at Bertie's or if he'll just travel here every day like I do. Not entirely thrilled about the intimidating woman or the man who mistook me for a footman. But I'm sure Bertie knows what he's on about.

10 August 1817

Dear Bartleby,

Letters have all been sent out. The applicants will arrive next week. I was surprised by the turnaround, but Bertie said his first letters had provided an idea of his anticipated timeline, so hopefully they will all be prepared. Today Bertie sat me down and explained what to expect with everyone here. He is treating it a bit like a house party, a bit like a training program, and a bit like an extended interview. Because of this, I'm to revert to my usual schedule of studies in the morning, but I'm to come over before lunch. He says he wants me to get to know all of the applicants. After lunch, the applicants will have some leisure time, and Bertie will give me my magic lessons during that period. Then, instead of assisting him with his casting, I will assist him with whatever exercises he puts the applicants through and I shall be taking notes at his dictation. I'll be eating dinner at home.

Isn't it strange that I was so lonely before and now I shall be simply surrounded by people all the time?

I'm quite excited to begin.

And I'm prodigiously glad that my magic lessons will resume.

11 August 1817

Dear Bartleby,

It was a bit of a comfort to go back to my old routine today. Charles sat with me during my studies and explained how royal appointments, like the Royal Spellcaster, work. They are not exactly lifelong appointments, but essentially permanent until the King or the Prince Regent decides they want someone new. The current Royal Spellcaster is quite old, apparently, which is why they're looking for a new one. But as he's still alive, we have some time to find his replacement. Anyway, it was good of him to explain it all to me.

Bertie made me fold a shirt from across the room with magic. I did not do a particularly phenomenal job on that one, I'm afraid. At one point he realized that I didn't even know how a shirt is meant to be folded. So he called in his valet, who showed me how it's done properly by hand. I had to learn that first before I could try the spell again. Still couldn't get it right. So Bertie told me to practice at home and try again tomorrow.

12 August 1817

Dear Bartleby,

Who knew a shirt would pose such challenges? The trouble is I can get it in more or less the right shape, but I can't get it to look crisp. It's all floppy and bunched every time. Practiced in the library during my leisure time last night until Gavin came in and said I really had to go to bed.

13 August 1817

DEAR BARTLEBY,

Still couldn't get the folding spell right, so Bertie is having me continue to practice at home, but gave me a different problem to solve during our usual lesson. This time I had to pour a pitcher of water into a bowl from across the room. Harder than you'd think because I was lifting the entire pitcher off the ground and then lifting part of it more in order to tilt it. Of course, I had to keep it centered above the bowl and Bertie didn't want me to spill it. I did spill it. Many times. Still not quite perfect. Have another spell to practice now.

I'm hoping these tasks are harder than they used to be and I'm not getting worse.

14 August 1817

DEAR BARTLEBY,

Pip came into the library while I was practicing the folding spell and watched for a bit. He even tried it as well, which was jolly good fun. We were laughing so much that Gerry came to see what the fuss was about. Then she joined in too.

It turns out that not one of us can fold a shirt from across the room with magic.

15 August 1817

DEAR BARTLEBY,

Bertie added to the shirt-folding assignment. Now, I not only have to fold it, I have to button it first. Lord, what a trick that turned out to be. Buttons are outrageously difficult to do with magic. It's so precise.

16 August 1817

Dᴇᴀʀ Bᴀʀᴛʟᴇʙʏ,

Gerry, Pip, and I had another go at my assignment. We gave up on trying to make it look nice and eventually gave up on the buttons altogether and turned it into a race with who could fold their shirt first. Lord, it was fun! Although I might have torn one of my shirts. Shall have to apologize to Charles about that. Fortunately, I do have more money than usual since I'm not shopping as much and I'm earning wages from Bertie. I suppose Parks was right after all.

Applicants start tomorrow. I'm a little disappointed I won't be home on Gerry and Pip's day off. We might have gotten a good amount of practice in. I made them promise not to cheat and do it without me.

I'm a trifle nervous now that the whole thing is about to start. I hope I don't make a cake of myself.

17 August 1817

Dᴇᴀʀ Bᴀʀᴛʟᴇʙʏ,

Glad to report: did not make a cake of myself. Met the applicants officially.

The severe woman is Miss Cornelia Locke. She looked to be in her fifties. She is pale, has grey hair that is pulled back tightly, and a perpetually annoyed expression. Her eyes are a rather nice shade of blue, but she is so often glaring with them that it's hard to be too complimentary. She is not very polite and I feel like a misbehaving child when she speaks to me. Not overly fond of her, I'm afraid.

Then, there's the local gentleman, Mr. Laurence Ayles. A pleasant-looking chap, really. Medium brown skin and dark brown hair, curly, but tighter curls than Pip's. Has an open sort of smile and large dark brown eyes that turn up a bit at the corners. Quite the opposite of Miss Locke—very friendly and very forthright. Reminded me of Gerry a bit, in the way that he doesn't seem to be afraid to say what is on his mind. Well, I suppose in that way he is like Miss Locke; she certainly isn't afraid of saying what's on her mind. Anyway, Mr. Ayles is about Gerry's age, or maybe Gavin's. He is between my height and Pip's. It's nice to be taller than somebody. He seems to be one of the friendliest. He might be my favorite of the group, and not just because he's the best looking.

The military gentleman, Major Carlton Wilburforce, is a very no-nonsense type, very gruff. His skin is pale and blotchy, he has watery sort of blue eyes, is tall, broad, has thin lips. He seems to appreciate efficiency and, in that way, he appreciates me. Not quite so intimidating as Miss Locke, but not quite so friendly as Mr. Ayles. Older than Father.

The man who mistook me for a valet is a solicitor, Mr. David Voss. He is slender and my height and, unfortunately, handsome. He has an olive complexion, dark blond hair, dark brown eyes and a very full mouth. Did not apologize for his error and truly seems to think I shouldn't be here at all. Therefore, I have decided to not consider him handsome.

Then there's the man with the lovely eyes, Sir Ronald Sinclair. He is of average height, about as tall as Bertie. His dark brown eyes are heavy-lidded, his mouth is full and pouting-like, his skin is a little tan (although not, I think, from the sun, given his aristocratic air), and his hair is black. Can confirm he is definitely interested in me. He didn't say anything, but he looks at me often.

Finally, the quiet woman, Mrs. Lydia Fossett. She is shy but seems kind. She has dark brown hair, sand-colored skin, a wide nose, and a small mouth. I'd guess she is rather pretty, but I'm not a particularly good judge of feminine beauty.

I'm still very glad to be a part of the process, but I don't mind only being there for part of the day. Most of them are nice enough, but Miss Locke and Mr. Voss are so very unpleasant. I don't much care for being looked at like I'm an intruder all the time.

Today was spent on introductions and giving everyone a tour of the house and the grounds and that sort of thing. I'm not sure if I've already mentioned it, but Mr. Ayles is not staying the night. He lives about three miles away and plans to walk or ride every day.

18 August 1817

DEAR BARTLEBY,

Lunch at Bertie's is another example of precedence not being followed when it comes to seating. Not that I mind, exactly. For then I might have to sit next to the same people every day. Which I suspect is Bertie's aim—to keep people from sitting in the same arrangement, I mean. Yesterday, I sat at Bertie's right—which earned me a glare from Mr. Voss. But today I was seated on the opposite end of the table with Mrs. Fossett on my side. We had a pleasant conversation. She said her late husband wouldn't have approved of her applying for the position, so she's glad the opportunity came up now instead of earlier. I told her about my studies and the work I do for Bertie.

After lunch, Bertie and I went to his study for my magic lesson. Bertie changed it up a bit. Since he's playing host now, he can't exactly watch me the whole time. He's going to alternate my practical lessons with theoretical ones. I'm still solving puzzles with spells, but some days, I have to do research and write a report on what spells I might need and what theories would support it. It is not quite as fun as trying the spells myself, but it does have a feeling of investigation. I find I like it more than I expected. I'm to work on one report each week and spend the rest of my lesson time practicing the assignments Bertie has given me until I can perfect them.

I did not finish the report today. I barely even got started in the writing. Bertie went back to the beginning with the assignment of moving a book to the shelf without damaging it and I had to pull out a whole pile of spell books to remember which ones I used. Then I had to look up all of the theories that applied. It will likely take me a few days just to get the report written.

After my lessons, Bertie had the six applicants do the same spells they had done for their interviews, only he had them all casting at the same time. I wondered why he would do such a thing, but it was very interesting to see how they reacted to each other. Some of them were focused and some were watching each other's methods. Some were faster and others were so careful as to be almost glacial in pace. Seeing them all working at the same time put their differences in sharp relief. Bertie stood next to me and made quiet observations, which I wrote down. Then, he strode to each spell and made observations so everyone could hear while I continued taking notes.

My hand was cramping by the end. I soaked it in balm before dinner, but now that I've written all this, I may have to soak it again.

19 August 1817

Dear Bartleby,

Sat next to Mr. Ayles today. I like him even better upon further acquaintance. He's very friendly and easy to talk to. I can't remember if I mentioned it before, but he has a very melodious voice. He asked how I like Tutting-on-Cress and we talked about my family. I then asked him a little about his family. He has two fathers and they live in a modest house close to the village. Apparently, he takes the same road that I do, but turns when he gets near the lake, whereas I go straight past it. In any case, we arrive and depart at different times, so it hardly matters. Pleasant to talk to and very nice looking. Not as blindingly gorgeous as Pip, but then, who is?

I fancy his friendly personality adds significantly to his appeal.

Kept working on my report today. I believe I have about half of it done, although it is hard to tell when it isn't even finished.

Bertie put the applicants through more spell tests and I took more notes.

20 August 1817

DEAR BARTLEBY,

Sat next to Sir Ronald today. Extremely flirtatious man. Fortunately, he was friendly enough, so I didn't entirely mind it. Asked many pointed questions about whether I was simply working for Bertie or if I was involved with him romantically and seemed relieved to learn I was living with my brother and that I was not married. Not at all subtle.

Thought I had finished the report but Bertie said I need to add citations. What a great bother.

21 August 1817

DEAR BARTLEBY,

Was seated between Miss Locke and Mrs. Fossett. Miss Locke had nothing to say to me except for occasional criticisms—my posture was poor, my questions were too familiar. Truly, she is like a governess.

Finished my report and the citations today. Thank God. Had no more time left to practice my spells, but I shall work on them tomorrow.

Bertie continues to drill everyone in spells. Some of them are getting a bit tetchy about it.

When I was leaving today, I was surprised to be joined by Mr. Ayles.

"Do you know, darling," Bertie said to the man as I was

putting on my gloves. "I worry about you walking all that way home by yourself after dinner. I fancy it is a trifle dark for you."

Mr. Ayles smiled. "It is no trouble, my lord. I grew up here, you know."

"Yes, but if something were to happen to you, I'd never forgive myself. Why don't you leave when Seb here does? And you can join us in the morning?"

"If it will not put me at a disadvantage?" Mr. Ayles ventured.

"Not at all, I assure you, my dear man. You get along with everybody. I have no worries about your tact or manners."

"Very good, my lord. Thank you," Mr. Ayles said. He turned to me. "Might I join you on your walk home, Mr. Hartford? It would appear I am leaving as well."

"Of course," I said, smiling.

We left together and walked down the road in the early evening light.

"How are you finding it?" I asked.

"A trifle strange," he admitted. "I like Lord Finlington, though. I trust his judgment in these matters."

"Is it difficult? Doing all of the spells in front of everyone?"

He smiled. "Not any more difficult than doing them alone. I try not to be distracted at any rate. I do not see myself as competing with them but proving myself to his lordship."

"But some of you will not be chosen to go to London."

"Yes," he said. "But if I am not chosen, I do not believe it is because others are better than I am, but because I was not up to his lordship's standards. So I'm competing with myself more than anything."

"That is a good way of looking at it."

"Thank you," he said, with another smile. "How are you liking your work as his lordship's assistant?"

"I like it," I said. "The notetaking can be rather dull. But I enjoy seeing so many spellcasters doing magic at once. Bertie is still training me in magic so it is nice to see professionals, as it were."

"I'm certainly not a professional yet," he said. "But I appreciate the compliment. I did not realize you were still in school. How old are you, if you don't mind my asking?"

"Twenty," I replied. "I was at Oxford but…er, I'm not anymore. Now I'm staying with my brother and his husband. They are seeing to my education. Except for my magic lessons. My sister was teaching me, but it was recently decided that Bertie would take over."

"Is that where you disappear to after lunch?"

"Yes," I said.

"I imagine it is quite an experience to have someone like Lord Finlington training you."

I need hardly tell you, Bartleby, that these days I am eager to talk about my lessons at the slightest provocation. So naturally I launched into an enthusiastic description. Mr. Ayles was very attentive, asked questions, and declared himself impressed with both Bertie for coming up with the lesson plan and me for following it.

It is too early to tell, of course, but I'm hoping I might have another friend. Or at least, the start of another friend. I don't wish to be too hasty. The nice part is that he lives in town. So after all this is over, I might still see him occasionally. I definitely enjoy his company and I would very much like to continue seeing him even when he is no longer an applicant.

22 August 1817

DEAR BARTLEBY,

Finally got to practice my shirt assignment today. Practiced for an entire hour. I can get the buttons done now, but not every time. I suppose I ought to tell Gerry and Pip about it so they can practice too. It doesn't seem sporting to practice when they promised not to.

Oh, and sat next to the major today. Not an unpleasant chap, really. Talks a great deal and doesn't listen much. But at least he is civil to me.

There was definite grumbling today when Bertie listed out more traditional style spells. It would appear he has segmented everything by weeks. Although I don't think all of them made that connection. Mr. Ayles did not seem bothered, nor did Mrs. Fossett. Frankly, those two are the most agreeable of the bunch. Is it silly of me to hope they're chosen to go to London for that reason alone? I don't much care who the third one is. But I would hate for either of them to be sent away when they're so very nice.

Had another nice chat with Mr. Ayles on the walk home. He realized Gerry is my sister and was full of compliments on her handling of the shop.

"I would tell you she's brilliant," he said. "But I don't want you to think I'm trying to get in your good graces. So in a month, I will be full of compliments."

I laughed. "I have no say in who is chosen, Mr. Ayles."

"Oh, I know," he said. "But I think his lordship values your judgment more than you realize."

I didn't know what to say to that. "It is funny to know that you've met my sister and myself but separately."

"I can't say I know her well," he said. "I imagine she'd recognize me if she saw me, but she may not know my name."

"I'll ask her when I get home," I said.

"Very good," he said, laughing. "I've been wondering for some time if you two were related. I saw you leaving her shop several months ago but hadn't seen you since."

I stared at him. "I remember that! I thought you looked familiar. You smiled at me."

He gave me the same open smile he had given me the first

time we passed each other. "I've been wondering about it actually. Since I only saw you the once. I didn't even know if you were still in town until I saw you during my audition for his lordship."

I marveled at this for a moment. How funny that I had found the man so attractive when I first saw him, completely forgot about him, and then here we were, talking about it.

He went on, "And are you acquainted with her shop assistant as well? Mr. Standish?"

"Oh, yes, Pip is a friend of mine," I replied. It is perfectly ridiculous of course, but I felt absurdly pleased to be able to say that.

"I like Mr. Standish very well too," he said. "He seems very kind."

"Yes, he is."

"Very pretty smile," he added.

"Very," I agreed. "You should try living in the same house with it."

He laughed. "Is it painful?"

"Positive torture."

We both laughed and he turned off at the road shortly after.

It would appear, then, that Mr. Ayles is of the masculine persuasion, Bartleby. Is it foolish of me to be a little delighted by that information?

23 August 1817

Dear Bartleby,

Sat next to Mr. Voss today. I was on the end so it was only him beside me. Lord, the man is rude. Completely ignored me the entire time. I tried starting conversations with him and he merely looked down his nose at me. I suppose he does consider me some sort of servant. But even if I were a servant, there would be no call to treat me like that.

Continued practicing my shirt assignment. Can now fasten the buttons every time. Still slow going, though. Sir Ronald came into the study looking for Bertie during my practice. I told him I didn't know where Bertie was, but he came in anyway and asked what I was doing. I explained about my lessons and the practice Bertie has had me do.

"How fascinating," he said. "Will you show me?"

I was rather proud of my work on the buttons, so I did. Only after I got to the third button, the first one came undone. I frowned and redid it and then the second one came undone. I finally realized Sir Ronald was using a Motion spell to undo them. He was laughing silently.

"I'm so sorry," he said. "I couldn't resist. The expression on your face was too adorable."

I was a little embarrassed but, well, as someone who has pulled many a prank, I had to admit it was a good joke. So I rolled my eyes and told him he was unlikely to find Bertie here.

He smiled. "Thank you for the reminder, Mr. Hartford. I had better go and find him. Oh," he said as he started to walk by me. He leaned down, pressed a hand to my lower back, and said in a quiet voice, "and when you learn to undo buttons as well as you do them, do let me know." His lips grazed my cheek and then he left.

I thought about the interaction all day. It didn't unnerve me, really, just made me contemplative. Which is, I daresay, very unlike me.

Mr. Ayles was kind enough to carry the conversation for most of our walk home and I was glad of it. Before he turned to head off in his own direction, he stopped me with a hand on my arm.

"Are you quite all right, Mr. Hartford? You seem a little quiet today."

"Sorry," I said. "Perfectly all right. In a brown study, that's all." He didn't look convinced, so I said, "If you don't mind me asking, what is it you lot do after lunch?"

He gave a small shrug. "A little more of the same of what we do at lunch, really. Socialization, but less structured. It has turned into a bit of a free period. Miss Locke and the major have formed a sort of friendship, so they tend to go off in conversation. I sometimes join Mr. Voss and Mrs. Fossett. Sometimes I take a turn around the garden. His lordship has splendid gardens."

"And Sir Ronald?"

"I'm not entirely sure what Sir Ronald does after lunch." He paused, frowning slightly. "Why do you ask?"

"I was just curious. He came and watched me practice a bit today."

"Did he—" He broke off and seemed to consider his next words. "Did he do anything inappropriate?"

"Good heavens. How did you possibly guess that?"

"Well, he does look at you a great deal," he said. "I've long suspected he was...interested." He frowned. "Are you all right?"

I laughed. "Oh, yes. It wasn't all that bad. He made a joke about buttons."

"But it bothered you?"

I thought about this. "Not exactly. I've been trying to make up my mind all day how I feel about it. You see, if I'd met him a few months ago, I'm sure I would have been pleased by the attention. He is quite good-looking. I've come to the realization that if I was interested, it would have been a rather intriguing offer. As it is..."

"You're not?"

I shook my head. "Not at all. Isn't that odd?"

He smiled. "Not particularly. But then, I admit I'm not overly fond of him myself."

"Why not?"

"From what I have observed of him, he is the sort of man

who sees things he wants and considers himself...entitled to them. For no better reason than because he happens to want them."

"That does sound about right."

"You're sure it didn't upset you?"

"Quite sure," I said, smiling at him. "But you helped me sort it out in my head. Thank you for that."

"A pleasure, Mr. Hartford," he said, returning my smile. "Good evening then."

We parted ways and I made my way back home.

Good God but Mr. Ayles makes everything easy to talk about.

24 August 1817

DEAR BARTLEBY,

Bertie gave me another report assignment and I worked on preparing the books for it. Did not get any writing done.

He is making all of the applicants do Motion spells now. A half dozen spellcasters levitating books and pillows. The room was filled with wind and movement. It was a little exciting. It felt like watching a performance.

The walk home was a livelier affair today as I was more in the mood for conversation. Mr. Ayles did not bring up what I had told him of Sir Ronald. I don't think I've mentioned it before, but Mr. Ayles cuts a very fine figure. He doesn't have Charles's height and muscle, but he looks as though he spends plenty of time outdoors and doing things.

25 August 1817

DEAR BARTLEBY,

Sat between Sir Ronald and Mr. Voss today. Not my favorite seating arrangement. Mr. Voss will not speak to me at all, so my only choice was to turn and talk to Sir Ronald. He pressed his leg up against mine the entire time. He even touched my leg at one point, although when I moved his hand away, he smiled a little and didn't try again. I'm beginning to see what Mr. Ayles meant about him.

Report is going better now that I know what to do. Also citing as I go, which should make the whole thing go a little faster.

More Motion spellwork. I think everyone is beginning to understand Bertie's method. They will have to resign themselves for Motion spellwork this week.

Had another nice chat with Mr. Ayles on the way home. Is it silly that I rather wish Gavin and Charles could meet him? I do not intend to call him my friend until I have their opinion on the man. I really don't trust my own judgment anymore. But he is so dashed pleasant. I look forward to my walks with him and am always happy to talk to him at Bertie's house. He listens as if he thinks what I have to say is important and interesting, which is very gratifying. He is funny and has interesting things to say himself. I'm wondering if I ought to ask Charles and Gavin about inviting him to dinner, but that might be too obvious. I'm not sure Mr. Ayles and I are at that level of friendship yet. I'm not even sure if we're friends. Although I'd really like to be. I hope I'm not wrong about this one.

26 August 1817

Dear Bartleby,

Sat between Mrs. Fossett and Major Wilburforce. They are so very different, it was amusing to be seated between them. I spoke mostly to the widow, but Major Wilburforce chimed in every now and again. Rather pleasant conversation overall.

Finished the report for Bertie.

Motion spells continue. I wonder if Bertie intends to

decide at the very end or if he is already making up his mind. To my eyes, they all look exceptionally talented.

Realized I only knew about Mr. Ayles's parents, so I asked him on the walk home today if he had any siblings and he said, "I am an only son."

"Really? I have three older siblings. I can't even imagine what it would be like without any."

"Rather lonely, to be honest."

I thought about all that time I was doing studies by myself in the library and how often I was left alone as a child and thought I might understand what he meant. "That must have been hard."

"Sometimes it was, yes. I…" He hesitated. "I haven't always been an only son."

"Oh, dear," I said softly. I slowed and laid a hand on his arm. "I'm so very sorry. What happened?"

He smiled and put his hand over mine. "No, nothing so sad as all that. I mean to say, when I was born, I was inaccurately believed to be a girl. So, for quite a while I was considered an only daughter. In any case, I later realized that it was not accurate to who I am."

I'd met a couple of people at Oxford who'd had this experience—one of my mathematics tutors, and Aubrey Dixon who was a year above me—but didn't know either of them intimately. At any rate, I was pleased to have a frame of reference. "Oh," I said. "I'm glad you were able to correct it, and relieved I was mistaken in believing you suffered some great tragedy."

"As am I," he replied with a grin. He squeezed my hand briefly and then took his hand away. "Father took care of all of the necessary paperwork associated with the discovery. And Papa was delighted when he got to take me to a tailor for the first time. He loves buying clothes," he added.

"You wear them well," I said. I felt myself blush and quickly pulled my hand off his arm.

"Thank you," he said with a laugh.

Do you know, Bartleby, Mr. Ayles has a very nice smile. It's a very open sort of thing. Very…genuine. He has a very *genuine* smile. I quite like it. I mean, honestly, his mouth in general is very fine. I've started wondering what his lips would feel like to kiss. But I'm certain I should not be thinking about such things. I mean to say, I should be sure of his character before I start imagining kissing the man. Is it not funny that I never had such scruples in Oxford? This place is changing me. I suppose it is a good thing, but I'm quite unnerved by the revelation.

27 August 1817

DEAR BARTLEBY,

Sat next to Miss Locke for lunch. We were getting along tolerably well, although she is still very cold in her address. Then she looked down and wrinkled her nose at me and said, "Young man, do button your waistcoat. Such dishevelment is a disgrace."

I looked down and saw that one of my buttons had come undone. I thought her assessment to be a little exaggerated, but I buttoned it and returned to the conversation. A few minutes later, I felt my waistcoat loosen slightly. I looked down to see two more buttons had come undone. I glanced up and saw that Sir Ronald was watching me, his smile sly. I felt my face get hot and hastily rebuttoned my waistcoat. It was just like the other day in Bertie's study. Every time I got one done, he'd undo another.

Finally, I got exasperated with the ridiculous game and simply said, "Oh, really!" I was, I'm afraid, louder than I intended. But it had the desired effect: my buttons stopped popping open. Everyone at the table quieted and looked at me.

"Everything all right, darling?" Bertie said.

I glanced at Sir Ronald, who was very carefully not looking at me.

"Yes," I said, turning back to Bertie. "Sorry. There's something wrong with this waistcoat, I'm afraid. Buttons won't stay."

Bertie's eyes cut to Sir Ronald briefly. "Very good, dear. If you're sure?"

I nodded and we returned to our conversations. I apologized to Miss Locke and asked her to continue with her fascinating opinion on the evils of waltzing. She seemed a little irritated to have been interrupted, but also gratified that I was still interested enough to listen. So that was all right.

Bertie pulled me aside after lunch to make sure I was fine.

"Yes," I assured him. "Sir Ronald has been flirting with me. That's all."

"Do you need me to talk to him?"

"I shouldn't think so," I said. "I'm not overly fond of him, but he hasn't done any harm as yet."

"Well," he said, "you will let me know, I hope, if he makes you uncomfortable?"

"Oh, yes," I said. "Don't worry. I went to Oxford, you know. Plenty of rotters there. I daresay I've had practice."

He smiled. "Very good, m'dear."

Sir Ronald very pointedly did not look at me during the Motion spellwork. So I suspect Bertie did talk to him after all. Part of me wishes the people here would stop treating me like a child. On the other hand, I do appreciate them looking after me.

On the walk home today, I asked Mr. Ayles what he likes to read. He is not particularly keen on poetry—must take care I do not mention this to Gavin. He explained that he likes to read magical theory.

"Really?" I said. "I don't think I've ever picked up a magical theory book outside of my schoolwork."

He laughed. "I daresay you're not the only one. But I do

adore it. I feel as though magic has so much untapped potential. I like to think that the more I read about it, the more I'll be able to reach its full potential."

"What do you mean?"

He considered. "I mean that many of the most recent magical theorists have been sort of stuck in what has already been discovered. They seem locked into an idea of what ingredients are best suited to magic work. But if everything truly has capacity for magic, why aren't we trying everyday items? Not everyone in England can acquire…I don't know… star anise, for example. I'd like to see a more thorough exploration of ingredients that are native to England or easily accessible to more people."

"I think I know what you mean," I said. "I feel as though I'm not so advanced as to try that sort of thing."

"From what you described about your lessons with his lordship, I'd say you're quite advanced," he said. "Thankfully magic is a broad enough science to appeal to people for different reasons."

I thought about what Bertie had told me once, about how everybody approached magic differently. "I wonder if you're like my sister in that way," I said slowly. "Bertie said once that she likes to take magic apart and see how the different pieces fit together—or something like that."

He gave me a wide smile. "That's an excellent way to put it."

I was a little flustered by the smile, so I asked him what else he liked to read. He said he likes to read up on plant-life, which is something I have never even considered reading about. He is, it would appear, mad for gardening. He went on a long discussion about how impressive plants are, how they seem to have a magic all their own. He adores Bertie's conservatory, but prefers being outside.

"Not that I wouldn't be opposed to having a greenhouse or a conservatory, myself," he added. "But there is something about gardens that gives me a sense of peace and belonging, you know?"

After dinner, I took a stroll about our garden and thought about what he said. I find I might appreciate plants a little better than I used to.

28 August 1817

DEAR BARTLEBY,

Sat next to Mr. Ayles at lunch today, which was very pleasant. I really do enjoy his company. We talked a great deal. It is funny, really, that I spend so much time with him but always feel as if I'm learning more about him. Did you know, for instance, that he is allergic to cats and hates cheese? I'll wager you didn't.

Worked on my pitcher spell for a bit. Sir Ronald came in while I was practicing.

"Ah," he said. "Not the little button spell. Pity."

I rolled my eyes. "If you're looking for Bertie—"

"As it happens," he said, shutting the door behind him. "I wanted to talk to you."

I crossed my arms and turned to face him. "Yes?"

"You were very familiar with that little farmer today."

"What?"

"At lunch."

"Mr. Ayles?"

He nodded.

I scoffed. "Well, first off, he's a gentleman. And second off, what of it?"

He moved closer to me. "I rather thought I had staked my claim."

"Did you indeed?" I said, feeling my face get hot. "Really, Sir Ronald. You do not own me."

Something flickered in his expression at my words.

I straightened. "I think you had better leave me to my

practice now, or I shall have to explain to Bertie why I haven't had time to finish."

He looked me up and down with his lip curled. "Insolent cub."

"Yes, well," I said. "That happens to be the reason I'm here at all, isn't it?"

"Perhaps someone ought to take you in hand," he said, cupping my chin.

I snorted. "You know you really went precisely the wrong way to flirt with me. I've never been impressed with that sort of talk. And I'm not interested, as it happens."

He dropped his grip on my chin. "I suppose you prefer farmer's boys and country bumpkins."

"I prefer gentlemen. And I'm not so inexperienced as to fall for the first titled prat who undoes my buttons."

"It would appear I was wrong about you," he said. "What a shame."

Then, thankfully, he left.

I did not mention the conversation to Mr. Ayles on the walk home. I did not entirely want to admit to him that Sir Ronald had been jealous of our conversation, for fear of him getting the wrong impression. Well, not the wrong impression. At any rate, I asked him a great many questions about himself on the way home, to keep him from asking me about my day. I asked him about his taste in clothes and he admitted he was not an expert on fashion, but that he looked to his papa for guidance most of the time. And I asked him what he most enjoyed learning about when he was younger and we talked about magical theory for most of the walk home.

I had thought I had successfully managed to distract him from my day, but when we reached the point where we split paths, he said with a smile, "I hope you will allow me to learn some more about you and your childhood the next time we walk. I don't mind being the focus of attention, but it hardly seems fair to you."

"I don't mind it," I said hastily.

"Well," he said, still smiling at me in a knowing way. "I don't wish to put you on the spot or anything, so I won't press. But you should know I have begun to store up a whole catalog of questions to ask you in the future, so please prepare yourself accordingly."

I laughed and we parted ways. I thought about what he said all the way home. Imagine a person storing up questions to ask me. I'm quite struck by it.

29 August 1817

Dear Bartleby,

Was seated between Sir Ronald and Mrs. Fossett today. It would appear I am now dead to Sir Ronald. He pointedly turned away from me at the table to talk to Bertie. I didn't mind. Mrs. Fossett is much better company, so I was glad I got to talk to her instead.

Practiced my shirt spell and had no interruptions. I think I may have successfully quashed his interest.

Had a nice talk with Mr. Ayles on the way home. Asked him what he hoped to do if he were chosen. That is, I was wondering what he planned to do with the additional income. It is not strictly a polite thing to ask a person, but he did not seem offended, thank heavens.

He smiled and said, "If I get this appointment, I should like to buy my parents some better comfort. We have lived a good life, but we do not have as many nice things as any of us would have liked."

"What will you buy them?"

"I shall take Papa to the tailor," he said. "What a delight that would be. He can order a whole bundle of new clothes.

And Father..." He considered. "Father will have a stack of books for his library."

"They sound like my brother and his husband," I said. "Charles is always exceptionally dressed and Gavin is forever reading something."

"They would probably get along," he said, grinning at me.

"Yes, I rather think they would. So that's your parents sorted out. What nice thing would you like for yourself?"

He considered. "I'm not entirely sure," he said at last. "I shall have to ponder the question a while and tell you later."

Then he flashed me one of his lovely open smiles and I felt myself blushing. Which is, quite honestly, a little unfair. Why is my family cursed with such a frustrating tendency to blush?

30 August 1817

DEAR BARTLEBY,

Bertie gave me the afternoon off. Practiced my shirt spell for hours. Gerry and Pip practiced with me after dinner. Currently: Gerry is the fastest at getting the shirt folded, Pip is best at the buttons, and my folds are the neatest. It is nice to know where I stand.

31 August 1817

DEAR BARTLEBY,

Pip promised to come by this afternoon to have tea with me and Bertie. It's his day off from the shop. At lunch I was seated next to Mr. Voss at the end of the table, which meant I had precious little by way of conversation. So I was quite eager to have a nice chat with my friend. I spent most of lunch trying to figure out if I could find a way to get Mr. Ayles to join us too, so Pip could meet him. Then I could get Pip to give me an opinion on the gentleman.

After lunch, I went into the study and Bertie gave me a new report to write. I left the door open so Pip might know he could come in as soon as he arrived, and then I began pulling books off the shelves.

I was studying one of the wind spells and trying to decide if it was too strong, when I heard Sir Ronald's voice outside my door.

"Well," he said, "what a delightful surprise. It looks like somebody finally cleaned you up, didn't they?"

I frowned. What an odd thing to say.

"And you're even prettier than I remember. Do you still make the same delicious little noises before you spend?"

I got up and walked quietly to the door and peeked out.

Sir Ronald was standing over Pip, gripping his chin so Pip had to look up at him, in much the same way he had done to me. Pip was standing as if frozen, his face ashen, his eyes wide, and his lips pressed tightly together.

"I would love to have you again. Who do you belong to now?" Sir Ronald said.

"Myself," Pip said, with what looked like tremendous effort.

Sir Ronald chuckled and kissed Pip's mouth. "Now, now, pretty thing. Creatures like you must belong to somebody. So tell me: Who is it?"

Pip closed his eyes at the kiss but did not move. He looked rooted to the spot. Sir Ronald reached up and brushed a hand through Pip's hair. Pip flinched and the pained expression that took over his face was one I suddenly realized I never wanted to see again.

Without stopping to think it through, I stepped out of the study and said loudly, "There you are, Pip! I've been wondering what kept you. Let's go out to the garden, shall we? Lovely day for a walk in the garden. Do excuse us, Sir Ronald."

Sir Ronald looked up in surprise and I managed to put my arm around Pip's waist to usher him out the front door.

Pip allowed himself to be walked outside. I led him out the door and around back toward the garden. But just as we turned around the corner of the house, Pip lurched forward and began heaving on the grass. I tightened my hold around his waist and threw my other arm around his chest to support him. He gripped my arm tightly and continued vomiting.

I felt completely helpless; it was all I could do to keep him standing. I had to get Bertie. I looked around to see if there were any gardeners about and spotted Mr. Ayles running toward us. I don't think I've ever been happier to see him, and that's saying something. I'm always happy to see him.

"Good heavens," he said, approaching us. He put one hand on Pip's shoulder and cupped Pip's forehead with the other. "What's happened?"

"Get Bertie," I said. "And Ayles?"

"Yes?"

"Please make sure Sir Ronald isn't around," I said as softly as possible.

He glanced at Pip and then nodded before running off.

Pip stopped vomiting shortly after, but he stayed hunched over, gasping, spitting, and retching. I didn't say anything. I didn't know what to say. I hoped holding him was enough. He was trembling all over. I was trying to determine if I should try moving him to a bench when one of them sailed into the air and landed behind us with a soft thump. Then Bertie was there, guiding us to sit down. Pip folded himself into Bertie's arms and buried his face in the crook of Bertie's neck. He was still trembling all over.

Bertie held him tightly. "What happened?" he said to me.

"Sir Ronald," I said. "He was saying…dreadful things. I think they've met before."

Bertie's face looked pinched. "Laurence, darling," he said.

"Would you be so kind as to see to it that Sir Ronald stays inside the house?"

"Right away, your lordship," Mr. Ayles said behind me.

I glanced back as I hadn't realized that he was standing there.

"Seb."

I turned back to Bertie.

"I need you to go inside and tell them to ready the carriage. Then I want you to go to my study, open my cabinet of tinctures, and grab one of the bottles with the lavender-colored liquid. Then get your things. You're taking him home."

I hurried to do as he said. I was very relieved to see that Sir Ronald was no longer in the front hallway. I asked one of the footmen to send for the carriage and asked that it be sent as close to the garden as possible. Then I found the bottle Bertie had described. The footman passed me my things and, when I asked him, handed me Pip's as well. I tucked the bottle into my waistcoat pocket and returned to the bench.

Nobody spoke as we waited for the carriage. Bertie continued to hold Pip, who sat unmoving in Bertie's arms, taking deep, shaky breaths. Finally, the carriage arrived. I tossed all of our things onto one seat and helped Pip get in. He sat down and leaned forward, his head in his hands.

Bertie put a hand on my shoulder. "Get him to bed. If possible, tell no one but Charlie what happened. Did you find the tincture?"

I pulled it out of my pocket.

He gave me a brief smile. "Very good, darling. Tell Charlie to give him two doses, just in case. I'll see you tomorrow."

I stepped into the carriage and sat beside Pip. I tentatively put an arm around his shoulders and he reached up and clasped my hand.

Bertie closed the door, and we rode home.

When we arrived, the driver hopped down and helped me

get Pip out, which I appreciated. I put an arm around Pip's waist again and offered him my free hand. He gripped it tightly. We made it halfway up the stairs without anyone but the servants seeing us, until Gavin met us as he was coming down.

"Good God," he said. "What's happened?"

"Can you get Charles?" I said.

Gavin's eyes were wide, but he immediately turned and hastened back upstairs.

Just as we reached the top of the staircase, Charles hurried down the hall and slid his arm around Pip's waist. "I have him now," he said to me.

I stepped away, but Pip still held my hand. He glanced up at me and gave it a squeeze before letting it go and allowing Charles to half-carry him to his room. I was almost to the bottom of the stairs when I remembered the tincture. I ran back up and knocked softly on the door.

Charles opened it. I held up the bottle. "Bertie said to tell you two doses."

He took it, his expression tight and full of understanding. "Go wait in my study, will you, Seb? I'll only be a moment."

I went back downstairs. I noted with relief that someone had gotten our hats and coats out of the carriage. I let myself into Charles's study and sat down. But I felt too shaken. I got up and paced the study, waiting.

A quarter hour later, Charles came in. He took one look at me and then strode to his shelf and poured a glass of brandy. He handed it to me wordlessly. I drank it, savoring the burning feeling in my throat.

Charles led me to a sofa and sat down next to me. "Tell me," he said.

I described the conversation I overheard, how Sir Ronald had touched Pip, how I had gotten Pip outside, how he had vomited and I had held him, how I had asked Mr. Ayles to fetch Bertie, and how Bertie had taken over and gotten us home.

Charles listened without interrupting. When I was finished, he said, "Are you all right?"

"Me?"

"That can't have been easy for you."

"I did feel rather helpless," I said. "I didn't know how to stop him from hurting. Does that…does that happen often? Will he be all right?"

Charles let out a long breath. "It has never happened exactly like that before. But he did have a very hard time of it when he first came to stay."

"What happened to him?"

"That's not for me to say, darling."

"Did Sir Ronald hurt him?"

"Many people hurt him." Charles passed a hand over his face, looking tired. "But please don't ask him about it."

"No," I said, thinking of the pained expression I had seen in Pip's face. "I would never."

"Come here," Charles said, pulling me into a hug. I was a little surprised by the gesture, and even more surprised by how much it comforted me.

"You did very well today," he said. "I'm proud of you."

Oddly enough, that was the thing that made me feel weepy. I pulled away and got out my kerchief. "I was only helping a friend. Anyone would have done the same."

"Oh, I'm not so sure about that. Are you?"

I considered for a moment, thinking of my friends at Oxford, trying to imagine how they would have reacted in my place. "Maybe not," I said at last.

He patted my knee. "You ought to take a nap, darling."

"Yes," I said. "That might be nice." I got up slowly and headed to the door. "Charles?" I said, turning.

"Mm?"

"What was that tincture for? The purple one?"

Charles looked sad. "It's to make him sleep, dearest. And to keep him from dreaming."

"Oh."

Tried to take a nap but couldn't fall asleep. So I gave up and read a book instead. It was almost time for dinner when the butler knocked on my door and told me there was a gentleman downstairs wishing to see me.

I was very confused, I need hardly tell you, Bartleby. I went down and found Mr. Ayles waiting for me in the drawing room.

"Mr. Hartford," he said. "I do hope you will forgive me for dropping in like this. I wished to see if your friend was all right."

I smiled. "I think he will be. Thank you."

He looked, for the first time since I'd met him, a trifle self-conscious. "Good," he said. "I'm glad to hear it." He paused a moment and then said, "You should know Sir Ronald has been sent away."

"Bertie talked to him?"

He nodded. "None of us even saw him leave, and his lordship did not give the particulars. He explained that he had determined Sir Ronald was not a good fit after all."

"Thank you for telling me."

"Of course," he said, with a smile. "And..." He hesitated. "Are you all right? You looked quite shaken earlier."

I scuffed my shoe against the carpet. "Yes, I'm all right. Didn't like seeing my friend like that. I'm glad Sir Ronald was sent away."

"As am I. And I'm glad you—"

The door opened and Gavin stepped in. He took in the two of us standing in the middle of the room with his usual solemnity. "Are you coming to dinner, Seb?"

"Yes," I said. "I'll only be a minute."

"I'd better take my leave," Mr. Ayles said. "I only wished to see that you were both doing better."

"I did not intend to rush you," Gavin said, stepping farther into the room.

"Not at all," Mr. Ayles said. "I was only stopping by for a moment. And I'd hate to keep you from your dinner," he said to me. "You've had a rather trying day."

Gavin glanced between us. "I don't believe we've met," he said. "Seb, would you be so kind as to introduce your friend?"

I blushed at his casual pronouncement of Mr. Ayles being my friend, but Mr. Ayles did not seem to mind it. I proceeded to make introductions.

Gavin shook Mr. Ayles's hand stoically. "Mr. Ayles," he said. "A pleasure. I believe I met your father…Mr. Robert Ayles. He came by when we first moved into the neighborhood."

Mr. Ayles smiled. "Father likes to be correct about things. That sounds like him."

"I'm afraid we've been remiss in getting to know everyone here. Well, I should say, I have been remiss. My husband is very social. And of course, my sister knows everyone."

Mr. Ayles laughed. "I expect she does."

"Would you like to stay for dinner?" Gavin said.

"Very kind of you, Mr. Kentworthy. But I'd better be off. My parents will be expecting me."

"It is getting dark out. Would you like to use our carriage?"

Mr. Ayles ducked his head. "No, thank you, sir. I don't mind the walk. Thank you all the same. I'll take my leave. It was a pleasure to meet you, Mr. Kentworthy. I'll see you tomorrow, Mr. Hartford."

Gavin waited until Mr. Ayles had left the room before turning back to me. "He seems quite nice."

"He is."

Charles came in at that juncture. "Aren't you two coming to dinner?"

Gavin swiveled around on his heel. "Yes. Just meeting Seb's friend."

"Oh, stop it," I said. "I'm not sure he is my friend."

"Why not? He certainly seemed like it. Came by to check on your wellbeing, didn't he?"

"Really?" Charles said, coming up to stand behind Gavin. "That's very interesting. Who was it?"

"Oh, stop it," I said again.

"Mr. Ayles," Gavin replied, leaning back into his husband's chest. Charles wrapped his arms around Gavin.

"Which one? I believe there are three."

"Mr. Laurence Ayles," I said automatically.

Charles's eyebrows rose. "Oh, indeed? What do you know of them, darling?" he said, looking at Gavin.

"Not as much as I should, probably. Good family, by all accounts," Gavin said. "And the son seems like a very pleasant fellow. Doesn't he, Seb?"

I sighed. "Shouldn't we go into dinner?" I said, stomping past them. I heard Charles laughing as I exited.

My word, but this is one of the longest entries I've written in a while. I'd better make that tincture Bertie taught me.

1 September 1817

DEAR BARTLEBY,

Dinner was a fairly solemn affair, as Pip did not join us. Although Charles and Gavin kept asking about Mr. Ayles. Then Gerry jumped in to pester me, too. Lord, they're so nosy.

Pip slept all afternoon and all night. He wasn't even downstairs at breakfast. Gerry left for the shop without him.

Gavin and I were sitting in the library while I studied when Pip finally woke up. I was reading a book on philosophy that Gavin had assigned for me. Charles opened the door and called for me. I looked up.

"Pip wants to see you."

I was so relieved to learn Pip was awake that I jumped out of my seat. When we reached Pip's door, Charles put a hand on my shoulder. "He may not want to say very much," he said. "He's a very private person, particularly when it comes to his past."

I nodded and went inside. Pip was still in bed, looking pale and drawn. But he smiled when I walked into the room.

"Ah good, Seb," he said. He pushed himself up to sitting and I hurried over to see if he needed help. He waved me off. "I'm all right," he said. "Before you ask. Just tired."

I stood next to his bed, feeling unsure of what to do.

He gave a small smile and held his hand out on the counterpane. Tentatively, I took it and he gave it a gentle squeeze.

"Thank you," he said. "For saving me yesterday. I don't know what I would have done if you hadn't been there."

"I wish I had done something sooner," I admitted. "I'm so sorry. I heard the way he talked to you and I didn't know what it was about or what to do."

He shook his head. "You couldn't have known. Everyone's been very...careful about explaining how I got here. I suspect the gaps of information are what made you hesitate. My fault really."

"Pip—"

He squeezed my hand again. "You were there when I needed you. Thank you."

I clasped his hand with both of mine. "Will you be all right?"

He smiled a beautiful dimpled smile. "With friends like you lot? Of course I will. One of these days I'll explain everything. Not today, though. It's too...raw."

"You don't need to."

"I know," he said. "But I want to. I'm slow to trust people, Seb. You proved yesterday just how trustworthy you are. You're a good friend."

I felt weepy again, which was awfully embarrassing.

Pip smiled and held open his arms. "Come here."

I was a little nervous about how to hug him—gently? Tightly? I followed his lead, returning his gentle embrace with my own. His neck was warm and clammy.

"Are you sure you're all right?" I said.

He laughed and fell back onto his pillows. "The tincture always leaves me feeling…off. And I fancy Charles gave me more than usual yesterday." he said. "But I'll be fine." He scrubbed a hand over his face. "It makes me feel all wooly-headed, though. I've never been fond of that. I weaned myself off of it as soon as I could so as to avoid that side effect." He dropped his hands to his lap. "By the way, who was the fellow you sent in for Bertie?"

"Goodness," I said. "I didn't think you'd have noticed."

"I didn't exactly get a good look at him or anything. I remember a hand on my forehead because that felt comforting. And I remember a voice I didn't recognize, then you sending him inside."

"Mr. Ayles."

"Any relation to the family who lives in Tutting-on-Cress?"

"Yes, Mr. Laurence Ayles."

"Oh! I've met him. I quite like him. Although I rather wish he hadn't seen me in that state."

"He was more worried than anything else. He and I walk home together, part of the way, that is. From the way he's talked about…some of the other applicants, I think he understood some of what was going on."

He looked at me consideringly. "Friend of yours?"

I scrubbed the back of my neck. "I'm not so sure of that yet."

"What do you mean?" he said, laughing.

I shrugged. "I'm not a very good judge of character. I'm

trying to be more particular about who I pick as friends. Currently, you're it."

"Me?" he said, raising his eyebrows. "What about Gerry, Gavin, and Charles?"

I shrugged. "They're family. They don't count."

"Bertie?"

"He's my employer. That's different."

Pip laughed. "Gerry's my employer and she's one of my closest friends. You know people can be both, right?"

"Maybe Bertie then," I said.

"Well, I'm glad I'm in good company," he replied. He paused, considering. "Can you do me a couple of favors, Seb?"

"Of course, anything."

"Can you talk to Bertie for me? If I know him at all, he'll blame himself for what happened. And he mustn't. He couldn't have possibly known... Anyway, tell him I don't blame him, but I may wait until everyone leaves to visit his house again."

"He left. Sir Ronald, I mean. Bertie sent him away. Mr. Ayles told me that last night."

"Oh," Pip said. He heaved a sigh. "Can't say I'm sorry to hear that. Though I wish I didn't need Bertie to keep protecting me."

"I'm not sure he sees it that way," I said.

Pip looked unconvinced.

I shrugged. "Well, they're all there as applicants to an important position. Bertie isn't just checking for their magical abilities, you know. He's making them socialize and everything. I think he's gauging their personalities, too. He wouldn't want to recommend a man like that."

Pip tilted his head. "I suppose you're right."

"You said two favors?"

He hesitated a moment. "Can you bring Mr. Ayles here tonight? I'd like to thank him."

I wasn't entirely sure I was ready for the level of teasing my family would inflict upon me. But I couldn't deny Pip such a request. I told him I would, then left so he could go back to sleep.

Bertie pulled me aside before lunch to ask how Pip was. So I was able to take care of Pip's first request right away. Not that it worked. Bertie took the blame anyway.

"You couldn't have possibly known they knew each other," I told him.

He sighed. "I know, m'dear, but it is an awful wrench. I've always done what I could to make Tutting-on-Cress a safe place for the darling man. I could never have anticipated being the one to—"

"He said he doesn't blame you. He was most insistent. And he was relieved to know Sir Ronald had been sent away."

Bertie smiled. "Isn't that just like him? Such a sweet thing. To be perfectly honest, m'dear, I have been contemplating sending that wretched man away for quite some time. I only wish I'd done it sooner."

"Why?"

"Well, I didn't like his behavior toward you. And I suspect you weren't the only one he attempted to seduce. I put a spell guarding the servants' quarters against him, but I couldn't be sure he wasn't talking some of them into going to his room instead." He sighed. "Well, he's gone now, thank goodness."

"How did everyone else take the news?"

He chuckled. "Well, no one seems to be sad at his leaving. However, I have now set a precedent for removing an applicant before the final announcement. So I fancy they are all on edge a bit."

With that, we went into lunch. I could see what he meant. The conversation had a feeling of forced jocularity. I was seated next to Mr. Voss and the man actually talked to me, which is something of a first. He still doesn't seem to like me very much. But I think he doesn't care to make that as apparent now.

After lunch, I pulled Mr. Ayles aside and asked him if he would walk home with me today, explaining that Pip wanted to thank him.

"I didn't do so very much," he said. "But I should be glad to meet with him."

So that was settled.

Did precious little of my report yesterday so I was still reading books today. The group is now finished with Motion spells and Bertie has moved on, to my surprise, to theory. Today, for instance, he drilled them all on the common Constitutional Properties. I almost laughed when I realized I knew the list better than most of them. Bertie is making them all memorize it now. They have to get it done by the end of the week. How funny that I should have only just mastered it myself. I said as much to Mr. Ayles on the walk home.

"It would seem your sister and his lordship are of the same mind when it comes to magical education," he said.

"You never had to memorize the list then?"

He shook his head. "I studied it, of course. And I daresay I know it fairly well. I couldn't recite any of it for you, but I can see why it would be useful."

"To be honest, I'm still not sure why it's useful," I said.

He smiled. "It is more important when one is creating new spells," he explained. "If I want to expand a spell for lateral movement, say, and adapt it to move buildings, I would need to know what items have the right Constitutional Properties for such a task. Then I can determine which ingredient is the strongest or most potent, or possibly a combination of ingredients. After that, it's all calculations for weight and so on. But having that foundation would give a person a definite head start."

"So you don't mind the assignment then?" I asked.

"Not at all. I consider this all to be very educational, if

nothing else. Any tips on memorization, since you've already done it?"

"Gerry made a chart with each item, its properties, and common spells that used them. Having the spells helped, even though it was more to memorize."

He considered that. "Context, I suppose. Yes, I can see how that would help. Thank you."

We were just coming in view of the house when I saw Charles and Gavin walking toward us. "Curses," I said.

"What's the matter?"

I sighed and turned to him. He stopped obligingly. "Listen," I said. "My family is outrageously nosy. Gavin was all intrigued after meeting you yesterday and now it appears Charles is curious about you, too."

He smiled. "I see."

"I had hoped we wouldn't need a whole lot of fuss for you to meet Pip. But it looks like they've taken it into their heads to meet you."

"Is that a problem?" he said. He looked like he was trying not to laugh.

"Well, it is rather embarrassing."

"I don't see why it should be," he said.

At this point, Charles and Gavin were within hearing distance, so I took a deep breath and prepared to be embarrassed.

Charles greeted us cheerily. "We thought we'd join you on your walk back."

I rolled my eyes. "Yes, thank you. That is quite apparent."

"It is good to see you again, Mr. Ayles," Gavin said. "Please allow me to introduce my husband, Mr. Charles Kentworthy. Charles, this is Seb's friend, Mr. Ayles."

Mr. Ayles proclaimed himself delighted to meet Charles. "Mr. Hartford speaks very highly of you both," he said, bowing.

"Do you really, darling?" Charles said to me. "How nice."

"Don't worry. It won't happen again," I said.

Mr. Ayles laughed and Gavin's mouth twitched.

Charles's smile broadened and he turned back to Mr. Ayles. "Pip explained that you would be stopping by. We would be delighted to have you for dinner, Mr. Ayles. Won't you join us?"

"Very kind of you, Mr. Kentworthy," he said. "But I would hate to keep my parents waiting."

"I have no desire to press you," Charles said. "But I'd be happy to send a message to your house telling them of your change in plans. Unless, of course, another evening would be better?"

Mr. Ayles glanced at me. I was blushing furiously and turned to avoid eye contact. So embarrassing. "I would be delighted," he said.

"Wonderful," Charles said. He turned and fell into step beside Mr. Ayles.

Gavin joined me behind them. "He seems very nice," he said to me in a low voice.

"He is," I said. "I'm quite sure I already told you that. You had no need to come all the way out here to verify it."

Gavin slowed his pace a bit and put his hand under my elbow. "Seb," he said. "I must confess I've been worried about you. You seemed so very upset about leaving your friends at school—"

"Yes, well, they weren't that good of friends as it turns out," I said.

"I know."

"I hate that you were right about them all along."

He huffed. "When you first came here it was enormously evident you had gained some very bad influences. I can't deny I'm relieved you came to that realization on your own, although I wish it hadn't been so painful for you."

I stuffed my hands into my pockets and said nothing.

"But the fact is you are a very social person. You like to

be around people. So I wasn't entirely pleased that you went from a whole group of terrible friends to no friends at all."

"I have Pip."

"Yes," he said with a small smile. "I know. But you're both so busy. I've been contemplating inviting people your age to tea, to broaden your social circle. But I wasn't sure you'd appreciate it."

"I certainly wouldn't!" I said. "Imagine having friends out of pity."

"Thought you'd say something like that. I'm sorry we embarrassed you by coming all the way out here. We were eager to meet your new friend."

"I've been trying to be careful about applying that word to people."

"I've noticed that, too," he said. "Mr. Ayles didn't seem bothered by it."

"No," I said, cheered by the observation. "He didn't, did he?"

"And Bertie spoke very highly of him."

"When?"

"When Charles wrote to ask what he thought of Mr. Ayles."

"Oh, spare me," I said. "What on earth did I do to deserve your nosiness?"

Gavin had the grace to look a little guilty. "Sorry," he said. "It is a dreadful family trait of ours, isn't it?"

"Not me," I said. "I'm not in the least bit nosy."

"Aren't you?"

"Well, all right. I'm sure I am. But I don't embarrass you in front of—"

He glanced at me, eyebrows raised.

I huffed. "Well, I don't."

"If you had come to London when I was still only friends with Charles, can you honestly say you wouldn't have tried to push me along? Gerry did her level best. And John only didn't because he decided he disliked Charles."

"John is such a prat sometimes."

"Too true," Gavin said.

Pip was waiting for us when we got home. He took Mr. Ayles aside in the drawing room to thank him in private. I don't know what was said between them, but they didn't talk for very long. When they came out, there was no awkwardness between them, so I think they got along very well. Hardly surprising, since they're both such agreeable people. But all the same, I was relieved.

I was dreading dinner, but thankfully I needn't have. Unlike me, Mr. Ayles was completely at ease with the whole situation. He got along with everybody. He was pleased when Gerry and Pip recognized him from his visits to the shop. He gamely answered all questions about how the application process was going, although he was far more polite about his fellow applicants than I have been.

"Miss Locke is the most thorough out of all of us," he said. "And the major's spells are always very powerful. Mrs. Fossett has remarkable instincts. But Mr. Voss is likely the cleverest. He's enormously talented."

"Oh, dear," I said. "Is he really? He's such a horrid man."

Mr. Ayles laughed. "He improves upon acquaintance."

"And what about you?" Gerry asked him.

Mr. Ayles leaned back in his seat and considered the question. "I'm not sure," he said.

"You're the steadiest," I said without thinking.

Everyone turned to look at me.

"What do you mean?" Gerry said.

"Er…" I glanced at Mr. Ayles who was smiling but had an unreadable expression in his eyes. "That is…well, Miss Locke is thorough, but she takes a very long time because of it. I reckon she lacks confidence. The major is powerful, but sometimes too powerful. He overloads his spells quite often. Mrs.

Fossett is instinctual, but she tends to rely too much on what she's done before. She isn't as bold when it comes to new spells. And Mr. Voss is clever, but he knows he's clever. Sometimes he botches his work because he's too confident. But you…you're consistently good. That is, you're not flustered by people around you doing different things and you don't get upset when your spells do go wrong. You know, steady."

I felt my face get progressively warmer throughout this speech.

"Thank you, Mr. Hartford," Mr. Ayles said. "That's a very kind assessment."

I nodded and carefully avoided looking at anyone.

Fortunately the rest of the meal passed without incident. Charles insisted on sending Mr. Ayles home in a carriage as it was dark. After he left, of course, they all turned to look at me, smilingly.

"He's very nice, Seb," Charles said.

"I like him," Gerry proclaimed.

"Seems like a very decent sort of chap," Gavin said.

Pip did not add to this commentary, but I could tell by the smile on his face that he felt the same.

I sighed. Truthfully, I was relieved but still rather embarrassed about the whole thing. Luckily, I had an excuse to go to my room early to write all of this since I didn't have time before dinner. Glad I still had the ingredients for the tincture as I will definitely need to soak my hand again tonight.

2 September 1817

Dear Bartleby,

Sat next to the major at lunch today. I now know far more about pheasant shooting than I ever cared to learn.

Finished my report. Glad I made citations as they made the rest of the report go a great deal faster.

I had no notes to take this afternoon because Bertie is

having the applicants write about their knowledge of magical theory. He told me to leave early, so I didn't get a chance to talk to Mr. Ayles today, which was a bit of a pity.

Charles and Gavin were preparing to go out riding as I approached the house. They reined in their horses.

"Everything all right?" Charles asked.

"Why shouldn't it be?" I said.

"You're home quite early."

"Oh, yes. Bertie didn't need me this afternoon, as it happens."

"Going riding. Care to join?"

It didn't take long for me to decide that I did. Another horse was saddled for me and we left.

"Gavin and I had Mr. and Mr. Ayles over for tea today," Charles said.

"You didn't!"

He smiled. "Very pleasant gentlemen. I'm glad you brought that family to my attention. I'd like to see more of them."

I was actually very curious about Mr. Ayles's parents, but I did not want to admit such a thing. So instead I said, "You two are acting like he's courting me. I wish you wouldn't. I've only known the gentleman for a few weeks."

"Would you like to be courted by him?" Gavin asked.

I didn't say anything.

"You are not usually so reluctant to form opinions about people," Charles remarked. "I seem to recall you pursuing other gentlemen with alacrity when you first arrived here."

I sighed. "Yes, well. That was before I discovered I'm a dreadful judge of character. I'm trying to be more fastidious now."

"I've been wondering about that actually," Gavin said. "How did you come to be friends with those chaps at Oxford?"

I shrugged. "How does one get to be friends with

anybody? It just happened."

Gavin leveled me with a look.

"I don't know," I said at last. "It isn't as if I sought them out or anything. No one would talk to me when I first got there. It wasn't until Parks dared me to do something to liven up the headmaster's address that anyone noticed me at all."

"What did you do?" Gavin said.

"I turned the lectern invisible."

"Ah," Charles said. "So that's how you got into the prank business."

I huffed. "Well, I am good at it."

Charles smiled but said nothing.

"Do you miss it?" Gavin asked. "Being at school?"

"Not particularly," I admitted. "I'm learning more interesting things here. I like working with Bertie. And Pip is a far nicer friend than anyone I met at school."

"I imagine Mr. Ayles is, too," Charles added.

I very pointedly did not reply to that. "You two and Gerry are rather nice to be around, when you aren't nosing into my business."

"Thank you for that," Gavin said drily. "I promise I'll stop pushing. Although I do like Mr. Ayles. Even if you aren't interested in courtship, I think you've found a very good friend with the gentleman."

I was prodigiously relieved to hear that, Bartleby.

"I, however," Charles said, grinning, "give no such promises. Furthermore, I don't think Mr. Ayles is opposed to courting you."

I looked at him in alarm. "What do you mean?"

Charles chuckled. "I mean the man looked at you a fair amount during dinner last night and he seemed very gratified when you complimented him. He likes to have your good opinion. And you very clearly like to have his."

"Come on," Gavin said. "We've tortured my poor brother long enough." And he kicked his horse into a canter.

I followed after him, grateful that he was making good his promise.

Charles laughed before following and beat us both to the house.

3 September 1817

DEAR BARTLEBY,

Sat between Mr. Ayles and Bertie today, and curse my family for getting the notion in my head, because I am now absurdly nervous interacting with Mr. Ayles. Fortunately, he's such a good-natured person and so very easy to talk to that I wasn't tongue-tied or anything. But I found myself worrying over things I'd said, hoping I didn't sound foolish. It was all very unlike me. I didn't care for it one jot.

After lunch, Bertie came in to see my progress on the assignments I've been practicing. I've got the pitcher spell down very well now. The shirt and buttons are coming along quite nicely, too. Bertie pronounced himself satisfied on both. He gave me my next practical assignment.

"You're going to pour tea, darling."

Except it wasn't just tea. Bertie wanted me to do the whole thing: tea, sugar, and milk. He even had me add freshly squeezed lemon juice—apparently it's a Russian style of drinking. You'd think the tea would be easy after I finished the pitcher of water, but it was a different weight and fragile. The milk was even smaller and lighter. And the lemon is giving me some real stick. It's very challenging and there are all sorts of components to it, so I daresay that will keep me busy for a while.

Once again, Bertie sent me home shortly afterwards as he was drilling the applicants on theory. I wonder how Mr. Ayles is getting on with his memorization. I shall have to ask him later. I'm rather disappointed to keep missing the opportunity to talk to him.

4 September 1817

DEAR BARTLEBY,

Strange to think that Sir Ronald has been gone for days. I don't miss him in the slightest.

Lunch was a trifle unexceptional. Was seated between Major Wilburforce and Miss Locke, and they talked a bit over my head the entire time. Partly because it was a topic of which I knew nothing and partly because they're both very tall.

Practiced the tea assignment some more and then left early again.

Charles called me into his study when I got home. Gavin was already in there, sitting on the edge of the desk with one leg hitched over the corner.

"I want to discuss your studies with you," Charles said as he ushered me to a seat. "You would have likely left Oxford at the end of this year, or thereabouts. So, your studies shall change to assessments of your knowledge rather than lessons. Any gaps we discover can then be rectified before the end of the year."

"May I continue with my magic lessons?" I asked.

He smiled. "I'll talk to Bertie, but I think he enjoys teaching you. So I imagine you can continue until you leave."

I felt hollowed out by his words. "Am I being sent away?"

Charles looked up in surprise.

"Don't be a goosewit, Seb," Gavin said. "No one is sending you away. I imagine Father will want to see you at some point so he can gauge your progress for himself. But as far as we're concerned, you're welcome to stay as long as you'd like."

"Oh," I said, breathing out in relief. "Good. Er, thank you."

"However," Gavin went on, "we should have a discussion about your future. Once you are finished with your studies and Father declares himself satisfied, you will be expected to know what you want to do next. I didn't when I was your age. I drifted about the house for years, unsure of what I would do until Mother sent me to live in London. John was a right beast about the whole thing until Charles proposed. To my mind, you have plenty of time to figure it out, but know that the longer you wait, the more likely it is Mother or Father will take matters into their own hands. And John will hound you on the subject as well. If you want to have a debut in London, Mother will likely be keen to take you. The Dukex of Molbury is a friend of ours and I know they'd be pleased to help usher you into society as well." He paused. "At one point, I would have been sure of what you'd like to do, but now I'm not so sure. If you're not interested in going into the Marriage Mart—and I wouldn't blame you—there are some career options that are suitable for a nextborn of your station."

I considered this. I had never really thought of the future at all. Some things I knew with certainty, however: I like working for Bertie, I like living with Gavin and Charles, and —dash it all—I like Tutting-on-Cress. Neither Gavin nor Charles said anything while I pondered all this.

"Do you think," I said at last, "that Bertie might consider me for employment long term?"

"I advise you to talk to Bertie about that," Charles said. "But I imagine he would be amenable to the suggestion."

"Thank you."

I am a trifle nervous about the prospect of discussing that with Bertie. But Gavin is right: I ought to have some sort of plan in place.

It occurs to me I have never had to make such a decision before. I mean, when I was at Oxford, I followed Parks's lead. Since I've come here, I've pretty much done whatever Charles or Gavin told me to do. I'm not really accustomed to making decisions, and this feels so very important. I daresay I won't sleep a wink tonight, thinking about how to phrase the question to Bertie.

5 September 1817

DEAR BARTLEBY,

Today's lunch was doubly awkward. I was still finding myself nervous around Mr. Ayles, only now I was also anxious about talking to Bertie. I was a bit of a wreck the whole time and frightfully jumpy. When I asked Bertie if I could speak to him after lunch, he looked very concerned.

"Is anything the matter, darling?" he said as soon as he'd closed the study door behind him.

"I had something I wanted to ask you," I said.

"To be sure, m'dear. Why don't we sit down?" He directed me to the sofa and sat beside me.

I took a deep breath. "Gavin told me yesterday that I ought to be thinking of the future. Or at any rate, should be considering my options."

"Good advice, but that isn't surprising considering dear Gavin."

I clasped my hands together and looked down at them. "I was wondering…that is, I know this arrangement is only temporary…but if I were to stay in town…I mean, in Tutting-on-Cress, for the foreseeable future…would you consider keeping me on as your assistant? You see, I don't know what it is I want to do, but I do know I like my work here and I like…my life here. But I shouldn't wish to be a burden on anyone."

"Why, darling," he said. "How delightful." I glanced up to see him smiling. I'd forgotten Bertie does that when asked a question. He always acts like it's a brilliant one. "Do you really enjoy working with me?"

I nodded. "I feel as if I'm always learning something when

I watch you do magic. I should like to keep learning, if you'll have me."

He chucked me under the chin. "Don't be silly, darling. I would love to have you stay on as my assistant. You take marvelous notes, you know. Excellent penmanship."

I let out a long breath. "Thank you, Bertie."

He chuckled. "Your poor thing. Were you really so nervous to ask me? If I wasn't satisfied with your work, you would have known." He leaned back against the sofa. "So, when considering your future, you decided upon Tutting-on-Cress? That's very fine. It is lovely, isn't it?"

"Pip said once it has a way of giving people exactly what they need."

He smiled softly. "Did he indeed? And has it?"

"I'm not sure," I said. "But I think I'm on my way to getting it, whatever it is. I rather think my chances are better if I'm around you and Gavin and Charles. Gerry and Pip too, for that matter."

He laughed at that. "What a darling notion. Well, I am pleased to know I shall still have your assistance for a while longer. Is there anything else you wished to ask me?"

"Just that. I'm still working on that tea assignment."

"Very good. Let me know if you have any questions, darling."

I left early again today and Bertie told me to take tomorrow off.

I feel rather disconcerted about having finally gotten my family's approval to consider Mr. Ayles my friend, and I'm just beginning to wonder about him becoming something more. But now I barely have a chance to talk to the gentleman. I hope next week is better.

I went back home and found Gavin in his study. I relayed my conversation with Bertie. "Might I stay here while I continue working for him?"

"Naturally," he said.

I hesitated and then added, "It is rather frightful thinking about the future all of a sudden, isn't it?"

He gave a small smile and folded his hands in front of him on the desk. "It can be, yes. I'll admit I had less direction than you do now. So you're well ahead of me in that regard."

"Had you planned to get married then?"

"Not at all. I was rather frightened of the prospect, to be honest."

"Really?" I said, taking a seat in front of his desk. "Even with Charles?"

"No, just the whole notion of marriage. I knew I didn't want to have children, but I also assumed that was expected of me. So I had come to the conclusion that marriage wasn't for me."

I had to laugh. "But you're so very domestic now."

He rolled his eyes. "If by 'domestic,' you mean having my own study in which to read without anyone bothering me, then yes."

"Oh, stuff," I said. "Look at yourself: you have all sorts of papers and things all over your desk."

He riffled the papers into a stack. "Yes, well. Menus have to be approved and whatnot, haven't they?"

I smirked.

"At any rate," he said. "Gerry was the one who persuaded me to reconsider my position on marriage. And Charles— well, when Charles proposed I realized I might be cut out for marriage after all. But I was convinced I would never find anyone..." He cleared his throat. "Anyone to love me enough to want to marry me." He was silent for a moment, looking as though he were lost in the memories. "Anyway, you're only twenty and have a respectable occupation. So, I daresay you're off to a good start."

So, Bartleby, it would appear I have decided to stay in Tutting-on-Cress for a while. Is it not strange?

6 September 1817

DEAR BARTLEBY,

Was granted the morning off for studies as well, so I practiced my tea spell a bit until lunch. At lunch, Charles announced he was taking the carriage with Gerry and Pip when they returned to work so he could do some shopping in the village.

"Would either of you care to join me?" he asked.

"I'm not sure I can," Gavin said. "I promised Mrs. Thornsby I'd approve the linen schedule for her today. And Aunt Lily asked me to come to tea."

Charles smiled at Gavin fondly. "Very good, my darling. Anything you need picked up in town?"

Gavin shook his head. "Nothing comes to mind."

Charles turned to me. "What about you, Seb? Care to join me for a little shopping trip? Get out of the house a bit?"

"I'd like that."

He grinned. "Lovely. We'll get you a new pair of boots, too. I fancy your current pair is looking a little worn."

We took the carriage together with Gerry and Pip into Tutting-on-Cress and Charles had the driver wait while he and I went shopping. He stashed all of our parcels in the carriage and sent it back home.

"You don't mind the walk, do you?" he asked. "I'd like Gavin to have the carriage to visit your aunt."

I assured him I didn't mind and fell into step. "Charles?"

"Mm?"

"Did you know when you married Gavin that you might also be taking on a whole lot of other people?"

He grinned.

"I know you said you like spoiling people," I went on. "But you're housing Gerry and Pip, as well as me. I'm fairly sure you're paying for all of our clothes, too." I hesitated. "Do you mind at all?"

He chuckled. "Not a bit of it, darling," he said. "We won't be having children, so I have no need to save for that eventuality. I have no doubt that the three of you will be settled in the next few years. I can easily afford to take care of you until that happens."

"Oh," I said. "Are you disappointed that you won't be having children?"

"Not particularly," he said. "Mind you, I do adore children, and I'm convinced Gavin would make a darling father. But I've known from the beginning of our courtship—quite frankly, before Gavin even realized it was a courtship—that he wasn't interested in raising a family. It would hardly be fair for me to do so with the intention of trying to change his mind. Besides, I love Gavin more than I love the prospect of parenthood."

"Oh," I said again. "That's good."

He smiled. "It is sweet of you to worry about it, though."

I shrugged. "Just something I've wondered about. Ever since Gavin mentioned I ought to be thinking about the future…I don't know…it occurred to me to wonder about it."

"Would you like to have children?"

"I'm not sure," I said. "I've never really thought about it much, to be honest. I like children."

"And you do like to keep busy," Charles said.

"Yes," I said, rolling my eyes.

"Children would definitely keep you occupied."

"Yes…" I said. "I suppose I would be like Mama and be in charge of the nursery and everything when I get married?"

"Most likely," Charles said. "Unless you marry another nextborn."

"Somehow I don't think my work with Bertie would support an entire family."

He chuckled. "Unlikely." He didn't say anything for a moment. "Mr. Ayles is a firstborn, you know."

I sighed. "Yes, thank you. I am aware."

"If you were courted by a gentleman who wanted children, would that please you or concern you?" he pressed.

I considered. "I suppose I could go either way on the matter."

"Not a bad perspective," he said. "Do you mind a slight detour, dear? I'd like to make a social call while we're in the vicinity."

"I have no plans for the day," I replied.

When we approached a small house, I asked him where we were going.

"This is Copperage Farm," he said. "The Ayles family property."

I stopped. "Oh, no. You didn't."

He smirked and slung an arm around my shoulders. "I did, darling. It was very underhanded and I do apologize. However, even if you are simply looking to know the gentleman as a friend, it would do well for you to know his parents, wouldn't it?"

"You're intolerable," I said, fussing at my coat and wishing I'd worn something a mite nicer.

A maid took our things and we were ushered into a cozy parlor where a gentleman was sitting. He was in his mid to late forties, had dark brown skin, no hair on his head, and bushy eyebrows. He was of a stocky sort of build, well dressed, and looked to be of a cheerful disposition. He smiled as we came into the room.

"Mr. Kentworthy," he said, stepping forward to greet us. "How nice to see you again."

"Mr. Ayles, a pleasure as always," Charles said. "We were on our way back from the village and thought we'd pay you a visit. I hope you don't mind."

"Not at all," Mr. Ayles said, beaming. "Please stay for tea."

"We would be delighted. Allow me to introduce my brother-in-law, Mr. Hartford."

Mr. Ayles took my hand warmly. "Mr. Hartford? My, it is a pleasure, young sir. My son has talked of you often."

"He has?" I asked.

"Oh, yes," he said. "Do, please be seated." He sent the maid to fetch some tea. "He has told us much about all of the friends he's made since he's been training with his lordship. I daresay he thinks very highly of you."

I felt a little flutter in my chest at the thought of Mr. Ayles speaking of me as if I was a friend, and, what's more, a well-regarded one. "That's very kind of him," I said.

The door opened and another gentleman strode in. "Algie," he said as he walked in. "Where are my—oh," he said, seeing us. "I beg your pardon. I did not know we had company."

Charles stood and I hastily followed suit.

"My apologies, Mr. Ayles," Charles said. "We dropped in unexpectedly. Your husband was kind enough to invite us to stay for tea."

He waved his hand. "No need for apologies, Mr. Kentworthy. You're welcome any time." Mr. Robert Ayles was of a less cheerful manner than his husband, and much more soft-spoken. But he did seem to be a good-humored sort of person. He looked a little older, with frizzy grey hair, keen eyes, and pale skin. A pair of glasses perched on the end of his nose. He noticed me and gave a friendly smile.

"Ah," Charles said, leading me forward. "Allow me to introduce my brother-in-law, Mr. Hartford."

Mr. Ayles shook my hand. "A pleasure, young man. I'm glad to finally meet you. I must admit we've been wanting to for quite some time."

"Oh, er, you have?"

We all sat back down again, Charles and I took a pair of chairs and both Mr. Ayleses sat together on a sofa. Quite frankly, Bartleby, it is too confusing trying to discuss two men with the same name. I shall henceforth describe them as Mr.

Robert and Mr. Algernon, but you ought to know I was thoroughly proper the entire time.

"Well," Mr. Robert said. "Our son talks of nothing these days but his experiences at his lordship's house."

"We've been excessively curious about both you and Lord Finlington," Mr. Algernon said. "Of course," he added. "I'm not sure we'll have an opportunity to meet his lordship. He is a rather grand person."

Charles smiled. "He's one of my oldest friends. I know he would be delighted to have your acquaintance. Perhaps when this is all over, you can all join us for dinner."

"Oh, that would be lovely," Mr. Algernon said.

"Very kind," Mr. Robert said.

"And the ball," I put in.

They all turned to look at me.

"Er, I believe there is to be a ball at the end of the process. Where Bertie will announce the three finalists."

"Yes," Charles said, smiling at me. "I do believe you're right, dear." He turned back to the gentlemen. "So you will have an opportunity to meet him soon."

"Delightful," said Mr. Algernon.

"How are your studies coming along, Mr. Hartford?" Mr. Robert said. "Laury tells us you've been learning magic from the viscount."

"They're coming along nicely, sir," I said. "Thank you."

The tea was brought in and Mr. Algernon poured out for everybody. "How long do you intend to stay in Tutting-on-Cress, Mr. Hartford?" he asked after everyone was served.

"Well—"

The door opened and Mr. Ayles, my Mr. Ayles—well, dash it all, Bartleby, I mean to say, Mr. Laurence Ayles—walked in. He stopped at the sight of us (I feel as though I ought to refer to him as Mr. Laurence to keep consistent, but, well, I do think of him as Mr. Ayles. You will indulge me, I hope, if I name people as I see fit.).

"Oh," he said, smiling. "Good to see you. No, please don't get up," he added as Charles and I prepared to stand.

"You're home early, aren't you?" Mr. Robert asked.

"Yes," Mr. Ayles said, walking across the room. He walked behind the sofa and leaned down to give each of his fathers a kiss on the cheek. "Today was the last day of theory. We had to recite the list of Constitutional Properties in private. His lordship was kind enough to have me go first, so I was able to leave sooner."

"How did you do?" I asked.

He grinned at me as he took a seat. "Very well, thank you. Your suggestion for the spells was most helpful."

"I cannot believe you memorized the whole thing in a week," I said. "It took me over a month to get it all done."

He accepted a cup of tea from Mr. Algernon. "Yes, well, I had a more pressing need, I expect." He flashed me a smile. "So I had an incentive to memorize it right away. And Father helped, of course," he added.

Mr. Robert chuckled. "I now know far more about Constitutional Properties than I ever wished to."

"Mr. Hartford," Mr. Algernon said after some silence had passed. "I do apologize. You never had a chance to finish your answer. How long do you intend to stay in Tutting-on-Cress? I understand your sojourn here is temporary."

I glanced at Charles, who was looking at me in that amused way of his. Curse him. "Well," I said. "As it happens, I believe I shall be staying here for quite some time. Bertie, I mean Lord Finlington, has agreed to keep me as his assistant for the foreseeable future. Charles and Gavin, my brother, have agreed that I may stay."

"That is good news," Mr. Algernon said. "It's always nice to have young people come into the neighborhood."

"Indeed," Mr. Robert said. "Most people your age gravitate toward London at this phase, at least for a short while."

"I have always wanted to go to London," I admitted. "But

I don't know that I'd like to go there for a Season…at this time. Besides, my father…er, well I'm not sure I'd be permitted. Alone, at least."

"He'll probably relent in a few years," Charles said, chuckling. "Give him time. He needs to forget your time at Oxford first."

"Trouble-maker, were you, young man?" Mr. Robert said.

"Oh, very much, yes," said Charles.

"Charles!" I whispered.

Mr. Algernon laughed. "Not to worry, Mr. Hartford. I was too, back in my day."

"Really?" said Mr. Ayles. "That surprises me."

"It shouldn't," Mr. Robert said.

His husband grinned. "Rode a horse through the library once. Almost got sent down for it."

"You didn't, Papa!"

"What about you, Mr. Hartford? What manner of trouble did you stir up?"

I was frightfully embarrassed by the direction of the conversation. "Well," I said. "I played a few pranks."

"A few?" Charles said. "This rascal was always sending my husband all sorts of stories. Let me think now, there were the bubbles in the fountain, the missing bust in the garden, the invisible lectern, the—"

"Yes, yes, Charles. I think they get the point," I said. "Father was not best pleased about it all. That's why I was sent here."

"And are you still up to your usual tricks, Mr. Hartford?" Mr. Algernon said.

"As a matter of fact," Charles said, "he is not. I daresay Gavin and I are quite proud of the young man he's turning out to be."

I looked at him. "Really?" I said quietly.

"Of course, darling," he replied.

"I'm not at all surprised to hear that," Mr. Robert said. "I find the most mischievous young men often grow up to be the kindest-hearted ones." He looked fondly at his husband. "I daresay there's something to be said about understanding human nature or what have you."

"Oh, really, Robert. You give me far too much credit," Mr. Algernon said, patting his husband on the knee.

Everyone turned to me as if I ought to say something then. I squirmed in my seat, uncomfortable with the sudden attention and completely unsure of what to say.

"Mr. Hartford," Mr. Ayles said. "Would you care to take a stroll around the garden with me? It is nothing to his lordship's, of course, but I think you'll find it very fine."

I blushed, but quickly set my teacup aside. "I would be delighted."

When we stepped out of the house, he said, "You looked a bit uncomfortable. I fancy all the talk about your pranks was not something you wished to discuss."

I shoved my hands into my pockets. "Oh, dear," I said. "Was it so very obvious?"

He chuckled. "That is one good thing about being an only child," he said. "No older siblings to tease me."

"Very lucky for you." I hesitated. "Thank you," I added. "That was considerate."

He smiled at me. "Don't mention it."

We walked in silence for a bit. The garden was very nice. It was less manicured than Charles's or Bertie's and there were vegetables mixed in with the flowers. Not that Charles doesn't have fruit and veg, but the kitchen has its own little garden plot by the chicken coop. Although I don't walk by it very often these days.

"This is a lovely garden," I said at last.

He grinned. "Thank you. I love it. I have plans, you know. I want to expand it. Look here," he said, taking my arm and walking me to a wide empty space. "There's this lovely area. Papa had it cleared out for a pond he thought to put in, but then he never did it. I would very much like to use it for my own purposes. I've been talking to his lordship about growing magical plants and plants good for spellwork. Can you imagine it? We could have mint and rosemary and mugwort. I could even fit a willow tree just over there. Maybe even a witch hazel tree. And his lordship gave me all sorts of suggestions for growing things like dragon's breath, frostblossom, and Oberon's Wrath. You know, plants that have to be treated and such. It would be marvelous."

He was so animated during this speech. For all the times I've talked to him and all the time I've spent with him, it occurred to me that I was seeing a new version of the gentleman, here in his own home. It was a nice sensation. I realized I want to see more of that version of him.

"Indeed it would," I said. "It's like your two favorite things blended together in one project, magic and plant-life."

"Exactly! I shall be able to experiment as much as I'd like. Everything from potatoes to cardamom—"

"Potatoes? What on earth can they do?"

"You'd be surprised. And all of the treated plants I can grow here would be useful as well. I want to see if using dragon's breath in my fertilizer will keep plants healthy during the winter and—" He broke off and chuckled. "Well, I have all sorts of ideas. I suppose I don't need to tell you all of them."

"I don't mind," I said. "You're not boring me."

"Thank you. I'm glad to hear it. But it would be better for me to save some topics for later conversations. Keep you in suspense, you know." He gave me a little wink.

I felt my face get hot and I turned away. "Well, I must say it's impressive that you have so many ideas. I confess I've only recently begun to think about my future. You seem to have a talent for it. Do you have any plans beyond the garden?"

His grin widened and he held out his hand. "Come with me."

Taking his hand shouldn't have been exciting, Bartleby. But it was.

He led me away from the garden and to a tall tree. There were wooden planks nailed to the tree like a ladder and at the top was a treehouse, partially built.

I looked up at it. "Did you build this?"

"Papa's been helping me, but yes. It isn't done yet, but it's stable to walk on. Fancy a look?"

I nodded.

He climbed up and I tried not to admire the view. I waited a moment before following.

As soon as I reached the house, he took my hand again and walked me inside. "We still have to finish the roof, you see," he said. "This side is done, but the other half needs more added. And I would like to give it more polish. You know, sand down the rough edges. That sort of thing."

"It's incredible," I said. "I've never been in a treehouse before. What do you plan to do with it when it's done?"

He smiled softly and didn't look at me as he said quietly, "Well, I should very much like to have it ready for when I have children."

"Oh," I said. "How funny. Charles and I were just talking about that. He and Gavin won't be having any children, and he asked me if I wanted them."

"Do you?" he said, turning to me.

It is strange, Bartleby, because I've sat next to the man at lunch and walked with him for weeks. But it wasn't until that moment, when he was standing so close, with his hand clasping mine in the dim light of the treehouse, that I noticed how lovely and dark his eyes were. I was flustered by the observation.

"Er," I said. "I think so. That is, I believe I could be happy either way. If I'm honest, I've barely thought about it at all. I suppose I've always thought I'd decide when I met someone. Find out what he wanted."

He smiled and gave my hand a small squeeze. "I should very much like a family. A large one. If I get this position—" He broke off and let go of my hand, stepping away from me to look out the window of the treehouse. I'm embarrassed to say that I felt the loss rather keenly. "If I get this position," he said. "I would be well set up to adopt a whole bunch of children. The house isn't all that big, but it's large enough to room four or five little ones comfortably."

"But wouldn't you be gone a great deal? In London?"

He shrugged. "His lordship thinks that most of the work would be in correspondence; there would only be a need to go to London once or twice a month. And besides," he added, leaning against the window with a wide grin. "I love the idea of coming home and having a small crowd of children running out to greet me. It—" He turned to me. "It sounds quite perfect, really. Having a family and husband to come home to."

I could picture it: Mr. Ayles walking down the long drive to his home, a whole bundle of children dashing down the road to meet him. The thought made me feel absolutely wonderful. I realized Mr. Ayles was looking at me very intently, which unnerved me rather.

I looked away and said, "Yes, I daresay it does." Then I continued airily, "It sounds as if you have your whole future worked out. I've, er…I've only just started thinking about mine."

He chuckled and the tension in the room dissolved. "Well, I'm an only child. I've known some aspects of my future for years. And besides," he went on, "I'm a little older than you. I can tell you I did not have all this worked out when I was your age."

"How old are you?" I asked, turning back to him.

"Seven and twenty," he said.

"Oh," I said. "You're about Gavin's age. Not that much older than I am."

"Indeed," he said. "It is a rather good age difference, I fancy." He smiled. "Come on, let's go back inside. I imagine the subject has changed by now."

As I climbed down after him, I felt as though a pleasant and important moment had been ruined. In fact, I felt a little guilty about it. So when I got to the ground, I put a hand on his arm before he could walk away. He turned back to me inquiringly.

"I do like your view for the future, Mr. Ayles," I said. "I'm sorry for being so…flippant earlier."

He gave me a soft smile. "No need to apologize, Mr. Hartford. I have a tendency to read people fairly quickly. I flatter myself that I am rarely wrong in my first impressions. But I often forget that others do not make such quick assessments. It is a bad habit of mine, I'm afraid. I tend to assume everyone else around me has come to the same conclusions I have."

"I have the opposite problem," I said. "I've been trying to be more cautious in my own assessments of people."

He tucked his hand around my arm and led the way back toward the house. "I think you do not give yourself enough credit, my friend."

My head whipped around at the word and he looked at me in bemusement. I felt myself flush.

"Did I say something wrong?" he asked.

"No," I said. "On the contrary."

He frowned a little, questioningly.

I sighed. "Well, I had several friends at Oxford, but it took me leaving Oxford to realize they are all quite horrible people. So I've been careful in applying the term to anyone. I was hoping I might consider you a friend but—"

He smiled. "You certainly may." He hesitated. "If I can be honest…"

"Please do," I said.

"I consider you my friend, but I would very much like to be more than a friend, eventually. If you have a mind to it."

I stared in surprise at his directness. "Truly?"

"Truly," he said. "Gradually," he added, smiling. "So that you can feel more comfortable with the notion. To decide if you like it."

"I think I already do like it," I mumbled.

He chuckled and pulled me toward the house. "I know we've only known each other for about three weeks, but as I said before, I tend to come to conclusions about people fairly quickly. I recognize that you may not feel the same way about me, at least not yet. So you need not even consider this an official...declaration. More along the lines of you knowing where I stand and how I feel. I'd hate for you to think I hold you in any less regard than I do."

"Thank you," I said. "I suppose it's only fair to tell you that I...hold you in rather high regard as well."

He grinned. "Thank you. I did hope that might be the case. I really don't mean to pressure you toward any particular decision. Only, I would be very grateful if you gave the matter some thought. There is no hurry; I know you've only just decided to stay in town. Regardless of whether or not I am selected for the position, I will still live here. I shall have less to offer, of course, in terms of financial security, but—well, it won't change the way I feel in any case. I've felt for a while now that you are exactly who I would like to spend the rest of my life with. As long as I can claim you as my friend, I'm not particularly concerned about when the rest of my life begins, if you understand me."

"I do. And I will," I said. "Think about it, that is."

"Thank you," he said, giving my arm a light squeeze.

We walked back into the house and it was very evident that the other three gentlemen had been talking about us, for they all turned and looked at us with a great deal of amusement and curiosity.

"The garden is lovely," I said to Mr. Robert and Mr. Algernon.

"Thank you, Mr. Hartford," Mr. Robert said, smiling at me. "I'm glad you enjoyed your stroll."

"Did Laury tell you about his plans for expansion?" Mr. Algernon said. "He is quite the visionary, you know."

I could feel a blush coming on. "He did," I said. "And he is." I didn't quite dare to look at Mr. Ayles when I said this.

"Well," Charles said, standing. "We won't intrude upon your hospitality any longer. Thank you, gentlemen. It has been a delightful visit."

We all bowed. Charles put an arm around my shoulders as we walked out.

He didn't say a word until we had gone down the road some distance.

"You two were gone a nice long while," he said.

I cleared my throat. "Yes, well, he wanted to tell me of his plans to expand the garden."

"Indeed? And what did you think of them?"

"His plans?"

He nodded.

"Well, they're very clever, of course."

"Of course."

"What did you talk about while we were gone?"

Charles grinned. "Well, we talked about the two of you a great deal."

I groaned. "God keep me from nosy older brothers."

He laughed and, mercifully, did not pursue the subject.

I should add that I'm gaining a frightful proficiency in Bertie's hand-cramp tincture.

7 September 1817

DEAR BARTLEBY,

Thought about the conversation with Mr. Ayles all night and I still can't get it out of my head. The fact is, I rather like the idea of being courted by the gentleman. He's so very kind and clever and good. He's very open and forthright about who he is. And of course, he's extraordinarily attractive. The life he envisions for himself—well, it's nothing like what I might have imagined for myself a year ago. I had rather hoped to find someone like Charles, a dashing and wealthy gentleman who could spoil me. But now? I'm not so sure that would actually please me. After all, I live in a grand house now and it usually feels far too big. I do not like how often I find myself alone in it. Whereas living in that little cottage with a man who likes my company and thinks of me as a friend…He might be gone a great deal, but it would be an easy distance to Charles and Gavin if I got lonesome, and I could possibly even still work for Bertie. Although I'm not sure how that would work with all of the children—

Well, anyhow, it all sounds quite lovely. But it also feels rather soon. I'm not even finished with my own schooling yet; I know I shall be done by the year's end, but all the same… I've only just made my first big decision about the future.

I would very much like some advice on the matter. The question is, who to ask?

Sat next to Mrs. Fossett today, asked her what she hopes to do if she gets the position. She said that she wants to use the position to improve magical education in the country. She particularly wants to see better opportunities for the lower classes and nextborns. Apparently, that's her true passion, which I thought was interesting. She has all sorts of ideas for what the Royal Spellcaster could do in that regard, so it would appear she's given it a great deal of thought.

Bertie gave me a new report to work on, so I was pulling books off of shelves all through my study period.

Afterward, he surprised me by giving me work in the study. I'm to fill out the invitations to the ball. He wrote out the first one and then gave me a list of everyone who is to be invited. It seems like he wants to invite not only the applicants and their guests, but a great deal of the local residents. I should add, Bartleby, that my name was on the list. Which is perfectly thrilling! I think it will be a very fine affair. Quite a good number of people are coming, so I did not finish the stack. Shall have to work on it tomorrow.

Mr. Ayles was kept later today so I left without him. I was disappointed as I do love his company. But as I haven't made up my mind regarding the discussion we had yesterday, it might be better that we didn't talk today.

Just remembered it's Pip and Gerry's day off. Going to see if they want to practice the tea spell with me.

8 September 1817

DEAR BARTLEBY,

Sat next to the major today. He thinks magic should be applied more particularly to the military. He would like to see more spells designed for that purpose. Personally, I find it rather frightful to think of magic being used as a weapon. I'm not exactly surprised by his goal, though.

Started writing my report and then I finished up the invitations.

Walked home with Mr. Ayles today. I was worried it would be awkward after my visit to his house, but as usual, he seemed completely at ease and I found myself able to talk to him as before. He did not bring up the conversation we had the other day. He must really have meant it when he said not to rush in my consideration. I would worry that he had regretted saying anything, but his manner was every bit as warm and friendly as before.

I told him I had enjoyed meeting his parents and he replied with a beautiful smile.

"I know I am terribly biased, but they really are quite wonderful, aren't they?" he said. "They adopted me when I was a baby. Hired a wetnurse and everything. They really wanted to see me grow up."

"So you've only ever known your life with them?"

"Exactly. As far as I'm concerned, it's the only life I've ever had."

"Will you—" I broke off because I realized I was about to ask him something related to our previous conversation and I wasn't sure if it was appropriate.

He glanced at me and put a light hand to my back. "Go on," he said gently.

"Er, will you be adopting children as infants, do you think?"

He smiled. "Possibly. Although I have looked into the matter a little and my understanding is that most people wish to adopt infants. So many older children are left behind. It would also be a trifle more difficult to leave an infant at home if I had to go to London. So I think I would primarily adopt children over the age of two or three. But I'm not set on that notion."

I nodded.

He withdrew his hand from my back. "It was a little different for my parents. They could only afford one child and they were both living at home. So raising me from infancy was an easier decision for them to make."

It struck me that it had been impolite for me to bring it up when I had no idea yet what I wished to say to him. I cast about for a change in topic. "What have you been doing in the afternoons this week?" I blurted. "That is, last week was theory. What is it this week?"

"Spell-building," he said.

"Really? How is that going?"

"Well, it is a trifle different than the previous weeks. We are to design some spells, but we are doing that on our own time. Then we will be showcasing them later."

"What spells are you designing?"

"We have to design two different spells. One is to be something useful, one is to be an illusion. We have to showcase our ability for both traditional style spellwork and Motion spellwork. And at least one of them must be something particular to ourselves."

"What do you mean, particular to yourselves?"

He grinned. "Actually, I suspect his lordship was inspired by you with that."

"Me?"

"You've been asking everyone this week what they plan to do if they are appointed to the position. His lordship has asked us to design a spell that reflects what we hope to accomplish if we are selected."

"I didn't realize anyone had noticed I was asking about that."

He chuckled. "I fancy his lordship is a very purposeful person. I believe it is by design that he has you join us for lunch every day. He likes to see the way people interact with each other. He notices things." He shrugged. "It is a good notion in any case. I would very much like to see what sort of spell Mrs. Fossett comes up with to advance education."

"What are you going to do? That is, what do you hope to accomplish?"

"It is harder to explain succinctly, I'm afraid. I feel as though magic is often out of many people's grasp. Partly due to education and partly due to lack of resources. One has to go to a spell shop to buy a spell. Your sister has very good pricing and, from what I can tell, she works to make sure every customer gets what they need, even if they can't strictly afford it. But she is a rarity in that way. For many people, magic is too costly to be really helpful. Magic has so much potential," he went on. "And people everywhere have great potential to do magnificent things with magic if only it was more accessible for them." He smiled. "It is not as easy to explain, I suppose, as better education or better military spells."

"I don't think that matters," I said. "Do you know what sort of spell you're going to do?"

"I have some ideas," he said. "But I'm still working on it."

"I guess I'll have to ask Mr. Voss and Miss Locke next."

He grinned. "I wouldn't be at all surprised if his lordship arranged the table particularly for that purpose."

"Do you really think he would?"

"It's a different question, coming from you. No one feels as though they're on the spot or they have to prove anything to his lordship in answering you. I think he recognizes that."

"I'm not sure Mr. Voss will tell me. It's difficult getting him to talk to me at all."

"I imagine he will be pleased as anything to tell you about his own goals and plans."

We reached the usual divide in paths home.

"A pleasure as always, Mr. Hartford," Mr. Ayles said, before bowing and heading home.

I stood and watched him walk away. I wonder if he will be right in his guess about where I will sit tomorrow.

9 September 1817

Dear Bartleby,

Received my invitation for the ball, which is hilarious since I'm the one who wrote it. But I'm glad to have it; it will be a nice keepsake. The ball is being held on the 19th of September. Charles told me at breakfast that he has already put in an order for my clothes. I didn't even think about it, so

I'm glad he did. Everyone at our house is going. I'm relieved, for it means I will have people to talk to. I expect the applicants will be surrounded by people asking them questions and getting to know them. So I can't imagine I will be able to talk to any of them very much.

Sat between Miss Locke and Bertie today. I glanced at Mr. Ayles when I saw who my neighbors were and he was grinning like anything.

Asked Miss Locke what she would do in the position. She told me it was an impertinent question, but then proceeded to launch into a sermon about how common magic is now, how it used to be this grand and well-regarded thing. She thinks it ought to go back to being grand and well-regarded. So her hope is to give the art and practice of magic more dignity and respect. It struck me as rather the opposite hope of Mr. Ayles's. And, in a manner of speaking, of Mrs. Fossett's. Both want to make magic more commonplace. I did not say this, of course. Bertie was busy talking to Mrs. Fossett on his left, but I fancy he was listening.

I had no work to do after I finished my report, so Bertie had me leave early. Walking home alone made me dashed contemplative. I kept thinking about Mr. Ayles and how much I liked his company and what I would say to him in answer to his declaration. I would very much like to ask someone's advice on the subject, but I'm not sure who would be best suited. If I go to Charles, he'll be terribly smug about being right all along. Gavin will likely have some helpful things to say, but he never does push me one way or another. Which I usually appreciate, but I think I should like to be pushed. Gerry is far pushier than Gavin, but I have a hard time talking to her about these things. I'm a little shy of asking Pip, but he is my friend. Isn't that what friends do? Perhaps when he comes home tonight I'll ask him.

10 September 1817

DEAR BARTLEBY,

Lost my nerve and did not ask Pip last night. So I still don't know what to tell Mr. Ayles.

Sat next to Mr. Voss at lunch and Mr. Ayles was smirking when we all sat down. He was also right about Mr. Voss being more inclined to talk, considering the subject matter. Mr. Voss, it would seem, wants to make magic bigger. No, that's a silly way to put it. He thinks it ought to be used for bigger things. For instance, instead of building bridges and houses and towers by hand, Mr. Voss wants more magic to be designed with that intention.

"Look at the state of the roads," he said. "Just think what we could accomplish if we applied magic to the problem."

It was fascinating, I hate to say it. I wonder what sort of spell he'll design to reflect that.

Practiced my tea assignment and I nearly have it down.

Left early again which meant Mr. Ayles did not accompany me home today either.

When I got home, Gavin came and got me and brought me into Charles's study. Charles was already at his desk. Gavin perched on the edge of it and had me sit down in the chair in front.

"Is something the matter?" I asked.

"Well, the main reason we wanted to talk to you is because we have some news," Charles said. He waved a letter at me. "This is from your father."

"Oh God," I said, feeling dread fill my stomach.

"Oh, for heaven's sake," Gavin said, flapping his hand at me. "Nothing so serious as all that." He glanced over his shoulder at Charles.

Charles folded his hands in front of him on his desk. "I believe you know Bertie plans to go with the final three applicants to London."

I nodded.

"He asked that we write to Mr. Hartford to see if you could accompany him."

"Father said you may," Gavin said.

"What?" I said, leaning forward. "I get to go to London? With Bertie? And—and everybody?"

"Yes," Charles said, smiling. "But of course, you will be going as his assistant. So you will likely be working."

"I don't even care! I really get to go to London?" I gave a whoop.

Charles laughed.

"I've been wanting to go for simply ages!"

"I recall," Gavin said. "You asked me to send for you in practically every letter when I was staying there."

"Yes," I said mulishly. "And you never did it."

He rolled his eyes. "At any rate, I wish to impress upon you the trust Father is giving you to behave yourself while you're there. You've—you've grown up quite a lot in the time since you arrived here. So I'm not exactly concerned, but London will offer a great many temptations. Please see to it that you don't do anything reckless."

"I won't," I assured him.

Gavin glanced at Charles again. Charles got up and stood next to him, putting his arm around Gavin's shoulders. Gavin said, "We also wanted to ask you…"

"Yes?"

He frowned. "Are you all right?"

"What?"

"You've been moody the past few days. Is anything the matter?"

"Oh," I said. "No, nothing is the matter. Just…I've just been thinking."

"About?" Charles prompted.

I sighed. "I'm not sure I want to talk about it yet."

"You know you can tell us anything, darling," Charles said.

"Well, I don't know how I feel about it yet. I feel like I need a push but—"

"Charles is definitely good for that," Gavin said. Charles grinned.

"I know," I said. "But I don't know if I want that big a push."

Charles laughed.

"If you're sure," Gavin said.

"I'm not sure of anything right now," I said.

"Well," Gavin said. "I can understand that actually. But mind you ponder it less moodily, all right? Or I will have no choice but to sic Charles on you."

I snorted.

Charles wrapped his arms around Gavin's chest. "I'm so glad you're finally learning how to put me to good use, dearest," he said, kissing Gavin on the cheek.

Gavin leaned back to gaze adoringly into his husband's eyes.

"Right," I said. "Can I go now?"

"Off with you, you rascal," Charles said, laughing.

I had better talk to Pip soon.

11 September 1817

Dear Bartleby,

Sat next to Mr. Ayles at lunch today. It was quite nice, as I've missed his conversation. I'm wondering if he was correct and Bertie was hoping I'd ask him about his plans, but I had already asked him. Instead I asked how his spell design work was coming along and we talked about that for most of the meal.

Pip showed up after lunch, which surprised me. He came with a delivery for Bertie from the spell shop and he stopped in to greet me. It seemed too perfect an opportunity, so I asked if I could leave early to walk back with him part of the way. Bertie didn't mind, of course.

"I hear you've decided to stay here for a while," he said, as we walked down the road.

"Yes," I said. "Bertie said I could continue working with him, and Gavin and Charles said I might stay."

"I'm glad," he said. "I take it you no longer feel quite so confined by living here as you once did."

I stuffed my hands into my pockets. "Not as much, no," I said. I was trying to figure out a way to work the conversation around to my dilemma, but nothing was coming to mind.

He glanced at me. "Is anything the matter?"

I sighed. "Well, not exactly. You see, I'm trying to make up my mind about something. I was hoping to ask for your advice, but I don't know how to go about doing it."

He grinned. "I'm all ears."

"Well, Charles took me to visit the Ayles family the other day."

"Ah," he said.

"And Mr. Ayles and I got to talking, apart from the others, you see. He, er, he said he considered me his friend."

"That's good," he said. "I seem to remember that being a concern of yours."

"Yes, it was a relief…"

"But?"

"Well, he also said that he'd like to be more than friends. He…er…sort of proposed."

Pip seemed to consider this. "Is that a problem?"

"I'm not sure," I said. "That's what I wanted to talk to you about. You see, I like him very much. He's quickly becoming one of my favorite people, really. He was telling me all about his plans for the future and they sound wonderful. Possibly perfect, even. He said he wasn't in any hurry. He told me to think about it. He even said it wasn't necessarily an official declaration, more along the lines of ensuring I knew how he felt. But…" I sighed and raked a hand through my hair. "I only just decided I'd like to stay here for a while. And I don't even know how long 'a while' is. That decision was the biggest one I've ever made. I'm not at all sure I'm ready to make another big decision so soon."

He smiled. "I can understand that."

"You can?" I said, feeling strangely relieved.

"Yes. I'm…" He paused. "I'm in a similar position, in a way." He stopped walking and turned to me. "I promised you I'd tell you about my history, Seb. But I've never really gotten around to doing it."

"You're not obligated to," I said.

"I know," he said. "But my past…well it's not a very nice one, but it is a part of who I am and it's a significant part of why I'm here in Tutting-on-Cress and living with Charles and Gavin."

"I always supposed it was because you work with Gerry," I admitted.

"That was the reason given," he said. "But there is a great deal more to it, I'm afraid." He let out a long breath. "When I lived in London, I…lived with a man who…well, he said he loved me, but he was actually very cruel. Only I didn't really know it for cruelty then. So I stayed with him for years even though I was miserable. And—oh, Lord, how to say this correctly," he muttered. He considered for a moment. "This man used me to make money. Initially, it was by teaching me to steal and sending me out to steal things."

I blinked at him. I hadn't realized Pip was a thief.

He smiled a little at my surprised expression. "It is a wonder, truly, that your family is as kind to me as they are."

"Not all that wondrous," I said. "But do go on."

He seemed to steel himself. "Sometimes, however, he also used me to make money by…sending me home with other people." He glanced at me to see if I understood his meaning.

I did, but I had no idea what to say. I finally settled on, "That's horrible, Pip."

He nodded, chewing his lip. "That man you saw talking to me at Bertie's…he was one of the people I was sent home with."

I clapped a hand over my mouth.

"He requested me quite often, as a matter of fact. That's why I…reacted as I did."

"I don't blame you," I said.

"Thank you," he said with a wry smile. "As you can imagine, I have not been in any particular hurry to…pursue romance, as it were."

"No, I should think not." I hesitated. "Will you? Eventually?"

He huffed. "Eventually, yes. But I need time yet." He began walking forward again and I fell into step beside him. "I am very fortunate to have friends like your family, and you, who take care of me, and accept me despite…everything. But I am doubly fortunate to be loved by a gentleman who recognizes that I need time. That it might be years before I'm ready. Quite frankly, I'm already in love with him, but it's too soon. I'm not…ready for his love yet. Thankfully, he knows this and his patience means more than I can adequately put into words."

It suddenly made sense why I've always seen Pip and Bertie looking at each other with such fondness, but never actually touching. "Thank you for telling me," I said. "I'm sure it cannot be easy talking about it."

"It isn't," he said. "Although, it is getting a little easier. I say all of that to tell you that if your Mr. Ayles is in earnest about not hurrying you, then you should accept that. If he is the kind and loving person you believe him to be—and frankly, I expect he is, from what I've seen and heard of him— he will be willing to wait. If you continue to be his friend and continue to strengthen your friendship with him, he will understand."

It was not exactly the answer I was hoping for. Pip was giving me advice, but he wasn't telling me what I should do, besides wait. I considered for a moment. "Should I tell him, do you think? That I need more time?"

He smiled. "I think it would put your mind at ease, if nothing else."

"All right," I mumbled. "Thank you."

He chuckled. "If you were hoping for me to tell you whether or not a future with Mr. Ayles is for you, then I am not the person to ask." He paused. "I might be the worst person to ask, in point of fact. I imagine any one of your siblings will give you a more distinct suggestion."

"I was hoping for something like that," I admitted. "I thought you might give me more advice than Gavin and less advice than Charles."

He laughed. "I can understand that. But if you want my advice, it is to accept your friend's patience." He looked up ahead. "I believe I should branch off here shortly if I want a shorter trip to the village. Unless there was anything else you wanted to talk about?"

I shook my head. "That was it. Thank you."

He put a hand on my shoulder. "Trust yourself, Seb," he said. "You have a bigger heart, a better mind, and keener instincts than you realize." And with that, he gave my shoulder a pat, and walked away.

When I got home, I was at a bit of a loss what to do with myself. I decided to pace around the garden for a bit.

Gavin found me on my third circuit. "You're home early," he said.

"Yes," I said. "Pip came by with a delivery for Bertie, and I asked if I could leave early so I could talk to him."

He looked me up and down. "I take it he didn't tell you what you wanted to hear."

I sighed. "He gave me advice. And it was helpful. But…" I huffed out a breath and began pacing to and fro on the path in front of him. "I don't know. I'm not accustomed to making so many decisions all at once."

"You have a decision to make?" he asked quietly.

"Well," I hedged. "In a manner of speaking. That is, yes?"

His eyebrows rose. "And it is concerning your Mr. Ayles?"

I glared at him. "He's not my Mr. Ayles."

Gavin didn't reply.

I sighed again. "Yes, it is. He…he wants to be more than friends. H-he said he'd like to spend the rest of his life with me."

Gavin didn't look surprised by this. He didn't comment either.

"The trouble is," I continued, as if he had asked me to. "I think I would very much like that, but I'm not sure I'm ready for it."

Gavin put his hands in his pockets and leaned against a small birch tree. He still didn't say anything.

"And," I went on, "he told me to give it some thought and that there was no hurry. Pip says to wait and think about it a while until I'm sure." I glanced at Gavin, who was still staring at me with a solemn and infuriatingly inscrutable expression. I ran a hand through my hair and went on, "I daresay that's very good advice, but I was rather hoping his advice would be more direct. That's the reason I didn't ask you before, because I expected you to tell me something like what Pip did. I'm afraid to talk to Charles about it because he'll tell me exactly what to do, and I'm a little frightened of that much directness. And I can't tell Gerry because she's a sister."

He snorted at that. "Why should that signify?"

I shrugged. "I don't know. I've never asked her for advice on this subject before."

"Rubbish," he said. "You've recounted many of your personal exploits to her."

"Well," I said, kicking at a bit of gravel. "That was more along the lines of bragging than asking for help."

He rolled his eyes. "First off, Gerry gives excellent advice. You might talk to her sometime if you want some solid but gentle guidance. Although I should warn you: she does push when she feels a person needs it. As for the rest, what is it you want to hear, Seb? Do you want me to tell you that Mr. Ayles seems like a lovely gentleman and he suits you very nicely and that I would be pleased to see you settled with such a decent person? That you clearly like him and he clearly likes you and that you seem very happy around him? That it would be nice to know that you are well taken care of, and living close by? For all that is true."

My heart lifted.

He continued, "Or do you wish me to say that you are too young? That you've only known him for a month? That you oughtn't be too hasty? For all that is true, too."

My heart sank.

"Well," he added, "in point of fact, you are at a fine age to get married. Many people get married at twenty. You are younger than either John or I was, but I took a long time out of fear. And you would, presumably, be marrying someone who is able to assume financial responsibility. In which case, you will not have to worry about earning enough money for a new family or anything. So I can't exactly say you are *too* young. Only that you are young."

He pushed himself off from the tree and walked over to me and put both hands on my shoulders, rather like Pip did. "Pip is right. You should think about it. He's also right that you shouldn't rush into it and that you should wait. However, I suspect you already know what you want in this case, and you're hoping someone will tell you that it's a good idea. I'm sure if you ask Charles, he will tell you exactly that." He gripped my shoulders and gave me a little shake. "Just because you made one error in judgment with your friends at school does not mean you are foolish or a bad judge of character. I would be very happy to see Mr. Ayles become a part of our family. And I am not overly fond of most people, as a rule." He paused. "If you feel that he will make you happy, then that is your answer. If you feel that you are not ready for marriage yet, that can also be your answer."

I frowned at him. "How can both be my answer?"

Gavin sighed. "If you are in love with the man, tell him so. If you are in love with him but do not wish to marry him just yet, tell him that too. I would hazard a guess that he will accept the second truth as easily as he will accept the first."

I pondered this a moment. "Oh," I said.

He let go of my shoulders and cuffed me on one. "Come on," he said, turning back to the house. "Let's go inside and have some tea. I'm exhausted just watching you exhaust yourself."

I huffed but followed.

I've been thinking it over all evening and I have come to the conclusion that Gavin may be right. And Pip may be right too. After all, Pip also said to trust my instincts. I think I know my answer to Mr. Ayles, but I need more time as well. Now to have the courage to tell him my answer.

12 September 1817

Dear Bartleby,

Mr. Ayles was not at Bertie's today. I had a moment of panic at not seeing him. I could barely contain my anxiety all through lunch (sat far from Bertie, so I couldn't ask him—sat on the other side of Mr. Voss, who spoke only to Miss Locke the entire time).

After lunch, I asked Bertie as soon as we were in the privacy of his study whether Mr. Ayles had been sent away, like Sir Ronald.

Bertie was bewildered by the question. "Good gracious, darling! Of course not!"

I heaved a sigh in relief.

He looked amused. "Although I'm sure the young man would be gratified by your concern," he said. "He wasn't feeling altogether the thing, poor dear, so I sent him home this morning."

"Oh," I said. "Is he all right?"

Bertie's smile widened a little. "I daresay he will be back in top form tomorrow. I shan't need you after your lessons, m'dear. So, if you care to call on him before dinner, I imagine he would appreciate the thought."

I glanced at him. "Have you been talking to Charles?"

Bertie gave a hearty laugh. "Yes, but I also have my own eyes, my sweet. Why do you think I encouraged him to walk home with you?"

I gaped. "You—you knew? All this time?"

He chucked me under the chin. "You blush so adorably whenever he looks at you, darling. And he lights up every time you talk to him. It did not take much imagination. Now," he said, "let us see how you are getting on with your tea assignment."

I showed him my progress. He made me pour several cups of tea, but finally proclaimed himself satisfied.

"You really are doing marvelously well, darling. Why don't you run along and see how your gentleman friend is doing, hm?"

I withheld the impulse to roll my eyes at him. "You know I'm not allowed to leave the house except to come here."

"I highly doubt Charlie will need much provocation to join you. Go along with you now. I'll see you on Sunday. Take tomorrow off."

I took his advice and went home to see if Charles would escort me to Copperage Farm and check on Mr. Ayles. As

Bertie predicted, Charles was more than willing. Nosy sod. But I was surprised when he sent for the carriage.

"It looks like rain, dearest," he said, glancing out his study window.

I grew even more anxious to get going, now that inclement weather was involved.

It did not rain on our drive to Copperage Farm. Charles smirked at my restlessness but did not comment. When we arrived, we were shown into an empty sitting room. Mr. Robert came in to greet us.

"How lovely to see you again, gentlemen," he said as he walked in. "I'm afraid my husband is out shopping at the moment."

"I do apologize for dropping in so unexpectedly again," Charles said, with a smile that looked anything but apologetic. "Seb was concerned about your son's absence today. We came by to check on him."

"Oh, isn't that nice," Mr. Robert said, giving me a warm smile. "I'm sure Laury will be only too happy to see you. He's in the treehouse at the moment. You're welcome to go back and look for him, if you'd like."

I thanked him and hurried out. I felt very nervous climbing up the ladder uninvited. I know Mr. Robert had given me permission, but it was Mr. Ayles's space. I cleared my throat loudly, hoping it would get his attention. When he didn't look out the doorway, I said, "Mr. Ayles? May I come up?"

But he still didn't come over. A rumble of thunder decided it for me. I didn't have much time. I took a deep breath and climbed the ladder.

Mr. Ayles was sitting in a dark corner of the treehouse. His eyes were closed and he was leaning against a long pillow and had a blanket draped over himself. An empty cup of tea had been put aside by his feet. There was a small spell set up next to him: a cut of reed, a scrap of fabric, a small pocket watch, a chalked sigil, and then a circle had been chalked around him. Something stirred in my memory, but I couldn't quite place it.

He didn't look up until I was fully in the room. To my relief, he smiled at me and leaned over to mutter the counter-spell incantation and rub out the sigil.

"Mr. Hartford," he said, pulling his blanket back.

"Oh, please don't get up," I told him, hurrying over. "I'm sorry to disturb you. Bertie told me you weren't feeling well. I wanted to see how you were."

His smile widened. "How nice," he said. "Please," he added, patting the floor next to him.

I sat beside him, leaning against the wall. "Are you all right?" I ventured.

"Oh, yes," he said. "Thank you. It is nothing serious. A slight headache and some pain in my back. I've taken reme-dies for it, but they rarely help much. Your sister's warming spell works a treat, though," he added, pulling the blanket down briefly to reveal a handkerchief draped over his waist. "It will go away by tomorrow. It always does."

I hadn't realized how close I had seated myself at his side. I felt unnerved and suddenly was unsure if I could go through with what Gavin had encouraged me to tell him yesterday.

"Were you worried for me?" he asked softly.

I nodded. "When you weren't there, I thought—I thought you might have been sent away. I didn't get a chance to ask about it until after lunch. Then Bertie said you weren't feeling well and—"

He smiled and reached up to brush my cheek with the back of his finger. "It was sweet of you to worry, although I'm sorry it caused you agitation."

It is a strange thing, Bartleby, that I should be so nervous around an attractive gentleman as I am around Mr. Ayles. I have shared intimacy with a number of men at this point, so he shouldn't affect me in such a way. And yet...he does. I cannot explain it. All I can say is when he touched me with his finger, it felt so intimate, I found myself unable to say a word.

"Did Father tell you where I was?" he asked.

"Yes," I said. "I'm sorry for coming up with no notice. I tried calling to you—"

He chuckled. "Sorry about that." He gestured behind me. "I had placed a quiet spell for myself. It helps me relax."

"Did you buy this one at Gerry's shop?" I asked, realizing why it seemed familiar.

"I did. She does excellent work."

I folded my hands in my lap and tried to think of something to say. I heard another rumble of thunder and glanced up at the wooden roof.

"You should probably go," he said softly. "I don't wish for you to be caught in the rain."

"Shouldn't you go, too?" I asked.

He shrugged. "This little corner is finished enough that I don't get wet. I'll be fine. I enjoy sitting in here and listening to the rain. I've always loved the rain. It makes everything smell divine, don't you think?"

I felt a pang at the thought of having him alone and not telling him my decision. I trusted the feeling and didn't leave quite yet. I looked down at my hands. "Before I go," I said. "I would like to tell you something."

"Yes?" His voice was quiet.

"It's about the conversation we had the other day."

Rain started to fall then, hitting the treehouse roof and the leaves in the tree.

He didn't say anything, so I chanced a glance at him. He was looking at me expectantly.

I took a deep breath. "I...I think your idea of the future sounds...perfect, Mr. Ayles. And...I rather think that I'd like to be a part of it. I very much enjoy your company, and the prospect of marrying someone I like so well is the best thing I could hope for. But," I added, closing my eyes, "do you think we could wait a little while? Before starting…our future? I feel as if I still have some things to sort out and get accustomed to. I'd also like to know myself better before I make such a big step."

He placed a hand over mine. I stared down at our hands before looking up at him again. He was smiling and, Lord, Bartleby, it was his most beautiful smile yet.

"Of course we can wait," he said. "For one thing, if I get the position, I will likely be very busy for several months. And I may be in and out of London. I would hate to start a marriage off like that. I would feel more comfortable when we both knew what the job might entail before we enter into such a commitment. That is assuming I get it," he added. "If I don't get it, I should like to sort out expenses so I can know how best to support you."

I let out a long breath. "Thank you."

He reached up with his other hand and cupped my cheek. "For another thing, I want to marry you when you are as sure as anything that you want to marry me. I don't mind waiting until that happens. We can make it a long engagement while you sort through everything. Years, if you need it. You're very much worth waiting for, Sebastian Hartford."

There was no proper response for that, at least not in words. So, I closed the distance between us and kissed him. Kissing him was like kissing no one I've ever kissed before. There was no rush, no urgency, no panting, or petting, or being pushed up against a wall. Not that I mind those things, of course. I've always quite enjoyed that part of kissing. But when I kissed Mr. Ayles—that is to say, when he kissed me back, with one hand still cupping my cheek and another clasping my hand—it was all tenderness and softness. It felt like he was taking his time, savoring the moment, or maybe even me, in a way. His gentle way of kissing me made me realize that he really meant it—that he could be patient and that he understood all of my concerns, without me even having to voice them.

The rain pattered heavily around us and I fancied it sounded the way my heart felt as it pattered in my chest.

Mr. Ayles pulled back first. He shifted the hand on my cheek slightly to rub my temple with his thumb.

"I rather think I missed my opportunity to go home dry," I remarked.

He laughed. "Do you regret it?"

I shook my head and kissed him again, briefly this time. "You should probably know," I said, "that I'm pretty sure everyone in my life knows how I feel about you. Even Bertie."

He grinned. "That is because you carry your heart on your sleeve, my love," he said. He kissed my cheek. "And because you blush so prettily."

I felt my face get hot. "Oh, Lord," I said, covering my face with my hands.

He chuckled and took my hands away, clasping them in his own. "I love it," he said. "It has made me wonder for weeks if your skin blushes so nicely elsewhere."

I raised my eyebrows in surprise. "Mr. Ayles, I don't think you ever said anything quite so flirtatious before."

"Are we not engaged now?" he said. "I think you can call me Laurence."

"Oh," I said. "Yes, I suppose I can."

He pulled our hands to his lap. "Will you tell them then?" he asked quietly. "Your family and his lordship?"

"That we are to be married?"

He nodded.

I let out a long breath. "Yes, I suppose I will. Lord, how much they shall tease me."

He chuckled and kissed my cheek. "Yes, I imagine they will. Oh! Will you give me your father's direction? I shall have to write and ask for his permission."

"Good heavens," I said. "I'd forgotten that bit." The thought of Father made all of my warm and happy feelings about Laurence almost evaporate. What will he think of me getting engaged?

"You think he'll object?"

I shrugged. "He doesn't think very highly of me, but I expect he'll like you just fine. Particularly since Gavin, Charles, and Gerry have all met you and like you. I'll be sure to tell Gavin so he can write to Father as well and vouch for you. I suppose he'll want to meet you. Father, I mean."

"I would love to meet him," Laurence said.

"He's very frightening," I warned him.

Laurence laughed and pulled at my hands to tug me over so he could kiss me on the cheek again. "Well, if I get selected to go to London, I will have a good amount of practice with talking to frightening gentlemen."

I gasped and turned so I could face him better. "I'd forgotten! I'm to go to London too!"

He beamed and let go of one hand so he could brush my cheek again. "I'm so glad. You were just saying how you'd like to go. Your father gave his permission?"

"I imagine it has to do with the fact that I'm going with Bertie. I'm sure he wouldn't allow me to go alone." I gave him a wary look. "Does it bother you to marry someone so irresponsible?"

"Are you irresponsible?" he asked, looking amused.

"I don't know," I admitted. "Father certainly seems to think so. Or he did when he sent me here. I honestly don't know what he thinks of me now. I feel as if I've changed a great deal." I considered a moment. "I suppose I ought to write to him about all of this. Will you be telling your parents?"

"I told them about our first conversation, so Father had likely already guessed when he sent you here."

I stared at him. "You did?"

"Oh, yes," he said. "They quite like you, and I've told them a great deal about our conversations. So they weren't exactly surprised. Of course, they'll want to know you better." He hesitated. "They'll be living here, you know. Even after we get married."

"I like being surrounded by people."

He glanced out the window. "It has stopped raining. Perhaps we should go inside."

"Charles is going to be so smug," I grumbled, but I stood up and offered him my hand.

Laurence took it, grinning. He left his blanket, pillow, spell materials, and teacup where they were and followed me out the door. I was a little worried about him climbing down when he wasn't feeling well, but he chuckled when he reached the ground and saw the concern on my face. He reached for my hand and bussed my cheek.

"You are sweet," he said. "I really am fine."

"I've never seen you laid up like that before," I said. "Does it happen often?"

"Often enough," he said vaguely. "Every month, actually. But only for a few days. You really needn't fret. I'm accustomed to it."

We walked back into the house hand-in-hand. I was kept rather busy trying to make sure Laurence was all right walking on the wet ground while also making sure I didn't slip and make a cake of myself. For his part, Laurence seemed to sense both of my intentions, for he appeared highly amused.

When we walked back into the house, Mr. Robert and Charles looked at us smilingly. They were sitting across from each other on a couple of chairs. Laurence's and my hands were still clasped together, so it was no secret what had passed between us.

"Looks as though you managed to avoid the rain," Mr. Robert said tactfully.

Laurence tugged me forward and pulled me to sit next to him on the sofa. He did not relinquish my hand, but placed our clasped hands on his lap. I felt a little embarrassed to be so open about everything all at once, but Charles was smiling at me so fondly, I didn't fuss.

"Yes," Laurence said. "Papa did a marvelous job on the roof, you know."

"He does have excellent craftsmanship. Very good at the details," his father said, turning to Charles. "I confess," he went on, smirking. "I expected you both to come in looking like drowned rats. This one," he said, pointing to Laurence, "used to love the rain. Always running around in it when he was little."

Laurence chuckled. "I used to get my pretty frocks so frightfully dirty."

Charles laughed, seemingly unsurprised by this tidbit.

"Would you gentlemen like to stay for dinner?" Mr. Robert said. "My husband will likely be home soon. I'm afraid we tend to eat unfashionably early, but we would be happy to have you."

Charles glanced at me. "It is very kind of you," he said. "And I would love to accept, but I believe we'd better be getting home. Can we take you up on your offer another day?"

"Any time," Mr. Robert said.

"And you must all come and dine with us as well," Charles went on. "As it is," he said, "I suspect these two have news to impart. And if I know Seb, he'll keep it to himself until I can pry it out of him." He grinned at Mr. Robert. "Best to get him back to my husband, who is much better suited for that task. A two-pronged attack will be more effective."

"Oh, Lord," I grumbled. "You two will be the death of me."

Everyone stood and Laurence cupped the back of my neck to give me a swift kiss on the lips. Which I'm positively certain made me blush to high heaven, if everyone's grins were anything to go by.

Thankfully, Charles did not attempt to pry anything out of me the whole drive home. But it was another matter entirely when we got home. Charles practically dragged me to Gavin's study. Gavin was in the middle of—well, I don't know what, but he had a whole bundle of papers spread out on his desk. He looked up at us, thoroughly bemused, when we walked in. Charles sat me down in a chair and then leaned back against the desk.

"Are you going to tell us now or later?" he said.

Gavin got up and stood next to his husband, who wound an arm around his waist.

I sighed. "You are insufferable. I suppose I'd better tell you now. Although I'm sure I'll have to say it all over again when Gerry and Pip get home."

Gavin's eyebrows rose. "You talked to Mr. Ayles then?"

"Oh, they were sitting alone in a treehouse in the rain for quite some time," Charles said. "So adorably romantic."

Gavin tutted. "Really, Charles. You are the most dreadful chaperone."

"Oh, I say!" I said, objecting to this line of thought.

They both looked at me expectantly.

"Very well. Laurence and I are going to be married." I paused. "I took your advice," I added, looking at Gavin. "I asked if we might wait a while."

"And?"

"He was perfectly fine with it," I said. "Just as you and Pip said he'd be. He said if he does get the position, he may be busy for quite some time, going back and forth to London and everything. If he doesn't get the position, he'd…er…like to make sure he can support me," I added, feeling embarrassed.

"He's got a good head on his shoulders, that one," Charles said. "I'm so happy for you, darling."

"Thank you. It doesn't change anything yet," I continued. "I mean, I don't know when we will get married. So I'll still be living here and everything. If that's all right."

"Of course it is, you goose," Gavin said. "Charles and I were engaged for a full year before we got married. You're young yet; it wouldn't be a bad idea to wait even longer, if you need it."

"That's what Laurence said, too."

"I'm wholly supportive of long engagements," Charles said. "Even if they aren't strictly fashionable."

"He wants to write to Father and ask for his permission," I said. "Do you think you could write to him too and, I don't know, put in a good word?"

Gavin smirked. "I'll be happy to. I imagine Gerry will write to Mother as soon as she learns of it, which will help your case." He paused. "You might write to him yourself, you know. He'll want you to be happy and you're the best person to assure him that this would make you happy."

"I intend to write him, but...I'm not sure what to say. I've never exactly had to tell him something like this before. What if he thinks I'm too irresponsible?"

"The fact that you intend to wait proves you're not," Gavin said softly.

"Have one of us read it over before you send it," Charles added. "If it will make you feel better."

"I will. Thank you." I glanced at Charles. "You're a good deal less smug about it than I thought you'd be."

Gavin snorted.

"Oh, just wait until we have them over to dinner, darling," Charles said.

"Damn," I said. "Curse my blasted ruddy mouth."

"When should we have them over?" Gavin said.

"There's no hurry," I said.

"I should like to do it soon," Charles said, ignoring me. "They invited us to stay for dinner today, but I knew I wouldn't get the news out of him until he came home. Do you think tomorrow night would suit?"

"Oh, really!" I said.

"Perhaps Sunday," Gavin said. "It would give them a little more time."

"And we can invite Bertie," Charles added.

"Would you two stop talking like I'm not in the room?" I said.

Charles kissed Gavin. "Sunday then."

I groaned and sank into my seat.

Charles laughed and leaned forward to tousle my hair. "You really don't think we're going to miss the opportunity to get to know our future in-laws better, do you?"

I groused at the tousling. Gavin rolled his eyes.

"I don't know what I shall write to Father."

"Do it in the morning, darling," Charles said. "Take time to enjoy your news."

"But don't fret about it," Gavin added.

I made the announcement at dinner, because Charles looked like he'd do it if I didn't. Gerry and Pip both offered their congratulations. Dinner was then spent talking about Laurence, how nice his smile is, how pretty his eyes are, how clever he is, how kind he is, and how grand all of his ideas are. By the end of dinner, everyone was referring to him as Laurence, so I rather suspect he's already been accepted as part of the family. And I have to say, Bartleby, it really is a very nice thing.

13 September 1817

Dear Bartleby,

I did not sleep a wink all night, torn between excitement over the reality that I am betrothed and the sickening dread of having to write to Father about it. When I woke up this morning, I had myself all worked up.

It must have shown on my face because as soon as breakfast was over, Gavin said, "Why don't you go get started on
your letter before you make yourself sick? I'll look over it and
send it along with mine. And see to it you send a message to
your gentleman with Father's direction."

I got up from the table, grumbling a little about Gavin
telling me to do things I already intended to do.

"Oh," he said, before I had left the room. "Once we finish
up your studies and Father declares himself satisfied, I'll start
teaching you the running of a household."

I turned on my heel. "Must I?"

"Well, of course, there's plenty of time," Gavin admitted.
"But you'll feel better about everything if you have a good
idea of what you're getting into, in terms of responsibilities."

"Besides," Charles said. "You will do a marvelous job of
keeping house, darling. It will suit you admirably."

Startled by this compliment, I left.

I sent off Father's direction to Laurence as soon as I got to
my desk in the library. But it took me ages to write out my
letter. First, I decided to soak my hand because I had written a
frightful lot yesterday, but that was really to stall for time, as
I'd been too excited to notice how much I was writing. Then
when I started actually writing the letter, I kept scratching out
words and changing my mind on how I wanted to phrase
things. I kept thinking that I ought to have worried about it
sooner and that Father may very well object to my getting
married at all.

Gerry found me while I was on my third messy attempt.
"Oh, good," she said. "I was hoping I might find you in here.
Do you know where my—" She broke off. "What on earth is
the matter?"

"I'm trying to write to Father about the engagement and I
don't know what to say."

She frowned in confusion.

"What if he says no?" I asked.

"Papa?"

"After all, I was sent down here as a punishment. What if he thinks—"

"Punishment?" she said. "Well, I like that. You think living with us is a punishment?"

"No, of course not," I said. "You know what I mean."

She sighed and pulled up a seat. "First off, you were not sent here as a punishment. Don't be such a goosewit. You were sent here because Papa wanted you to stop playing pranks and he wanted to get you away from bad influences. And, from what I understand, he hoped you might learn responsibility."

"Gavin said our making it a long engagement was proof enough that I'm responsible."

"I'm inclined to agree with him," she said. "Here, let me see what you've written."

I grudgingly passed her my messy letter.

She glanced over it quickly and then said, "The trouble is, you've always been too afraid of Papa to recognize that all he really wants is for you to be happy."

I rolled the pen between my fingers but didn't say anything.

"Why are you so afraid of him?" she said after a few moments of silence.

"He doesn't like me very much."

"What are you talking about? Of course he does."

"He's never said anything to me that wasn't some sort of lecture."

"Well, that's because—"

"And I'm not talking about my time at Oxford," I said. "Even before then."

"Nonsense," she said. "When we were growing up, he was always around, playing games, taking us riding. How can you forget all of that?"

"When *you* were growing up, you mean," I said. "By the

time I came around, he'd stopped doing all of that."

"But—" She broke off and considered. "Even if that was the case, you can't possibly think it was personal to you. I daresay Papa thought you were surrounded by siblings and didn't need him."

I shrugged. "Perhaps."

"You really believe he dislikes you?" she said softly.

"I suppose I've always felt he was indifferent to me. And then I went to school and mucked it all up. I'm quite sure I'll never have his good opinion now."

"I'm quite sure you're mistaken."

"That's easy for you to say," I said. "You're perfect and can do no wrong."

She gave a very indelicate snort. "Rubbish. Do you have any idea of the scolding I got when I told them I was going into trade? Neither Papa nor Mama was pleased. It took me months to talk them around to the notion."

"Really?"

"Yes," she said. "But when they came to the realization that I was still being cared for, that I wasn't starving, that someone was helping me with the financial aspects of the shop, and that someone else was coming to work alongside me, they relented."

"Oh."

She sighed. "If you were to tell Mama and not Papa about it, what would you say?"

I considered this. "I would tell her that I've been working with Bertie for the past few months and that I met someone while I was working—"

"Very good," she said. "That's a nice start. It adds that Bertie knows him too. Go on."

"I would say that...this gentleman is someone I've spoken with nearly every day and that you all have met him and like him. And that I like him very much, and he has quickly become one of my favorite people. And that he has proposed?

And," I added hastily, "I would say that I'm not actually getting married yet; that we've agreed to wait a little while. Until I have a better understanding of who I am and what I want, and when he has a better understanding of his future and career."

She beamed. "There's your letter."

"Really?" I said. "But—"

"Listen," she said. "Why did Papa give you that journal for Christmas? Do you remember?"

I thought about it. "He said I needed more introspection."

"Don't you see? He worries about you. I know he can be a little gruff in his worry, but, honestly, aren't we all?"

I tilted my head in acquiescence.

"I write to Mama regularly," she went on. "And never has she said that either she or Papa are disappointed in you or dislike you. They love you, you clodpole," she said. She reached forward and grabbed both sides of my head and then pulled me toward her so that she could kiss me on the forehead.

I batted her away. "Ugh," I said. "Charles does that. Why do you people always treat me like a child?"

She laughed. "You're the littlest, dear. You must get accustomed to it."

"I daresay you'll do it even when I'm married and have children of my own."

"Oh, yes," she said blithely as she stood. "I most certainly will. I expect Charles will too."

I sighed. "Insufferable."

She leaned against the table. "You want to have children then?"

I felt myself flush. "Well, Laurence wants children. Lots of them, I think."

"Does he?" she said, grinning as if she was trying not to laugh. "What else does Laurence want?"

"He wants to expand his garden to grow magical plants

and things he can use in spells. And…er…he's building a treehouse for the children to use. He wants to get the Royal Spellcaster position so he can make magic more accessible to more people."

"Capital," she said. "I shall have lots to discuss with him when his family comes to dinner," she said, walking away.

"What?"

"They're coming to dinner tomorrow night, along with Bertie," she said. "Didn't Charles tell you? He sent over the invitation yesterday, I believe."

I groaned and laid my head on the desk. She tousled my hair and then left.

I sat that way for a moment, being vaguely irritated with my nosy siblings, but also feeling strangely comforted that everyone had taken the news of my engagement so easily. In fact, they had taken it more easily than I had. With that in mind, I sat up and wrote out my letter, just as Gerry had advised. I added everything I could think of about Laurence so Father might recognize how much I liked him and how well I knew him. Then I took it to Gavin before I had a chance to second-guess myself.

He looked over it, as promised. "This will do very nicely," he said. A corner of his mouth quirked. "I didn't know he didn't like poetry."

"Blast," I said. "I had forgotten I wrote that."

He rolled his eyes. "Shall I send it with my letter?"

"Would you mind?"

"Not at all."

I hesitated. "What did your letter say?"

He gave me a wry look and handed it to me.

It was, well, frankly, glowing with praise of both myself and Laurence, not to mention a nice bit about his family. The part that made me feel a little wobbly was where Gavin described Laurence's financial situation. There were details I didn't know and hadn't thought about, like how much

Laurence has per year, how much the house and farm are likely worth, and the prospective new position and what that might do for his financial and social standing. I studied the letter for a moment, long after I'd finished reading it.

"Seb?" he said gently.

I stirred and handed it back to him. "Thank you," I said. "I really do appreciate it." I turned abruptly on my heel and walked to the door.

"Seb!" he said again.

The door opened and Charles stepped in. He glanced at me and then at Gavin. "Is everything all right?"

"Ask my addlepated brother," Gavin said.

"I'm fine," I insisted. I looked up at both of them. They were each staring at me in a mixture of concern and consternation. Well, the consternation was really from Gavin. Charles was simply concerned. I sighed. "It's just—well, I'm sure it is what Father wants to hear and I don't mean to sound ungrateful but—" I felt tears welling up, which was really just too embarrassing. I pressed on, simply to get it all out. "Well, I mean, telling him about the Ayles family and h-how much Laurence has per annum. It all sounds so dreadfully businesslike. As if it were some sort of transaction."

"Oh, Seb," Gavin said, sounding less irritated and more sad.

Charles surprised me by pulling me toward his chest and wrapping his arms around me.

I gave a little sob and felt thoroughly silly about it. "It didn't feel businesslike when he asked me."

"The best ones never do, darling," Charles said.

I pulled away so I wouldn't get his coat dirty. I rubbed my nose with the back of my hand. "Sorry," I said. "So silly."

Charles reached up and rubbed his thumb under my eye. "Not at all. This is the less romantic part about marriage, I'm afraid. Laurence and your father will have much to discuss on that subject."

I sighed. "It seemed simpler yesterday. The only concerns then were my own fears. And he—he makes them seem less worrisome, somehow."

Charles smiled. "As he should."

I rubbed my eyes. "It's fine. I'm sure it's all perfectly normal. Just gave me a shock. That's all."

"You look a little tired," Charles said.

"Thank you very much."

"Did you sleep at all last night?" Gavin said.

I shrugged. "I've had better nights."

"Go have a lie-down," Charles said. "We'll call you when it's time for lunch."

I did as Charles suggested while Gavin sent out our letters. After lunch, Charles sat down with me in the library and went over the list he had made of everything I have learned in the past few months.

"Now that we all have a better notion as to your future," he said, with a smirk. "I have some ideas for lessons that might be more specific to you."

"I thought I was nearly done with school," I protested.

"I'm perfectly satisfied with all of the work you have done thus far," he said. "But since we have the opportunity, it would be good to take advantage of it."

I leaned against my hand. "Oh, very well then. What do I have to learn now?"

He grinned and patted my shoulder. "Not to worry, darling. I have it all planned out."

"Of course you do," I said. "You just like to see me busy."

He pulled over a pile of books. "You and I will be talking about estate management. Gavin will explain to you the running of a house, how to be a good employer, and clever ways to economize." He paused, looking fond. "He really is a genius with that, you know. Even though he doesn't need to be."

I rolled my eyes. "Yes, yes, you're very much in love. Do get on with it."

He smirked. "Bertie plans to teach you a great deal of at-home remedies and spells that are useful for housework."

"That doesn't sound too bad," I said.

"Gavin and I have also talked to our head gardener, cook, butler, housekeeper, and my man Jennings. You will spend some time with each of them after your return from London."

"What on earth for?"

"They will teach you the basics of gardening, cooking, maintenance of the house, repairing clothing. That sort of thing."

"Must I?" I said. "They do have servants. And anyway, if Laurence gets the position—"

"If he does, then you will simply be armed with a great deal of knowledge that will allow you to better understand your household staff," he said. "If he does not, well, dearest, I really want you to be prepared for that possibility. You're lucky I'm not adding childcare into your curriculum."

"Oh, good heavens, please spare me," I said.

"As I said," he said, chuckling. "This can all wait for your return from London. Bertie tells me you will be leaving in a little over a week. So you can take that time off from studying."

I glared at the pile of books he had set up. "Can we move those until after I get back?"

He smiled and picked up the books and shoved them onto a nearby bookshelf. "Better?"

"Thank you."

"Also," he said, leaning against the table. "Gavin and I have been talking. We think you've been marvelously good about staying in the estate for the past few months. We've decided to lift that particular edict."

I stared up in surprise. "I can go wherever I like?"

"Well," he said, with a smile. "Don't leave town or

anything without talking to us. But you are now engaged. If you wish to go to the village or..." He grinned. "You know, take a stroll down to see your betrothed...you needn't ask for permission first, or garner an escort."

I blushed at this but didn't say anything.

"Not that I mind going with you," he added. "As a matter of fact, I very much like all three of the gentlemen at Copperage Farm. But I expect his parents will provide sufficient chaperonage, should there be a need. And I imagine you will want to visit by yourself upon occasion. I want you to know you're free to do so."

"Thank you," I said, more feelingly than the last time. I glanced up at him. "Did you ask Father for his permission to marry Gavin?"

"I did."

"What was it like?"

Charles laughed. "He was stern, but he was predisposed to like me, I think. Your mother had already met me, which helped a great deal. I expect Gavin's letter will do much to further your young man's suit."

I mulled this over. "I imagine I shall have to go back and introduce Laurence and everything."

"I imagine so, yes."

I ran a hand over my face at the thought.

Charles patted my shoulder and left.

I was restless most of the day. Tried reading a bit, but couldn't get comfortable.

Gavin eventually forced me to go on a walk with him. I hate to admit it, but it helped.

14 September 1817,

Dear Bartleby,

Got to Bertie's house a little early today because I had no

schoolwork to do and, quite frankly, I was feeling restless again. Bertie was delighted when I walked in.

"Oh, how lovely," he said. "I want to talk to you."

He took me into his study and sat me down.

"First things first, my sweet. I hear congratulations are in order?"

"Charles told you?"

He smiled. "He did, but so did your darling betrothed."

"Oh," I said. "That's all right then."

"I'm delighted for you both, m'dear," he said. "You two will get on very nicely."

"Thank you."

He considered me for a moment. "And I'm going to make a suggestion, if you don't mind, darling."

I looked at him in surprise. "Of course I don't."

"Well, I recommend you talk to him about continuing your work with me. I will be delighted to employ you for as long as you desire, for you know I love working with you. I suspect he will anticipate you staying on. However, knowing you as I do," he continued, with a wry smile, "I imagine you'll fret about it at some point. So you might as well discuss it with him."

"Oh," I said. "You're right. And Charles said something about my lessons changing."

"Yes," he said. "That was another thing I wanted to discuss. We will be a little more purposeful in our lessons, after we return from London. I have a great many things I would like to teach you. Some of it will not be as exciting, but I promise to try to keep it as interesting as possible for you."

I nodded.

"Of course," he went on, "your future husband is a very skilled spellcaster, so you won't exactly need to worry about it. But I imagine you will want to be able to do things without asking for his help."

"Yes, I definitely would." I smiled a little. "It is odd to hear him referred to that way."

Bertie chuckled. "Best get accustomed to it, my sweet. Now, the last thing I wanted to discuss with you: this week will continue much as last week did. That is to say, I'm having them work on their own spells at this time. I believe they've all told you about that?"

"A little, yes."

"Excellent. Well, you and I will have our work cut out for us in preparing for the ball. I will greatly appreciate your help in getting everything ready. The day before and the day of the event, I will need you for most of the day. Is that all right?"

"Of course it is."

"Wonderful! I'll send you back home in time to get ready, of course. But it will be all go around here, the closer we get to the day. So I thought it best to prepare you."

I nodded again.

He clapped his hands together. "Delightful! After lunch, we'll sit down and coordinate our plans for the week. I'll give you a list of things I should like you to take care of or look into for me."

At lunch, I was seated between Bertie and Laurence. Bertie looked very pleased with himself and Laurence simply looked pleased.

"How are you with public affection?" Laurence asked in a low voice when we sat down.

"I don't think I mind it," I said.

"Lovely," he replied, and leaned over to kiss my cheek.

"Well!" Miss Locke said indignantly.

I blushed and looked down at my plate. Laurence reached under the table and gave my hand a squeeze.

"Oh, yes," Bertie said in a blithe tone. "Have you all heard the marvelous news? These adorable little lovebirds are engaged. Fancy such romance occurring during this process! I am so delighted!"

Everyone offered their congratulations, although Mr. Voss

looked perturbed.

"I daresay that put Ayles forward in the running, did it?" he said.

"I beg your pardon!" I said. Laurence squeezed my hand again.

"Well," Bertie replied, unruffled, "I must confess his inter-actions with Seb gave me a good indication of his character, much as the rest of yours have. But no, Mr. Voss. I will not be making my recommendation based on my assistant's personal affairs."

I felt myself blush again and looked back down at my plate.

"I will be making it," Bertie went on, "as I have already explained. You all must prove you have the skills required, a cool head in the face of stress, the ability to converse easily and work well with others, and a clear goal in what you hope to accomplish in the position. This is not simply a spellcaster of elevated rank. It is a government position and a royal appointment. All five of you would be excellent choices, but my mind is very nearly made up already."

Everyone stared at him in surprise at this statement.

"You're not going to tell us then?" Mr. Voss said.

"No, I shall not," Bertie replied. "As I said, it is very *nearly* made up. I am giving you all a chance to amaze me before the announcement."

Naturally, everyone was quite shaken by this. Well, that is to say, all of the applicants were quite shaken. Which I suspect was Bertie's intention. Even Laurence looked a little solemn. Although when I caught his eye, he smiled and gave me a wink. So I imagine he's taking it with his usual calm. Lunch was, as you might imagine, not quite as lively as usual.

After lunch, Bertie gave me a long list of things to look into. Most of it is business in the village, which he said I could take care of tomorrow.

"If I were you," he said. "I would go there before coming

here. It is a little less busy in the mornings, I find."

Seeing as my mornings are now free, I said I would go before lunch tomorrow. He then walked me through the whole house explaining where things will be set up, including the refreshments, the musicians, the seats, and the spells.

"The applicants have all provided me with descriptions of their spells," he said. "So we shall be accounting for those as well."

It took hours to go over. When it was time for me to go home, Bertie sent for the carriage and told me to go fetch Laurence. "I expect he'll be in the garden, dear."

He was, and he was talking with Mrs. Fossett, which surprised me a little. But they both smiled as I approached.

"Bertie said we're all driving home together," I told him.

"Family dinner," he explained to the widow.

She laughed. "Ah yes. Those are always interesting."

"What are you going to do with Bertie gone?" I asked her.

She shrugged. "Much like we usually do, I expect," she said. "We'll have dinner. Everyone will likely gossip about you two and then we'll all ruminate over who his lordship has chosen. I shall give you a full report tomorrow," she said, giving Laurence a pat on the arm.

"Please do," he said, reaching for my hand. "I hope Voss isn't too unpleasant about it."

She rolled her eyes. "For all his cleverness, he's very nervous. He wants it so badly, you know."

"Doesn't everyone?" I asked.

She smiled at me. "Not exactly in the same way. We all want it, of course. But if Mr. Voss or Mr. Ayles were to win the position, I'm confident that they'd help to push my goals a little, for we're all much of the same mind. I would like to be selected, of course, but his lordship has warned me that the position is technically for firstborns only. There is precious little chance I will be appointed, even if I am recommended by his lordship. So if either of them were to get appointed, I'd be pleased. "

"Oh," I said. "That's a shame. My sister said something similar."

"Is that why she did not apply?" Laurence said.

"One of the reasons," I said.

"Maybe I'll ask her about it tonight. Well," he said to the widow. "I'll see you tomorrow then."

"Enjoy your dinner," she said.

He grinned at her in response and we walked back to the house for our things. Before we reached the door, he pulled me closer and gave me a soft kiss on the lips. "Prepare yourself for a lot of teasing, my love," he said. "You know that is what tonight will be about."

I sighed. "I know it. At least they like you. I'm glad of that. Even if they do enjoy tormenting me."

He chuckled. "It's all out of love."

"So you say."

We walked into the house for our things and the carriage was brought around. Bertie did not tease us on the drive over, which was a relief. He asked Laurence about his parents for most of the trip.

When we arrived, however, we were both the center of attention. Laurence's parents were already there and everyone had settled comfortably in the sitting room. There was a pointedly empty space for us to sit together on the sofa. Laurence led me to it without hesitation while Charles introduced Bertie to Laurence's fathers. I suspected they were a little in awe of Bertie, due to his title and station. But Bertie is so easy to be around, everyone was at ease very quickly. Well, except me, because they would keep referring to us as "the lovebirds" and whatnot. Laurence seemed to enjoy it, for he took my hand and held it in his lap. Which is something I'm beginning to suspect he's fond of doing. He responded to all inquiries and commentaries in his typical calm manner. He even took it in stride when Gavin accused him of disliking poetry.

"I apologize," he said, laughing. "I have not the sensibility for poetry. It goes over my head far too much, I'm afraid."

"I shall forgive you," Gavin assured him solemnly. "If you will promise to try more."

"Oh, Gavin," I said.

Laurence assured Gavin he would. Charles asked Laurence which books he did like and then the conversation devolved into talk of gardens and plants and botany. It was quite over *my* head, I need hardly tell you.

Thankfully, we were called in to dinner before it went on for too long. For once, I was grateful that Charles and Gavin don't pay any attention to proper seating because it meant I got to sit next to Laurence, which I'm fairly sure would not ordinarily be permitted. Bertie and Mr. Algernon hit it off beautifully. They talked with Charles for most of the meal. And Mr. Robert and Gavin seemed to find a lot of common ground. Gerry pounced on the opportunity to talk to Laurence about his plans for his garden and growing magical plants.

Pip, who was seated on my other side, smiled at me. "Is it as bad as you feared?" he asked.

"Not so much. It is very nice that everyone gets along so well," I admitted.

"I'm glad," he said. "For you know this will be a regular occurrence from here on out."

I looked around the table at all of the cheerful conversations happening. It made me feel warm and comforted to see my family getting on so splendidly with Laurence and his family.

"I don't think I will mind that," I said to Pip. He beamed at me, dimpling.

After dinner, we all moved to the drawing room. Laurence sat tucked up next to me on the sofa and laid one hand on my leg. "That's a very fine pianoforte," he said. "Do any of you play?"

"Gerry plays," Gavin said.

"Will you do us the honor, Miss Hartford?" Laurence said.

"I should be delighted." She got up and played a couple of pretty melodies. Gerry is exceptionally good on the piano. Mama had hoped it would help push her along in the Marriage Mart. When she was done, she sat back down and everyone told her how well she did.

"Laurence will be too modest to say anything," Mr. Robert said. "But he plays, too."

"And very well," Mr. Algernon put in.

"Not very well," Laurence said.

"Oh, do play for us," Gerry said.

He grinned and sat at the piano. I had no idea he could play. I have never considered playing the piano an attractive activity, but it was surprisingly appealing to see Laurence do it. He was wrong: he did play very well. He played a couple of songs, like Gerry had done, before returning to sit beside me. He laid his hand on my leg again and I got distracted thinking about how nice his hands were.

I was pulled out of that pleasant line of thought by Mr. Robert saying, "Laurence sent out his letter this morning. So I hope we will hear from Mr. Hartford soon."

I tensed. Laurence looked at me questioningly and moved his hand over mine.

"I have written to him as well. As did Seb," Gavin said, glancing at me. "I anticipate my father giving his blessing."

The conversation moved on and continued in an easy-going manner until Mr. Algernon said, "Well, this has been a delightful evening. I do hope you will allow us to return the favor soon."

"Gladly," Charles said, grinning.

Everyone got up and made for the door. Laurence held me back. "Are you all right?" he said, when the room was empty.

I shrugged.

He cupped my cheek. "Angel," he said softly. "What is it?"

I stuffed my hands in my pockets and looked at the floor. "It's silly. Just—Gavin showed me his letter before sending it out and—well, it was unpleasant having to think about the financial part of this arrangement. I rather wish we didn't have to talk about it."

He leaned forward and kissed my cheek. "Don't worry about it. It is mostly between your father and I."

"I know," I said. "It's such a silly thing to be upset about."

He cupped the other side of my face. "Sebastian."

I looked at him.

"It means more than I can say that you care so little about money." His thumbs stroked my cheeks. "But I'm afraid my finances will always be a bit of an issue. That is, if I don't get the position."

"Bertie said I may continue working for him. Would that help?"

He smiled. "It might. But I would prefer it if you worked for him only because you enjoyed it, not because we needed the funds."

"You don't mind then? Me continuing to work for him?" I asked. "He suggested I talk to you about it and be sure."

"Why on earth would I mind it?"

"Well—"

"Laury," Mr. Algernon said, stepping back into the room. "The carriage is ready for us."

"I'll be there in a moment," Laurence said. "We'll discuss everything later, all right?" I nodded. He kissed me and then leaned his forehead against mine. "Try not to worry about it," he said.

I followed him out. Charles grinned at me and threw an arm over my shoulder. Bertie gave the Ayleses a ride home in his carriage, which was very kind of him.

When they left, everyone turned to look at me.

"He really is wonderful, Seb," Gerry said.

"Yes, he is," Gavin said. "And if you're fretting about Father again, don't."

I sighed. "I know. That's what Laurence said too."

"As someone who has actually talked to Mr. Hartford about such things," Charles said. "I can tell you that money was the least of his worries."

"That's different," I said. "You're wealthy."

Charles pulled me around to face him and put his hands on my shoulders. "He wanted to know if I could support your brother," he said. "If he asks Laurence the same question, I expect Laurence's answer will be the same as mine. You should also know the first question he asked me was whether or not I loved Gavin."

I looked up in surprise.

Charles smiled. "The second question was whether or not I would make Gavin happy. The third question was whether or not I could support him."

"Oh."

"And," Charles went on, "you should note that was his exact wording. He wanted to know if I could support your brother in every sense, that is, financially and emotionally."

"Oh," I said again.

Charles tousled my hair. "Now, try to turn your mind to something more pleasant, will you, darling? Tell us something about tonight that made you happy."

I smiled. "Laurence called me 'angel.'"

Charles grinned.

"Good God," Gavin said. "He really does have much to learn about you, doesn't he?"

Gerry smacked Gavin's shoulder. Charles tousled my hair again and we all trooped upstairs to bed.

It's all well and good, Bartleby, for them to tell me not to fret. But how can I help it? What if Father says no?

15 September 1817

DEAR BARTLEBY,

Started at the village today, picked up everything on Bertie's list, and talked to all of the vendors about things to be delivered later. He told me to charge everything to his account. There were quite a lot of things to carry, even with the later deliveries, so Pip stepped away from the shop to help me take everything to Bertie's.

He asked if I was excited for the ball and I told him I was.

"Are you?" I asked.

He shrugged. "I've never been to one. So I'm more nervous than anything else."

"What are you nervous about?"

"Well, I don't wish to dance, for one thing. Gerry and Charles offered to teach me ages ago, but I have no interest in it."

"Really?" I asked. Then I wished I hadn't. "Does it make you uncomfortable?"

"It would if it were with a stranger," he said. "It seems easier to turn down a dance out of ignorance of the steps. I can hardly say I don't wish to dance with anyone besides a small group of people. I don't want to appear to be a snob. I'm already quiet by nature, a trait people often equate to snobbery."

I thought of Gavin and how he always seems so put out, even when he isn't. "I can see what you mean," I said. "But it won't just be dancing. The food will be good. The applicants will be performing spells for everyone, which should be fun. And Bertie will be making the announcement."

"I am looking forward to that," he said. "Any ideas as to who will be chosen?"

"No," I admitted. "They're all very good. I know who I'd like to be chosen, of course."

"Other than Laurence?"

"Yes, well, mostly him. But I should like Mrs. Fossett to be one of the three who goes to London. She's so very nice. I've wanted both of them to be selected since the beginning really. Even before...Laurence and I...er..."

He chuckled.

"I imagine Mr. Voss will be selected," I said. "Much as I dislike him. He's very unpleasant, you know. But he is very clever."

We chatted amiably until we reached the house. Bertie was busy with the applicants so Pip walked back. I organized all of the purchases before lunch.

At lunch, Bertie seated everyone in exactly the same spots. I'm guessing this will be the arrangement until it's all over. Can't say I mind it. Mr. Voss was seated on Laurence's other side and very pointedly did not speak to him. So Laurence and Bertie and I talked for most of the meal with Mrs. Fossett, who was seated on Bertie's left.

After lunch, I showed Bertie the purchases. He seemed quite pleased. He had me sit down with his cook to go over the menu while he worked with the applicants. I felt very nervous being given such a responsibility. But the cook explained everything very well and told me what questions she still needed answers to. So that was all right. Bertie came and found me later and I was able to show him my notes. He sent me back to the cook with his answers.

Then he had me follow along as he talked to Miss Locke about her spells. She walked us through where she would be casting them, how much space was required, and any ingredients she needed. Bertie had her give me a list of anything that needed to be purchased. I'm to go back to the village tomorrow.

That took a while, so afterward, I was able to walk home with Laurence. It was the first time we'd walked home together since I accepted his proposal. It was both very different and not different at all. He held my hand as we walked down the road, which was nice. But we talked as we always do. When we got to the part where we branched off, he pulled me in for a long kiss. It was a touch different from our past kisses, I should note. There was a little bit of tongue involved. All right, so I'm the one who started that, but Laurence seemed amenable to the notion. We were both a little breathless when we finally broke apart.

He smiled and reached up to brush my cheek with his fingertips. "You're so beautiful," he said. "Do you know?"

"Well, I've always argued I'm the handsomest of my siblings. But do please tell me more. I should very much like some support for my argument."

He laughed, giving me a swift kiss on the lips. "Good night, my love."

I watched him walk away, pleased that I could enjoy the view now. Then I walked home. Must have still looked a mite flushed because Charles gave me a knowing grin when he saw me. Impudent man.

16 September 1817

Dear Bartleby,

Today was very similar to yesterday, only I didn't need Pip's help, and I only had to stop at Gerry's shop. That part was very nice, as I got to visit with Gerry and Pip for a little while first. Then it was lunch, same seating arrangement. Bertie had me talk to the housekeeper and head butler about the ball and I showed him my notes as before. We followed Major Wilburforce around while he talked through his spells and gave me a list of ingredients to purchase. After the major, Mr. Voss did the same thing, so I have a slightly longer list of things to get tomorrow.

Laurence and I walked home together again and I asked him if he was nervous about the ball.

He shrugged. "I've never performed a casting in front of

so many people," he said. "So that will be different. But I'm not sure I'm nervous, exactly." He gave me a sidelong glance. "I'm a little more nervous about you discovering I'm not a particularly good dancer."

"What?" I exclaimed. "That's impossible."

"Why is it impossible?" he said, laughing.

"Because you're good at everything."

"That is categorically untrue," he said. "Although your confidence in me is very sweet."

I bumped his shoulder. "Are you really as bad as all that?"

"Quite dreadful," he said. "I daresay you will be very disappointed."

"You'll still dance with me, won't you?"

"If you'd like me to," he said, looking apprehensive.

"You don't want to dance with me?"

He stopped walking and framed my face with his hands. "Please forgive me for what I'm about to say, my love."

"Oh, dear."

"I quite detest dancing."

"What!"

"But I will dance with you if you really want."

"I want to show you off," I said, a little petulantly. "Isn't that one of the nice things about being betrothed?"

He grinned and kissed the tip of my nose. "I regret to tell you that dancing with me is quite possibly the worst way to show me off. That is, if you want me to do you proud."

I muddled over this. "But I do so adore dancing. One dance?"

He leaned forward and repeated, "One dance," against my lips.

I was about to put my arm around his waist when he pulled away and began walking again, taking my hand. "Now, if you want to know what *I* am looking forward to," he said.

"Yes?"

"I'm looking forward to taking you on a walk in the garden."

"Oh," I said. "I suppose we haven't done that yet. It didn't occur to me that was something you wanted to do."

He smiled and squeezed my hand. "I particularly want to do it at the ball."

"Why?"

"You'll have to wait and see."

I grumbled. "I cannot believe I've engaged myself to a man who doesn't like to dance."

"I know," he said. "I am sorry, angel. I shall endeavor to make it up to you."

I felt a little buoyed by the term of endearment, so I stopped grumbling.

When we reached our usual break off point, he pulled me into the most searing kiss we've had yet.

"Is that you making it up to me?" I panted when we finally broke off.

He laughed and leaned in to me. "A little," he admitted.

"You're off to a good start," I said, drawing him close for another kiss.

He smiled against my lips and then pulled away.

"Oh, that's just unfair," I said as he started to walk away, still facing me. "Are you trying to frustrate me?"

"Your brother will never forgive me if I make you too mussed before we're married," he said with a grin.

I huffed. "You seem to be forgetting that I went to school. And did things! Plenty of times!"

"Yes, well, I prefer to keep you on your toes," he said, still walking backward.

"I think you're trying to turn me into a respectable person," I said, half shouting. "I'm not sure I like it!"

"You're not fooling anyone, angel," he said. "You adore it." And then he turned around and walked off.

Do you know, Bartleby, I rather suspect Laurence knows I like it when he calls me that.

17 September 1817

DEAR BARTLEBY,

I cannot believe we are so close to the ball. Started at the village again today to get the supplies for the major and Mr. Voss. Then we had lunch. After that, I talked to the head gardener and stablemaster and took notes for Bertie. Never realized how much coordination goes into planning a ball. Did you, Bartleby?

Then Bertie and I walked through Mrs. Fossett's spells and Laurence's. I have more ingredients to get tomorrow, so I'm to start earlier than usual. I've now walked through all of the applicants' plans, but I still don't know what they're really doing. I'm very much looking forward to seeing the spells in action.

I'm fairly sure Bertie scheduled Laurence last so we could walk home together. We didn't even talk this time. Just walked hand-in-hand and enjoyed a nice companionable silence. I'm not particularly keen on silence as a general rule, Bartleby, but I think I can stand it with him. We shared another lovely kiss and this time I pulled him closer to me, which was very pleasant.

When I got home, Gavin took one look at me and said, "Do I need to start looking into a chaperone for you two?"

I rolled my eyes. "Oh, leave off. We are engaged, aren't we? Besides, I got up to far worse things in Oxford and you know it."

"And that's supposed to make me feel better, is it?" he said, but I could tell he was joking, even though he looked as solemn as ever.

I remembered what Laurence had said the previous day

about Gavin never forgiving him if he got me too mussed before we got married. I suppose it did not occur to me that we might not share intimacy until our marriage. This realization then brought about two more realizations: the prospect of a long engagement had a decided downside, and I wasn't entirely sure what intimacy with Laurence might be like. I stewed over the matter for a moment and then went to find Charles.

He was still in his study, thankfully, although it seemed as though he was preparing to step away when I walked in. He looked at me with some surprise. "Good evening, darling. Something on your mind?"

"Yes," I said, a little hesitantly. "Is that all right?"

He grinned. "To be sure."

I closed the door behind me and sat down in one of the chairs in front of his desk.

He leaned back in his seat as if to prove to me that he was in no hurry and said, "Now, what can I do for you, my dear?"

"I wanted to ask your advice on something."

"Yes?"

I took a deep breath. "Well...do you remember when we visited Copperage Farm...er...the last time...and Laurence made a comment about his frocks?" I glanced at him.

"I do."

"You didn't seem particularly surprised by the comment. Why not?"

"Well, it was more that his comment confirmed some observations I'd made. I've been to their house several times now and I've noticed on my visits that there are a couple of small portraits that look remarkably like a younger Laurence."

"Oh," I said.

"I take it you knew all of this about him, however."

"Yes. He told me shortly after we met. That's what I wanted to talk to you about. You see...well, it occurred to me...just now...that when we are married and...well, intimacy with him might be a little different than with other men I've been with."

"Yes, I expect it will be. Is that a concern?"

"Only because I don't know what to do. I..." I looked down at my hands for a moment. "I'm still sort of coming to understand that aspect of who he is. But I thought you might have a better notion. That is, you might be able to give me a book or something that can tell me what to..." I let out a breath and tried again. "I would very much like our wedding night to be pleasant for him. But I haven't the faintest idea what he will like."

I peeked up at Charles and saw that he was smiling at me fondly. "I shall be pleased as anything to direct you to some good resources, darling."

"Oh, good," I said on a sigh.

"You are correct in assuming that intimacy will be different with him. However, I believe such information might be better given closer to your wedding."

"Oh, for heaven's sake," I said. "Laurence is perfectly respectable, which is rather unfortunate, really. So we won't actually do anything before—"

Charles laughed. "I'm sorry, darling, I did not mean to suggest a lack of trust. I meant to say if you learn everything now, you might forget later or, worse, you will work yourself into a nervous state trying to remember it all."

"Oh," I said. "Yes, you're probably right."

"So, we shall leave that conversation for a later day. In the meantime, there is some advice I can offer you now. The first thing you should know is the best way for a couple to find compatibility in bed is for them to share mutual respect." When I started to roll my eyes at this, he held up a hand. "No, no, dear. This is important. Believe me. I know you have had quite a bit of experience, but I would hazard a guess that at least one of your partners, if not most of them, did not really respect you."

He paused for a moment while I considered this. I thought of Warrow and the way he used to talk to me and the flippant way with which he'd push me up against the wall to kiss me. It had always seemed very exciting at the time—well, the wall part, not the insults—but then I started thinking of the way Laurence kisses me and how very different it is. I started to see what Charles might mean. So I nodded my understanding.

He went on, "I suspect you and Laurence will have no problems where that is concerned. You seem to have a genuine regard for one another. That will go a long way toward making things comfortable for you two—both in and out of bed. Now, the next thing you need to know is that I can provide you information on what he *might* like, but that will not necessarily be correct. Every person is different. What brings one man pleasure might be distasteful to another. I will give you what information I have, but when you are married, the best thing you can do is talk to him first."

I frowned a little. "That is not particularly romantic, Charles."

He chuckled. "Oh, I don't know. More romantic, I think, than guessing at what will please your husband and being incorrect. Don't you agree?"

I puzzled over this for a moment.

Charles leaned forward and folded his hands together on the desk. "You wanted my advice, darling. This is it: if you respect and love the gentleman, as I believe you do, you would do well to ask him what will give him pleasure. If he knows, he will undoubtedly be happy to tell you. If he doesn't—for I wouldn't be at all surprised, my dear, if you were the more experienced between the two of you—then it will likely be a great comfort to him to have a husband who is willing to listen and learn."

"Oh," I said quietly. "I hadn't even thought of that last bit." I let out a long breath. "Thank you, Charles."

He gave me a broad smile. "You are most welcome, darling. Does that clear up some of your concerns?"

"I think so. I'm not really accustomed to talking beforehand. That will be strange."

He laughed as he stood up. "Personally, I've always found that part to be rather enjoyable, really."

"You have?"

I stood up and he put an arm around my shoulders as he walked me toward the door. "Oh, yes. A nice glass of wine, perhaps. The anticipation of an enjoyable experience. It can add to the whole event if it's done properly." He paused as he reached for the door handle. "Just imagine, dearest, how it will feel for you to tell him *exactly* what you like."

I blushed just thinking about it.

He chuckled and opened the door. "There now. You see what I mean?"

We went to dinner. Gavin saw my face and glanced between the two of us before letting out a sigh of relief.

"Thank God," he said. "I thought he might come to me for advice on the subject."

Charles took Gavin's hand and pulled him close. "Not to worry, darling. I told him quite a while ago he could come to me with any such questions."

I wiggled out from under Charles's arm before he leaned forward to kiss my brother.

18 September 1817

DEAR BARTLEBY,

I was surprised when I got downstairs to breakfast to find someone new sitting at the table.

"Ah," Charles said when he saw me. "Here he is now. Your Grace, please allow me to introduce Sebastian Hartford. Seb, darling, this is the Dukex of Molbury."

I had heard the Dukex of Molbury mentioned several

times during my stay in Tutting-on-Cress. I daresay I'd heard of them before then as well, as they're something of a prominent figure in society. But I had no idea what they were doing at our breakfast table. The dukex did not stand up but turned their head slightly to the side. Charles beckoned me forward, so I stepped into the dukex's line of sight.

They were an older person—I would guess in their late fifties or so—who was round and handsome. They had bright blue eyes and full, upturned lips. Their suit was made out of very fine material and their posture and bearing added to their overall elegant appearance. They looked me up and down in a careful sort of way. Then they held out their hand, knuckles facing upward, and said, "It is a pleasure to meet you at last, Mr. Hartford."

I hesitated for a moment and then bent down to kiss their hand. Charles put a plate of food at my usual seat, so I sat down.

"The dukex is staying with us for a couple of days," Gavin explained. "They're Bertie's cousin, you see, so they're coming to the ball."

"Oh," I said, glancing across the table at them. "I wrote out all the invitations. I don't remember anyone outside of Tutting-on-Cress being invited."

The dukex gave a small smile. "Mine was discussed via correspondence with Bertram," they said.

The dukex's presence seemed to put everyone on edge for some reason. I suppose I, too, was a little nervous being in front of someone so grand. But I was also dreadfully hungry, so I started eating.

"Another busy day ahead, darling?" Charles said.

I nodded.

"For goodness' sake, Seb," Gerry said. "Do stop inhaling your food. We have a guest."

"I have to get to Bertie's," I explained. "Sorry," I added to the dukex.

They smiled at me again. "Perhaps if I escorted you in my carriage, you would be at more leisure to eat."

"That's all right," I said. "I have to go to the village first and I usually walk. Thank you all the same."

"Well, in point of fact," they continued, "I had looked forward to the opportunity to meet you. Considering you are so very busy, this may be my best opportunity."

I blinked at them. I very much wanted to ask why they wanted to talk to me but was quite sure it wouldn't be appropriate. I glanced around the table. Everyone looked nervous about how I might respond. I hated the idea of disappointing them all, so I took a deep breath and said, "That's very kind of you, Your Grace. I'm sure I would be happy to accept your escort."

Everyone relaxed and I felt as though I had passed some unspoken test.

The dukex smiled and said, "Very good." Then they turned to Pip and Gerry and asked them how the shop was doing. I was relieved because it gave me a chance to eat my food. By the time breakfast was over, it had been decided that the dukex would take Gerry, Pip, and I to the village, and then they would take me from the village to Bertie's. The carriage ride to the village was just as awkward as breakfast had been and when we got to the shop, I went through my errands for Bertie as quickly as possible, feeling uncomfortable with the dukex waiting.

When the two of us were back in the carriage heading to Bertie's house, the dukex wasted no time in starting the conversation. "I gather you are enjoying your time here, Mr. Hartford?"

"Yes," I said, still mystified by how it was their business. "I am."

"From what Charles and Gavin have told me, I understand that you do not intend to go to London for a debut."

"No," I said. "I wasn't sure…well, I wasn't sure I'd like it. Much as I want to go to London."

"Why not?"

I shrugged. "I didn't want to leave everyone here. At one point, I thought it would be very nice to enter into society and everything. But the thought of leaving Gavin, Charles, Gerry, Pip, and Bertie…and anyway, I work for Bertie and I enjoy that quite a lot. I thought it might be a suitable occupation while I sorted out what I really wanted."

"My word," they said. "Your time here really did make an impact, didn't it?"

"What's that supposed to mean?" I blurted, without thinking.

"I meant no offense, child. I only meant your family was quite worried about you at the beginning of the year. My visit is mostly to lend my support to Bertram's project, but I also wished to gauge your progress. You see," they continued before I could say anything. "If you didn't seem to be doing as well as everyone had hoped, I had every intention of offering to take you back to London with me."

"Why?"

"Well, there are a few months before the Season begins in earnest. Plenty of time to prepare you for a launch into society."

"No, I mean, why would you offer that…Your Grace?"

"I did as much for Gavin and Geraldine. It seemed only right to offer it to you as well. Since everyone was so worried about you, I wanted to help in my own way. I had learned that you were a social sort of person but had fallen in with some bad influences. I learned that you were frequently in trouble at school, but that you seemed to have a strong talent for spellcasting. I learned that you had a strong resemblance to your siblings, which suggested you would be as pretty as they are." They shrugged. "And Gavin had mentioned how much you wished to visit London. A Season in town seemed like a reasonable solution. After all, a pretty nextborn who is accomplished in a particular talent, such as spellcasting, and who is of a social disposition, might thrive in a different setting."

"Oh," I said. We sat in silence for a few moments while I thought about what they'd said. The fact was they were completely correct. Going to London for the Season had sounded thrilling once. Even a few months ago I would have leaped at the opportunity, regardless of how intimidating the dukex was. I was struck by my own certainty that I no longer wanted it.

Finally, I took a deep breath, and said, "That is very kind of you, Your Grace. But I think my answer is still the same."

They tilted their head and waited for me to continue.

"I know I would have loved to go to London and...and everything, if you had asked me a few months ago. Or when I first got here. I'm sure I would still enjoy it, but I'd miss everyone here. Now. And...well, I'm engaged, you see. So I don't know that it makes sense for me to go out into society at this point. I probably ought to have mentioned that sooner," I added.

They chuckled. "I'd heard about your betrothal. Congratulations. I am looking forward to meeting your fiancé. As I understand it, he is one of the contestants?"

"Yes, Laurence Ayles." I considered for a moment. "If you knew I was engaged, why did you still offer to take me to London? If you don't mind my asking?" I added, "Your Grace."

"It is good to have options," they said simply. "Besides, your stay here clearly helped you to grow, but I confess to some concern that your blooming was done in so...isolated an environment. You grew up in a small town, went to university, and then moved to another small town. And now you intend to settle here. I worry that such a limited experience of the world will not bring you contentment."

The carriage pulled to a stop and I looked out to see Bertie's house. I felt a small amount of panic because I hadn't had time to think through what the dukex had said.

They laid a hand on my arm. "I will be staying here for a few days. In fact, depending on who is selected, I may travel back to London with you and Bertram, so you'll have a chaperone. Take some time to think it over." They gave my arm a pat, stepped out of the carriage, and then offered a hand to me to help me down. "If your answer is still the same," they said as they walked me inside. "I will understand. But you are very young. It would be prudent to make sure that the life you are choosing is, in fact, the life you want."

We walked into the house and the conversation ended when Bertie greeted his cousin.

Then I was very busy. I didn't even see the dukex leave. I was all over the house and the gardens, checking to see if anything needed to be purchased or repaired and reporting back to Bertie. He had the applicants practicing their spells for him, but I didn't get to watch. Laurence left before I did. I realized when I got home that yesterday was likely our last walk home together, and it made me a little sad. I almost wrote to him about it, but that seemed too soppy.

I really hope Laurence gets the position, Bartleby. He wants it so very badly. And he shall do such grand things with it. Not to mention, I hate the idea of him being worried about money for my sake.

Dinner was a bit more formal with the dukex staying with us. They didn't bring up the conversation we had, but I've been thinking about it all day. The fact is, Bartleby, I'm quite sure of my choice. But what the dukex said put me in a dreadful muddle. Everything they said about me was quite correct. Am I being too hasty? I feel as if I ought to discuss all of this with Laurence but I'm not sure how I'd do it. Would it even make a difference if I choose to stay after all?

19 September 1817

DEAR BARTLEBY,

I just got home from the ball and I really ought to go to bed now. But there is so much to write about. Let me see if I can sort it all out.

First off, the day was very busy, just as Bertie warned me. I was running around for hours, trying to get everything ready, coordinating with the staff. I helped set up what felt like a million cooling spells. We didn't activate them, mind. Just placed everything and got it all ready to go. The same had to be done for the refreshment tables. I barely had time for lunch. I missed the usual time with everyone else because I was rushing about so much. Bertie made me sit down and eat at one point. Laurence came in to keep me company, which was nice. He looked a little more solemn than usual.

"Is anything the matter?" I asked him.

"Stop fussing and eat your lunch," he said, but he put his hand on my leg, so I knew he wasn't cross or anything.

I ate as ordered while Laurence explained that Bertie had pulled all of the applicants together this morning and essentially explained to each of them what their strengths and weaknesses are.

"It wasn't anything we didn't know," he said. "But it was sobering to hear it coming from him. He wanted to make sure we all understood why we might be chosen and also why we might not be chosen."

"Are you worried?"

"It isn't really in my nature to worry overmuch, but I am a trifle nervous," he admitted.

"Well, that is a responsibility I can easily take on," I said. "I definitely worry too much all the time. So I daresay we can put that task under my name."

He grinned and kissed my cheek. "Nothing has changed really. I'm still exactly where I was yesterday, only now I will understand the reasoning behind his decision. So that is something."

I finished my lunch. "Thank you for keeping me company."

"Of course," he said. "I won't be around very much today. And I don't know how much we will see of each other tonight."

I turned in my chair to face him. "I'll miss our walks."

He smiled and stroked my cheek. "Well, regardless of how everything turns out, I imagine I shall be able to come fetch you after work sometimes and walk back with you."

"Really?" I said, brightening. "You would do that for me?"

"Sweet Sebastian," he said. "You dreadfully underestimate how much I enjoy your company."

"What a lovely thing to say," I said. "I hope you continue saying things like that."

He grinned. "I think we can easily put that task under my name."

I kissed his cheek and then hurried back to work.

Bertie walked through the whole house with me later to make sure everything was right. When he pronounced himself satisfied, he sent me home in his carriage to get ready.

Charles practically pounced on me the moment I walked in the door. He was already dressed, as was Gavin, who kept tugging at his cravat. As I was going upstairs, Pip came out of his room looking stunning, as usual.

"Ah, lovely," Charles said to him. "Would you send Jennings in here, darling?"

Charles set his valet on me, which was odd considering the fact that I do have my own valet. But apparently Jennings ties the best cravats. After I was dressed, Charles made me stand in front of him so he could inspect my look and ensure it met his standards. I was relieved when he said I looked a picture. And, I own, I did look very fine.

Gerry was the last to come downstairs and she looked gorgeous, which was unsurprising.

Charles seemed very pleased as he ushered us into the carriage. It was a tight fit, with six of us, but we managed. Charles, Gerry, and the dukex kept up a breezy conversation the whole ride, and I didn't even notice until we were halfway there that Gavin, Pip, and I were barely contributing at all. Pip had already told me he was nervous, so I wasn't entirely surprised by his silence. And Gavin has always been a rather private person. Only I tend to forget that. Anyway, it occurred to me that I'm normally not this quiet and then I recognized that I was nervous for Laurence and then that got me in a tizzy.

Gavin noticed and said, "Stop fretting, Seb."

Charles gave me a sympathetic smile. "I'm sure he'll do just fine, darling," he assured me.

"Of course, he will."

Gerry tucked her arm around mine and I'm embarrassed to say it did make me feel better.

We reached Bertie's house and all got out. Charles and Gavin walked in together, then the dukex offered Gerry their arm, Pip offered me his, and we all walked in.

I was a little amazed by how grand everything looked, even though I helped coordinate it. The chandeliers were all lit, the cooling spells were making all of the rooms deliciously airy, and everyone looked very elegant. Bertie greeted us at the door, which was expected. But he also had all of the applicants lined up next to him so they could meet people as they came in. Most of them seemed to like all of the attention. Mrs. Fossett, poor thing, did not look very happy about it.

Laurence looked a little tired from it all, but he beamed when he saw me and gave my cheek a stroke with his finger before turning to the next guest. Fortunately, the next guest was Gerry, who teased him by saying, "Is that how you're greeting everyone, Laurence?" He laughed and stroked her cheek as well.

Once we were all inside, Pip wandered off on his own, while Gerry introduced me to a great many people. It was all a bit of a blur, really. She seemed to take an immense amount of pleasure in adding that I was engaged to one of the applicants. I was a bit embarrassed by her talking about it so much. After all, Father has not given his consent yet. But everyone congratulated me and many people were quite eloquent on what a good person Laurence is. I rather liked that.

We eventually met up with Pip again, he had found Gavin and the dukex and they were standing by the wall next to Mr. Robert Ayles.

Pip hailed me with a glass of punch. "You're right," he said. "The refreshments are wonderful."

The music started up and Charles walked up to take Gavin on the floor. I rather wished Laurence could dance with me, but he was still meeting people, so I contented myself with watching. Mr. Algernon came by and claimed his husband for a dance. Laurence finally joined our group as well, coming up behind me and wrapping his arms around my waist.

"Can we dance now?" I asked as the set ended.

He kissed my jaw. "If we must, my love. Promise me you'll still want to marry me after?"

I rolled my eyes and grabbed his hand to pull him forward.

I do so hate to admit it, Bartleby, but Laurence was absolutely correct. He is a terrible dancer. He knew the steps well enough, but there was no grace or form to it. It was almost funny. When it was over, he gave me a rueful smile.

I sighed. "Oh, all right. You're lucky I like you more than I like dancing."

He grinned at that and kissed my cheek. "How nice of you

to say," he said, taking my hand. He walked me off the dance floor with much greater speed than he had walked onto it.

His parents looked very amused when we rejoined them.

"I did try to teach him, Mr. Hartford," Mr. Algernon said. "Poor Laury is simply not a dancer."

"No," I said. "I suppose he was due to have at least one fault."

Mr. Algernon laughed and Mr. Robert smiled.

Laurence lifted our clasped hands to kiss my knuckles. "He said he likes me more than he likes dancing," he said in a bragging sort of tone.

"And I really love dancing," I said. "I daresay you squeaked by on that contest."

Charles was standing nearby and seemed to overhear my statement for he laughed and said, "Very well, you rascal. Let's take a turn, shall we?"

So then Charles led me in a dance, which was very fun. After that my cousin's wife, Julia, danced with me. Then Bertie, which was a surprise, but very nice. He's an excellent dancer, by the way. I enjoyed some refreshments while Bertie whisked Laurence off to meet people.

Then it was time for the applicants to perform their castings. We all gathered at the foot of the grand staircase in the foyer.

Miss Locke went first. She made a little speech about how magic has gotten too common and ordinary. If she were appointed as Royal Spellcaster, she would exalt magic to its proper grandeur. Gerry muttered under her breath at that.

Then Miss Locke cast her first spell. It was, I'm afraid to say, very impressive. She made the whole room go quiet, so you couldn't even hear people breathing or moving. Then we could hear music lilting into the silence. It was as if a whole orchestra was playing, but I knew the orchestra had been told to take a rest during the castings. She had the magical music play a few short songs, but there was definite range, and I was impressed despite myself.

Her second casting turned out to be her illusion spell. It caused her to appear as if she were floating in the air, high above us—but in point of fact, she was invisible and had made a mirror image of herself. A little unsettling if you ask me. I noticed Pip watching the image with a critical eye, and I remembered Bertie telling me he could sense magic in a way other people couldn't.

I leaned over to Pip and whispered, "Is something the matter with it?"

He shook his head slightly, but whispered back, "She doesn't seem confident. Nerves, probably. See how the image is flickering?"

I looked up and saw he was right, although I would never have noticed if he hadn't pointed it out. Once I noticed the flickering, it made the image even more unsettling. But we all clapped.

Next was Major Wilburforce. He made a speech about how magic can be used for military purposes and how it has untapped potential. His first spell made a suit of armor march forward into the crowd. It marched all around the room and then strode back to its place by the wall. I rather liked that one, because it looked so funny, but I'm not sure I like the idea of using it against real people. It seems awfully frightening, going against a whole battalion of not quite alive soldiers. Although, as Gavin pointed out when I said this later, it would mean fewer of our people getting killed in battle, which was probably the point.

The major's illusion spell was quite frightening. He made the whole building look as though it were on fire. And it wasn't just flames—I could swear the paint was curling and the tapestries were shrinking behind all of the smoke. Quite a lot of people screamed, a few people fainted, and a couple even ran for the door. But I noticed the major looked unfazed, so I knew it was part of his spell.

I glanced at Pip again, and he smiled at me and leaned over to whisper, "I remember your Mr. Ayles saying that man was very powerful... He's overpowered his spell a wee bit. The fire is burning through a lot faster than it should."

I looked closely and could see what Pip meant. It was as if the fire was burning at twice the normal speed. When he was done and everything went back to normal, we all applauded. The applause was a little louder for him, and I suspect it was partly because everyone was so relieved to not actually be in danger.

Mr. Voss was next. His speech was also about magic's untapped potential, but he wanted to use it to improve things in the country. "Magic can indeed be grand," he said. "We should enhance our understanding of it and use it for grand projects."

His first spell was an expansion of a wind spell. He made a narrow gust of wind blow in a very controlled course all over the room. The wind carried a few light objects so we could see its progress. I could tell he had tight control on it for he had it pass right over our heads and I didn't even feel it. His illusion spell was a whole show, practically. We could see a whole image of spellcasters using magic to build a bridge. It was incredible. I was very annoyed by how awed I was, but I grudgingly applauded him when it was over because, dash it all, it was very good.

I looked at Pip, hoping to hear something else, but he shrugged and said, "He has excellent control. That was arguably the best so far." Can't have everything, I suppose.

Mrs. Fossett then took her turn. She talked about improving magical education and providing it to more people. Her first spell was a large-scale warming spell. It was frightfully impressive. She only had to place a single spell and the whole room was positively roasting. I could tell it had a large scope because I could see people everywhere tugging at their cravats and fanning themselves. Can you imagine it, Bartleby? Casting one spell for an entire room? She really ought to publish that one even if she doesn't get the appointment.

Her illusion spell was very sweet. She made smoky, shadowy people appear in the air and then they all started to dance. I could see facial expressions and hairstyles. And the dance was very precise. It was a whole set practically. It was superb! I was very pleased when I got to applaud her.

I looked at Pip with hope and he said, "That's one of the ones you like, isn't it?"

I nodded.

"She's very good," he said.

Finally, it was Laurence's turn. His speech was about making magic more accessible to everyone, regardless of station and financial situation. His speech was a little different because he went on to say that even if magical supplies are affordable, it will not be helpful to people if they do not have the proper education, so he talked up Mrs. Fossett's goals as well. Which I thought a very nice thing to do.

His first spell involved the most bizarre ingredients: a potato, a feather, some string, and a piece of plain broadcloth. When he cast the spell, I realized it was an alternative sort of levitation spell, for he had a painting come unhooked from the wall and float all over the room before gliding back and gently setting itself back on the wall. After having trained with Bertie, I can appreciate the control that took. And to imagine he did it with such ingredients!

But I must confess—and I'm saying this only to you, Bartleby—I was a trifle worried his spell was…I don't know…a little less flashy than the others. Pip seemed to know what I was thinking for he leaned over and said, "That was much harder than it looked." Which made me feel better.

Then Laurence did his illusion spell, and all he did for it was light a match. He muttered an incantation as he lit it and the whole room went dark, including all of the candles, so all we could see was his face. Then, with the match still burning, he swirled it in a smooth motion in front of him and the light from the match split up into hundreds of little lights. Those lights flitted across the room and over our heads. When one got close to me, I realized that it was shaped like a butterfly. All of the little butterflies fluttered around the room, alighting atop various things as real butterflies would before taking off and fluttering somewhere else. Then, Laurence recited another incantation, and the butterflies all swirled together and swooped around him and then, almost as one, flew through the windows. The amazing thing was, we could see them all flying out the other side. Then the lights came back on inside. The applause was very loud that time.

Bertie joined Laurence on the stairs and beckoned the other four to come up as well. Bertie made a little speech about the future of magic in our country being in our hands and that we had witnessed castings by some of the most talented and powerful spellcasters in the country. He said he knew all of them would go on to do great things, regardless of whether they were chosen. And then, finally, he announced the final three who would be going to London:

Mr. Voss, Mrs. Fossett, and Laurence!

Bartleby, I've never been so proud of someone (other than myself). My hands stung from how hard I was clapping. Afterward, there was a mob of people clamoring to congratulate them. I rather desperately wanted to get to Laurence and tell him how proud I was, but I also didn't quite have the nerve to push through all of the people. To my surprise, Mr. Robert found me, put an arm around my shoulders and guided me through the throng.

When we reached Laurence, he was already hugging Mr. Algernon, and then he turned and hugged Mr. Robert with equal fierceness. Mr. Robert turned so that Laurence could see that I was there too and Laurence grabbed me and pulled me into a searing kiss. He broke off, laughing. Frankly, Bartleby, I very much wish I could preserve that moment forever: Laurence's arms around me, with the most perfect and beautiful joy all over his face. Of course, I couldn't actually stand there forever, so I stepped away to let other people congratulate him.

I found my family, and we and the Ayleses toasted to Laurence's success. Charles wrapped one arm around my shoulder into a crushing side hug.

Finally, the music started up again, and people drifted back to the dance floor and the refreshment tables. I stepped over to one of the windows to see if any of Laurence's butterflies were still outside, but it was all darkness and my own reflection in the glass. When I turned back around, Laurence was walking toward me. He reached his hand out and I closed the distance between us to clasp it.

He pulled me close. "Come out to the garden with me?"

It was a little chilly outside without our coats. But I didn't mind the excuse to curl my arm around Laurence's and press up against his side. When we rounded the corner of the house, my breath caught in my throat.

The butterflies were still there, fluttering around the garden. The lanterns had been lit for the party, but they were all out, like the lights inside had been during Laurence's spell. It looked enchanting. Laurence pulled me forward again and led me right to the center of the garden. I held on to him but looked up and around me, a little wonderstruck at the sight.

"Laurence," I whispered. "This is incredible. You should show Bertie—"

"He knows," he said. "I told him they would continue for a while."

I looked back at him and he was watching my face, a soft smile on his lips.

"Is this why you wanted me to walk in the garden with you?"

He nodded. Then, without a word, he unwound his arm from mine and wrapped it around my waist. His other hand reached up to cup the back of my neck and I could feel his fingers winding into my hair. He pulled me close and kissed me, rather like he had in the treehouse—softly, tenderly, slowly. I'll admit, I kept trying to make it more intense, but he smiled against my lips and pressed gentle fingers against my jaw, wordlessly telling me to slow down, and then continued to make me feel cherished.

I very much wanted to keep that moment forever too.

When we finally broke off the kiss, he leaned his forehead against mine.

"I'm so proud of you," I said. "I didn't know I could be so proud of somebody else."

He smiled and stroked my cheek, fingertips skimming over my skin. "I'm so glad I could share this with you. This... moment. This accomplishment. It makes it even more special."

"I don't want to keep you from your admirers," I said after a moment's pause. "But can we sit here for a minute?"

With an arm still around my waist, he led me to a bench and we sat down together. He reached for my hand and we sat in silence for a long moment, watching the butterflies dance across the darkened flowers.

"It's so beautiful," I said softly, as if noise would scare them away.

"I've been practicing for ages," he said. "The spell inside was meant to be impressive. But this part—" He squeezed my hand. "This part was meant for you."

I regret to say I suddenly felt very weepy. I hastily wiped my eyes, but Laurence cupped my cheek. "Angel," he said softly.

I looked at him. "So embarrassing," I said.

He smiled. "Not at all." He framed my face with both hands and gently rubbed under my eyes.

"I love you," I said.

His thumbs stilled and his smile was slow and broad. He kissed me again, and curses if it didn't make me a little weepy again. He pulled away and then kissed my cheeks that were now absurdly damp.

"I love you too," he whispered.

I pulled his hands away from my face and clasped our hands together, looking around the garden again. "I should probably tell you," I said in an airy tone. "I love it when you call me 'angel.'"

He chuckled and lifted our hands so he could kiss one of mine. "I know you do."

"Also," I went on. "You're the only person who calls me 'Sebastian' and doesn't make me hate it. The only people who ever call me that are my parents and my horrid oldest brother."

Laurence rested his head against my shoulder. "That is good to know," he said. "I like your name. It's lovely."

I snorted. "It's not lovely when it's usually followed with, 'Why can't you grow up?' or 'You're such a disappointment' or something."

He hummed thoughtfully. "That is something we shall have to work on, I think."

"What, me getting scolded all the time?"

"No," he said. "You associating your name with getting scolded."

"Oh."

A butterfly landed on my knee and I don't know how there were details on its wings and body, but there were.

"How did you do that?" I asked him.

"Hm?" I felt his head shift. "Oh, the butterflies? I've been working on some similar spells for ages now. I adapted it when his lordship first told us about the ball and the castings we would have to perform. I was delighted when he said one of them could be an illusion spell."

A breeze drifted by and I shivered. "And now we get to go to London together."

"Come on," he said, nudging me gently with this shoulder. "Let's go inside."

"I rather hate to leave this," I said as he pulled me to my feet.

He smiled. "My love, regardless of what happens in London, this—" He gestured around us. "—will always be available to us. To you."

I kissed him and let him lead me back inside. We found our little group and joined them.

"It's a good thing you came in when you did," Charles said with a grin. "Julian here was getting ready to go looking for you."

The dukex rolled their eyes. "Don't be absurd, Charles. I was doing no such thing."

Bertie was standing next to Charles and smiled at me. "Did he show you the garden, darling? Isn't it lovely?"

"Very," I said.

"Do you mind if I have a look?" Pip said to Laurence.

"Not at all."

Bertie and Gerry followed Pip out the door.

"How long will they last?" I asked Laurence. "The butterflies?"

"Another hour or so."

I wrapped my arm around his and leaned my head on his. Charles noticed and smiled. "Are you getting tired, darling?"

"What? No, of course not."

Gavin rolled his eyes. "Give it an hour," he said to his husband.

Charles smirked and led Gavin away for a dance. Laurence's parents followed them to the dance floor. Laurence led me to a sofa by the wall, where we could sit together while we watched everyone. I scrunched myself against the side so I could lay my head on his shoulder. I noticed that the dukex took a seat on Laurence's other side. I was relieved when they struck up a conversation with him and both seemed to get along.

However, I'm ashamed to report, Bartleby, that I actually fell asleep sitting next to Laurence. I woke up when Charles attempted to pick me up. I was dreadfully embarrassed and apologized profusely to Laurence, who seemed to think the whole thing both amusing and adorable.

"All right," Charles said, laughter in his voice. "Kiss your young man good night, Seb. Let's go home."

I did as I was told—it was no hardship—and then Charles put an arm around my back and walked me out to the carriage.

Bertie has already told me to take tomorrow off. So I imagine I shall be busy packing and preparing for my trip to London. I'd better stop thinking about it or I won't fall asleep at all. Too tired to even soak my hand.

20 September 1817

Dear Bartleby,

Woke up this morning feeling wonderful, as if the butterflies from last night had all migrated into my stomach. Laurence is one of the three finalists and we get to go to London together. I cannot believe it! Only I *can* believe it. He is so very talented, you know. And Mrs. Fossett and Bertie will be there too, which will be very nice. Mr. Voss might keep it from being a merry sort of party. But with the other three in attendance, I daresay I can withstand even his unpleasantness.

I slept in since last night was such a late evening. Fortunately, most of the household seemed to sleep in late. To my surprise, Charles had been up at his usual time. He looked fresh and cheery when we all sat down to breakfast. He had already eaten, but kept us company.

We all talked about the ball and the castings. Gerry admitted she was very glad Miss Locke did not get selected. "Her views on magic are old-fashioned and dreadful," she said.

"I can't say I'm displeased that the military fellow wasn't picked either," Charles said. "I'm sure magic will be integrated more and more in the military. But I don't like the notion."

Then the talk turned to how impressive the castings were, particularly the last three. Everyone talked a great deal about Laurence's spells, pointedly telling me as if I had been the one working the magic rather than him. But it was nice. I think they are almost as proud of him as I am.

After breakfast, Gavin asked me to come to his study for a moment. He had me sit down in a chair and that sat down in the chair next to me, which was surprising. He looked unusually nervous.

"Father wrote back," he began.

I felt my heart clench in my chest. "Oh Lord. Did he refuse to give his blessing?"

"Oh, for heaven's sake," Gavin said. "Don't be silly. Of course he didn't. But he hasn't given his blessing either yet. I daresay he will, for he sounds inclined to like your Mr. Ayles, but..." He took a deep breath. "He wants to talk to you first. And meet Laurence. He, er...he said he'd be staying in London in order to catch you while you're there."

I felt the blood drain from my face. "You're not serious."

He sighed. "Don't look so stricken, Seb. It's a good thing. Laurence makes a wonderful impression and I'm sure he will impress Father immediately. Even if he isn't selected, the fact that he has made it this far speaks volumes to his talent and genius. I daresay he has a promising career ahead of him, regardless of how London goes."

I knew Gavin was right, but I couldn't shake the fear gripping me. I haven't seen Father in months. And quite frankly, I haven't minded. The man genuinely terrifies me. The thought of having to meet with him on my very first trip to London makes the whole venture seem significantly less appealing.

Gavin put a hand on my arm. "Stop worrying," he said. "He is very pleased with how well you've done since you moved here. He was relieved when I told him you intended to stay on, even though you were no longer required to."

"He was?"

"Yes," Gavin said in an exasperated tone.

I was fairly sure this had more to do with Father being relieved to have someone else to foist me onto, but I didn't say so. Instead I said, "Do you know when he wants to see me? Am I supposed to go find him or will he seek me out?"

"He didn't say. If I were you, I'd write to him when you arrive and give him Bertie's address. Then he will know you have arrived safely and will know where to find you."

"Thank you for warning me."

"Don't lose sleep over it. I just didn't want you to be shocked when he showed up or sent a message over for you to call on him."

"That would have been dreadful," I agreed. I considered a moment. "Do you think I should go tell Laurence?"

The corner of Gavin's mouth twitched. "I reckon Father told him as well. But I imagine it will make you feel better to talk to him."

Taking that as permission, I fetched my things and left the house. I considered telling Charles, as I've never walked there alone. But it felt so freeing to go by myself. I also didn't really want to hear him tease me about being so nervous.

On the way there, I thought about my conversation with the dukex; it had been the first opportunity to really think about it since before the ball. Throughout the evening, it never occurred to me to imagine a future without Laurence.

Even the promise of balls and dinner parties in London, exciting though it may be, wasn't nearly as appealing as the prospect of sitting in a quiet garden surrounded by glowing butterflies.

This thought made me feel both giddy and a little strange. Have I really changed so much in such a short time? Or was I like this all along and merely distracting myself with other ideas? I was in a bit of a tizzy over this line of thought and nearly went back home so I could stew over it some more. But I very much wanted to see Laurence, and I had a silly hope that he would be able to talk me down from my swirling thoughts.

As I drew closer to Copperage Farm, I started to panic slightly at the thought that they might all be in bed—after all, it had been a late night for them too. But then I saw Mr. Algernon walking through the yard with another person, I'm guessing a servant. He waved when he saw me approaching.

"Good morning," he said cheerily.

"Good morning," I said. "I hope you don't mind my coming so unexpectedly."

Mr. Algernon grinned and stepped forward to put an arm around my shoulders. "My dear Sebastian, I hope you know you can come here anytime you please. We always love to see you."

With that, he led me into the house, but not to the sitting room. Instead, he took me to the residential side of the building and down a narrow hall. He rapped smartly on a closed door.

Laurence opened the door and smiled at me. "Good morning," he said. He was dressed less formally than usual, with a loose-fitting shirt with rolled up sleeves, trousers, and no waistcoat. He looked rather rakish, actually. I was momentarily distracted by his forearms. I do love a good forearm.

Mr. Algernon gave me a gentle push into the room. "Mind you keep the door open, Laury," he said, and walked away.

Laurence rolled his eyes at the command but did as his father requested, leaving the door slightly ajar for the sake of propriety. He kissed my cheek. "This is an unexpected surprise," he said. "Are you here to help me pack?"

"Not exactly."

He narrowed his eyes slightly and gave me a brief once over. "You're worried about something."

It took me a moment to remember the initial reason for my coming there. "Gavin just told me that Father will be in London and he wants to see me. Us. Both of us. He wants to talk to both of us while we're there."

Laurence smiled. "Yes, I know. He wrote to me the other day and informed me of it. Granted, he wasn't sure if I would be selected to go to London. But he did give me his direction and his club information, in case I were to come. I intend to call on him as soon as my interview at the palace is over."

"You've known all along?"

He gave a huff of amusement. "Come sit on the bed while I pack."

I did as requested, feeling an absurd little thrill at sitting on his bed.

"Yes," he said, as he pulled clothes out of his wardrobe. "I have known for days. I talked to his lordship about it and he assured me we could stay in London until I had a chance to meet with Mr. Hartford. He mentioned they were both members of the same club, so he might be able to bring me as a guest."

I sat, dumbfounded at this. "I'm the last person to know then?"

He smiled and gave my cheek a light stroke with his thumb. "I'm afraid you might be. I didn't know you weren't aware of it, to be honest. But I didn't tell you about his letter to me because I didn't want to worry you."

"Gavin said he didn't give his permission yet."

"No," Laurence said. "He didn't, but he didn't withhold it

either. Obviously, I've never had to go through this process before, so I have little by way of comparison. But his answer was about what I'd expect and more or less what I'd hoped for."

"It was?"

He began folding things and placing them in a trunk. "Yes. He said your brother had many good things to say about me, that he liked what he had heard, that he wanted to know a bit more about my financial situation. He said he thought the match sounded very promising, but he would like to meet me in person so as to come to his own conclusions." He shrugged. "I can't deny that I would like to have his personal approval." He glanced at me. "You're nervous about seeing him?"

I nodded. "I had rather hoped we'd have this conversation at home. You know, with my mother there. I suppose you might as well know that I'm not my father's favorite, by any stretch of the imagination. I don't think he likes me very much at all, really. I know I'm a disappointment to him. The idea of having to plead my case in person is terrifying. And now I might have to do it alone. What if I ruin everything?"

Laurence crouched in front of me and took my hands in his. "You will not ruin everything. If he really disliked you, he might have disowned you."

"He sent me away," I said.

"To stay with your brother," he said. "If he had truly given up on you, he would not have sent you to a place where he hoped you might learn and grow. He loves you, angel, and he wants to see you happy. That is why he wants to see us—both of us," he added. "Think of it this way. If he didn't care for you, then he could have sent his decision by letter. He could either have approved the match so as to stop having to take care of you himself or he might have rejected the match out of maliciousness."

I tilted my head in acknowledgement. He made a good point.

He reached up and eased his thumb between my eyebrows, encouraging away my frown. "If you want my opinion..."

"Always."

He smiled. "I think you have not forgiven yourself for whatever mistakes you made in the past. You really ought to, you know. From what I've seen of your family, they all have forgiven you. They like you quite a bit."

I sighed. "The dreadful part is that they knew of my mistakes for years. They were always telling me to stop. I never listened. And now I feel I have a great deal to atone for."

He cupped my cheek. "I am a firm believer in not holding a person's past against them, particularly when they've changed or are in the process of changing."

This statement brought back into sharp relief the dizzying thoughts I'd had on my walk over. Softly, I said, "Laurence, I'm not even sure of who I am anymore."

"That is one of the many reasons we are waiting, my love. You said you had things to sort out. I don't mind waiting for you."

"I've already changed so much since May. What if..." I looked down at my hands, feeling a very sudden and very solid fear.

He still had one hand over both of them. He lifted it to cup my other cheek and tilt my face toward his.

I took a deep breath and closed my eyes. "What if I change even more? Will you still love me?"

"Sebastian, look at me."

I opened my eyes.

"I love you because you ask me about my family, my tastes, and my dreams. You listen and you remember what I tell you. I love you because I can tell you things that matter and you accept those truths with the same ease with which you accept a cup of tea. I love you because you will hold your friend up when he is retching. I love you because you don't like fish but you try to pretend you do and you always pick around it so as not to cause a fuss. I love you because your emotions play out so beautifully on your face and I adore that I can practically read your thoughts sometimes. I love you because you would rather marry me when you know yourself better. I love you because you keep trying to be a better person.

"Of course you're going to change," he went on. "And so will I. People are always changing. They're meant to. No one is ever a constant. And if they are, then they shouldn't be. Will some of the things I love about you change as you grow? Possibly. But it's also just as possible—I would hazard a guess, even more possible—that the more I come to know you, and the more we learn about ourselves and each other, and the more we give ourselves grace to change, I will find more reasons to love you, not less."

It is likely obvious to point out, Bartleby, that I was definitely crying at this juncture. I had no response for this speech. Nothing felt adequate. I folded forward to rest my face on his shoulder.

Laurence cupped the back of my neck with one hand and moved to sit next to me on the bed. He pulled me fully into the embrace. I wrapped my arms around his back and he stroked gentle fingers through my hair. I don't know how long we sat like that, but he didn't try to move me or rush me.

Finally, I sighed and said against his neck, "I'm a bit of a mess, I'm afraid."

"Not to worry," he said cheerfully. "We all are." He reached into my waistcoat pocket and pulled out the kerchief tucked in there. "Besides, you're clever enough to never be without your handkerchief. I like that about a person."

I sat up and he dried my face, which made me feel a little

embarrassed, but I hate to admit that I rather liked it too. "Sorry about all this."

He flashed me a smile. "Don't be. I like taking care of you. I don't like to see you crying, of course, and I do wish you'd be gentler with yourself. But my shoulder is always yours for the taking."

I kissed him. It was not, it must be confessed, my best kiss with him, for I poured a great deal of my own fears and sorrows and yearnings into it. So I kissed him urgently, desperately, as if to prove to myself that he meant all those things. Laurence let me for a little while, and then he pushed me backward onto the bed so he was leaning over me, pressed fingertips to my jaw, and took control of the situation in the way that he does. I surrendered to the pace he set and allowed it to comfort me. I don't know how he manages to do that every time, but he does. It's a magic all its own.

The kiss was halted by the sound of a throat being cleared. We looked up to see Mr. Robert standing in the doorway, smiling amusedly down at us. He walked away without saying anything.

I closed my eyes, embarrassed. Then I sighed and said, "I suppose I'd better leave you to your packing, hadn't I?"

Laurence cupped my cheek again. "I wish I could resolve all of your worries for you. You carry too much."

I ran a hand up and down his forearm. "Oh, I don't know," I said. "I imagine I'm simply balancing out having carried too little for too long."

"I doubt that," he said. When I gave him a questioning look, he said, "I suspect you've always carried these fears. Although I suppose you may have distracted yourself from them, if stories of your school hijinks are anything to go by."

This felt startlingly accurate, so I decided to change the topic. "In any case, I knew I'd have to face my father eventually. I just didn't know it would be so soon."

"I'll make a point of taking you to London another time, when we don't have so much riding on the trip."

"Really?"

He grinned. "Well, I would very much like to actually enjoy the city. I can't imagine there will be much time for that."

"True," I agreed. "That will be a lark, won't it? Going to London together? Just us?"

He kissed me briefly. "Yes, it will."

I left him to his packing and walked home. I'm still not entirely reassured about the conversation with Father, but I suppose it is unavoidable. My valet had the packing well in hand, so there wasn't much for me to do and I couldn't focus anyway. I went on a ride around the estate to work out some of my nerves. Tomorrow, we go to London.

21 September 1817

Dear Bartleby,

The journey to London was long, but not as long as it could have been. We left early in the morning and took three carriages—two for us and one for all of our luggage. The dukex rather insisted that Laurence and I join them in their carriage. Mr. Voss and Mrs. Fossett joined Bertie in his. I admit I was nervous about riding the whole day with the dukex, but the conversation was pleasant among the three of us. I enjoyed being able to lean against Laurence whenever I wished. He would often take one or both of my hands in his, whether he was engaging in conversation or reading a book. It was delightfully companionable. I kept expecting the dukex to object, but they never did.

I learned that Bertie is a proponent of speed spells when traveling. This isn't exactly surprising, but many people don't bother because they can be devilishly difficult to get right, and very easy to get wrong. Oftentimes, people injure their horses or ruin their carriages because they've tilted the kerchief or the feather just slightly off-balance. But Bertie made all three applicants come out of the carriages to watch him cast the spells. I watched too because I've never seen one done before. With the speed spells (Bertie had to recast about halfway through the trip), we made it to London before dinnertime.

I had thought we'd all be staying with Bertie while we were in London. But it turned out that Mrs. Fossett has a cousin who lives in London, and she had decided to stay with her relation. The dukex explained that without the widow in residence, Laurence and I couldn't stay in the same house together overnight without a chaperone. Because of that, Laurence, Mr. Voss, and I were to stay with the dukex so they could keep everything proper. They even encouraged Bertie to stay with us rather than opening up his own townhouse. We dropped Mrs. Fossett and her luggage off first, and then we went to the dukex's townhouse.

The dukex's townhouse was very fine. Quite frankly, it was practically palatial, and quite large for being in the city. It was even bigger than our house back home. The family house, I mean, not the Tutting-on-Cress house. I rather wonder what the family townhouse is like, but I'm staying with the dukex, so I'm not sure I shall find out.

Bertie informed us we'd all be taking dinner at Nesbit's Club. Apparently, Bertie and I are both members. I didn't know, but it would seem all the Hartfords are members.

"Mr. Hartford undoubtedly signed each of you up when you were old enough to go," Bertie explained. "And speaking of Mr. Hartford, darling," he added, "I've taken the liberty of writing out a little note for him with my cousin's address, along with a bit about your schedule while you're in town." He held it up. "If you would like to send it to him instead, you are more than welcome. Charlie informed me Mr. Hartford wanted to meet with you and dear Laurence. He also said that you were a touch nervous at the prospect, so I thought it might be helpful to you if I sent that information. But I will understand if you wish to be the one to do it."

I stammered that I was perfectly fine with Bertie sending it. He smiled and assured me it would go out immediately and then went to get dressed for dinner. The dukex got us all settled into our rooms.

I dressed and then went downstairs to wait until it was time to leave. As I came down the stairs, I heard a light melody being played on a piano. I followed the sound, passing a sitting room where Mr. Voss was biding his time, and into a wide ballroom. It was dimly lit, just a few candles. Laurence was sitting at the piano, playing softly. He smiled when he saw me and tipped his head to the side. Reading that to be an invitation to sit next to him, I approached and slid beside him on the bench. I watched his fingers gliding across the keys, mesmerized.

"You asked me once," he said softly, "what I would buy for myself if I earned the position."

I looked at him.

He smiled, closed his eyes, and continued playing. "I should very much like to buy myself a new piano."

I kissed his cheek and then leaned against him, imagining evenings like this, in the semi-darkness, sitting together while he played.

I felt a hand on my shoulder and we both looked up to see the dukex standing behind us, smiling softly. "Much as I hate to break up this sweet picture, children, the carriage is ready for us."

We followed them out the door. Mr. Voss was already in the carriage next to Bertie and looking a little irritated at having to wait for us, but he didn't say anything.

When we arrived at the club, Bertie explained to me how to sign in a guest. I took Laurence in as my guest and Bertie took Mr. Voss in as his. The dukex did not need to be signed in. I'm not sure if that's because they're already a member or if they're so important that they're allowed in everywhere. Bertie began giving us a small tour of the club. As we were going through the card room, I heard my name called. I turned to see a group of men about my age sitting at a table. I recognized some of them as former classmates and the one who had called my name was Robert Parks.

He beckoned me over. I glanced at Bertie, who said, "Oh, do go ahead if you like, dear. We'll order dinner and you can join us as soon as you're ready."

I nodded and wound my way around the tables. I felt a mixture of emotions at seeing my former friend. It was, on the one hand, rather nice to see someone I knew in a strange and new place. On the other hand, it was a person who I wasn't sure of my feelings for anymore. I decided the best way to find out was to talk to him.

"Good God, Hartford," he said as I approached. "It has been an age. Sit with us, won't you?"

"I can't stay long," I said, taking a seat opposite him. "What are you doing in London?"

"I've been here for a month, old boy," he said. "London is corking! Did you just arrive? We'll have to show you every-thing," he went on, not waiting for an answer. "The races, the gambling dens, Covent Gardens. It's famous!"

The chair behind me bumped into mine. I murmured an apology over my shoulder and scooted my chair farther up and out of the way as the person behind me took a seat at his own table.

"Parks is on his way to joining the Beggar's Club," one man piped up. "Hasn't a crown to his name these days."

Parks grinned and shrugged. "Who cares? No one gives a fig for gambling debts anymore."

I was a little struck by the prospect that I might have been in much the same way if I had gone to London while still friends with the man. It made me feel a little unnerved to realize it. So I said nothing.

"Father wants to send me on the Grand Tour," he continued. "Should be a lark."

He waited for a reaction, so I said, "That sounds very fine. I hope you enjoy yourself."

He smirked. "Well, how have you been keeping yourself?"

I frowned. "I wrote you letters detailing it all. You never wrote me back."

He scoffed. "Oh, come on, Seb. No one writes letters anymore."

I sighed. "Well, I'm doing fairly well. Still living with my brother and his husband, which is very nice. And now I'm working for—"

"Any new pranks lately? Trying to get ideas, you know."

"No," I said. "Rather lost my taste for them actually."

He gave a snort. "I hardly believe that. You should see the ones Maring here has done. We've been having such laughs. Got a whole set of trays to roll across the carpet like wheels. Smashing!"

"Parks!" another man said, joining the group. "New blood arrived. In the dining room."

"Who?" Parks said, looking eager.

"A solicitor and a farmer."

They all laughed at this.

"Lord, what a joke," Parks said. "This place is dropping in quality every day. A farmer? Are you sure?"

"They're with some other people of title. A viscount and a dukex. Don't know either of them, though."

I felt a little sick at this summary of my companions. Had I been that horrid when I was at Oxford? God, I hope not.

"Can't do anything to the viscount or dukex, of course, too risky. We've been playing tricks on new fellows," Parks said to me. "It's great fun. Already got one bloke to quit the club because of it. Glad you're here now. You can help us with this new lot."

"Certainly not," I said.

"Oh, don't be a prat," he said, dismissively. "It's even easier here than at school. And you were always the best at pranks, don't mind telling you."

"Well, I was never intending to hurt anyone. I don't plan to start now," I said, preparing to get up. My chair hit the one behind me, so I swiveled in the seat, a bit annoyed that I couldn't make a dignified exit.

"God, are you boring now? How dull."

A hand settled on my shoulder and I looked up to see Laurence. "Just came to check on you," he said. "Dinner's being served."

I was relieved to see him as it gave me an excuse to leave.

"Who's this then?" Parks demanded as I stood.

I sighed. "This is Mr. Ayles. Mr. Ayles, this is Mr. Parks, an old schoolmate of mine."

Laurence's eyes narrowed in understanding. He gave a neat little bow. "A pleasure, Mr. Parks."

"Which one are you then?" one of the other men asked. "The solicitor or the farmer or—?"

"Not one of the titles," Parks said, casting a critical eye on Laurence's clothing. "My money's on the farmer."

I clenched my fist. Laurence eased my fist open with his fingers and slid his palm against mine, interlocking our fingers. "You would be correct, Mr. Parks," he said. "If you'll excuse us?"

Parks noticed Laurence's hand in mine. "Ah," he said. "This your latest fling, Hartford? Don't suppose he told you, Mr. Ayles, but this fool spreads his legs for every bloke who looks his way."

"As it happens," Laurence said, "I know that not to be true."

"Do you indeed? Too bad Warrow isn't here then, isn't it?

He could tell you a tale or two. Tell me, Hartford, have you told your country lover about the time Warrow had you in the—"

"Sebastian's always been very honest about his past," Laurence cut in. "It's one of the things I most admire about him."

Parks snorted. "I rather think you're the only one in his acquaintance with that particular sentiment. Hartford here is an amusing chap sometimes. Good for a laugh. But admirable?"

"My word," Laurence said. "You've known him for years. How can you possibly know so very little about him?"

Parks leveled him with a look. "I know this idiot better than he knows himself. I'm the only reason he has any friends. I'm just wondering what you're hanging around him for. It's not as if he has any money or status. If you're angling for a wealthy husband, Ayles, you're definitely barking up the wrong tree."

"That's enough," I said. "You can say what you like about me. But I won't have you insulting my friend. You don't even know him."

"Why would I want to know him? What use could I possibly have for a farmer?"

Laurence laid his other hand on my shoulder before I could reply. "Well, this has been quite an elucidating conversation, Mr. Parks. If you will excuse us, I don't want to keep Lord Finlington waiting."

Laurence led me out of the card room and Parks said loudly to our retreating backs, "If you had any brains, farmer boy, you'd go after the viscount instead."

Laurence gave my hand a reassuring squeeze but said nothing.

Bertie looked relieved when we approached the table. "Lovely," he said. "I was just about to go fetch you both myself. My word, darling," he said to me. "You do look peakish. Bit of a long day for you, I'm afraid. Why don't you sit down and—" He looked behind me and stood. "Well, this is a delightful surprise. Mr. Hartford, how wonderful to see you."

I felt as though a bucket of frigid water had been dumped over my head. I didn't want to look, but I knew it was inevitable, so I turned slowly to face my father.

"Good evening, Sebastian," he said. Then he bowed to Bertie. "A pleasure, as always, sir. Your Grace," he added, to the dukex.

"Do join us, Mr. Hartford," the dukex said.

Father bowed again and took the other seat next to me. It was very unnerving. Bertie introduced Mr. Voss and Laurence. Father greeted them both with the same level of courtesy, not giving away the fact that he and Laurence had been in communication. I chanced a glance at Laurence, who squeezed my hand before letting go to turn to his food.

Bertie took control of the conversation, explaining all about our purpose here, even though Father already knew about it. For his part, Father was all politeness, asking Mr. Voss and Laurence about their experience in the application process and their families and histories. He barely spoke to me, as a matter of fact. Well, that is to say, he did. But it was in the same conversational tone with which he spoke to the others, asking about my experience working for Bertie, and how the trip had been. I was so nervous that I was very abrupt in my replies, although he didn't appear to mind it.

We made it through dinner without mishap and it wasn't until we were all sipping brandy that things started to go wrong. I felt it first—a little tickle around my ankle. I stole a glance under the table but saw nothing. And then I started to feel a small amount of dread.

"Everything all right?" Laurence asked.

Then, Voss lurched up. "Good heavens!" he said.

"What's the matter?" Bertie said, standing.

"I felt—"

"Oh," Laurence said, frowning and peering under the table.

"My lord," Voss said. "I'm sure I don't mean to be rude about this fine establishment, but—"

"It's Parks," I said.

"What?" Voss said, clearly irritated about being interrupted.

"Excuse me," I said, and left the table.

They were all still in the card room and very clearly pleased with themselves.

"Oh, look who comes crawling back," Parks drawled when he saw me.

"Stop it," I said.

"I'm sure I don't know what you—"

"Leave off on whatever prank you're pulling, Parks. Did you really think I'd be foolish enough to fall for it?"

Parks raised an eyebrow expressively.

"Is your little man afraid of the little mice?" one of the others asked.

I took a step back and considered them all, thinking furiously. There was no spell set up on the table and there wasn't enough space under the table for a spell to have been set up on the floor. So, one of them was performing a Motion spell of some kind. Parks was leaning back, with one elbow hitched over the back of his chair and the other arm draped over the table, fingers curled loosely around a glass of wine—couldn't be him. Two of the men were still pretending to be playing cards. Another fellow, the one Parks had commended for his pranking, had both arms under the table, but I had a feeling that Parks wanted me to believe it was him. The last fellow had one arm under the table and was leaning against his other arm on top of the table.

Without stopping to think it through, I picked up the glass of wine in front of Parks and dumped it on the other man's lap. He sprang up with a yell, dropping a handful of feathers and string onto the table as he did so. All of the others laughed at him.

An older woman approached the table and asked, in consternation, what was going on.

"This idiot poured wine all over my friend," Parks said. He was trying to sound angry, but he was having a hard time keeping a straight face as his friend wiped uselessly at his trousers.

The woman turned to me. "I'm sorry, Mr. Hartford, but as the manager, I'm afraid I cannot—"

"As the manager," my father said, coming up behind us, "you'd do well to expel this entire table from the club."

The manager looked from Parks to my father to me, at a loss.

Bertie approached at that juncture. "Ah, Mrs. Ridley. So very good to see you. It has been a long time, hasn't it? Now, my dear lady, I'm sure I can straighten this all out. Would you be so kind as to step over here for a moment?" With that, Bertie smoothly maneuvered the manager to the other side of the room and began talking to her in a low voice.

"You owe me a new set of trousers," Parks's friend wailed at me.

"I rather think Parks is the one for that," I said.

Parks scoffed. "Don't be an idiot, Hartford."

I leaned forward and braced my hands on the table. "Listen here, Parks," I said. "I spent two years doing every blasted thing you told me to. I was your own personal bloody court jester. And what did I get for it? I was ridiculed and disrespected by practically everyone. Despite the fact that you were always the one in charge, I was always the one who got in trouble. I was the one who had to explain to the dean. I was the one getting scolded by my family. I was the one who was sent down."

"Well, that's on you, I should think," Parks said, looking dignified. "If you're foolish enough to—"

"Yes, I was rather foolish, wasn't I?" I said. "Foolish to spend years hoping to get in your good graces. Foolish to ever consider you a friend, or think of you as anything other than a rotten, pompous, horrid ass." I looked around the table and then turned back to the man with the wine stain. "Sorry about your clothes. But if you'll take my advice, you'll stop taking orders from a prat who doesn't care a jot about you and won't give two figs if you lose your place in one of the finest establishments in London."

I pushed myself away from the table and turned around. I didn't quite have the courage to look at Father, but Laurence was beaming at me, Voss looked confused, the dukex looked thoughtful, and Bertie looked proud.

"Come along, darling," Bertie said. "We'd better get you home. Dear Ridley here is going to sort everything out."

Bertie turned, and the dukex and Voss followed after him. Laurence took my hand and followed as well. I still hadn't looked at Father to gauge his reaction, but he followed us all the way out of the club. Once we stepped outside, I felt a hand on my shoulder.

"Your Grace, I wonder if Sebastian might be spared for a little while tonight? I would very much like to escort my son to your house."

Of course, the dukex didn't mind. The other four left together and Father hired a hansom for the two of us. He didn't speak right away, and I was working myself into a nervous state wondering if I was meant to start the conversation. I was agonizing over it for several minutes when he finally spoke.

"You handled yourself very well in there," he said. "With that friend of yours."

"He's not my friend," I said. "I'm embarrassed that I ever considered him as such." I paused. "But thank you...I'm sorry for causing a scene at your club."

"I rather think the manager will be relieved to know she

merely has to worry about a wine stain on the carpet and will not have to quell any rumors about a rat infestation."

I let out a long breath. "That's good."

"Nesbit's often pays far more attention to names than character, I'm afraid," he said. "It is most unfortunate. It makes the quality of the place somewhat lower, in my mind. Your friend, Mr. Ayles, however, seems like a very respectable person. I'm glad your social sphere now includes people of his ilk rather than the Parks boy's."

My heart was tight in my chest and I barely dared to breathe. "You liked him then?" I asked quietly.

"Well, I hardly know him so well as to say that," he said. "I should prefer to meet with him privately to get a better opinion. But I like the way he spoke up for you and…" He paused. "I rather liked the way you spoke up for him."

I frowned. "How did you—?"

"I was sitting behind you in the card room when you first arrived. I hope you will forgive me for listening in on a private conversation. I was curious to know if the meeting with Mr. Parks had been arranged."

"It certainly wasn't," I said, a little heatedly. "Although I suppose you figured that out."

"Yes, it was pleasantly evident. I would like to have a better chance to talk to you," he went on. "As his lordship pointed out at the beginning of dinner, this has been a long day for you. A long trip, a visit to a new city and a new house, as well as an excitable confrontation with an old acquaintance. It is hardly an appropriate time for a lengthy conversation about your future. As I understand it, his lordship has some tasks for you while you are here, but you will be at leisure day after tomorrow."

I nodded even though it was dark and he was unlikely to be able to see very well.

"I believe you know the address to our townhouse?"

"Yes, sir," I said.

"Very good," he said. "Come by when you have finished breakfast with your companions."

The hansom stopped and I looked out to see the dukex's townhouse.

"Thank you, Father," I said.

"Good night, Sebastian."

I got out of the cab and walked into the house in a daze. I was surprised to see the dukex waiting up for me, still in their dinner clothes.

"Are you all right, child?" they said. I nodded. "I imagine Mr. Hartford has already commended you for your speech at the club."

"Yes, he did…sort of."

They put an arm around my shoulders and led me up the stairs. "Well, I gather you are not accustomed to being praised, so I imagine there is no risk to overdoing it. You were quite impressive. It isn't easy standing up to someone you once relied on."

I swallowed. "Thank you, Your Grace."

"Am I right in assuming Mr. Hartford wishes to see you after the interviews are complete?"

"I'm going to see him day after tomorrow."

They squeezed my shoulder. "Try to get some rest, poppet. I imagine tomorrow will be quite a big day for everyone." They led me to my room, which was a relief because I'm not sure if I'd have been able to find it.

I changed out of the dinner clothes. I felt too confused and muddled from the evening's events: Parks's insults, Father's vague approval, and even the dukex's surprising offer of comfort. I didn't know what to make of it all.

A gentle knock sounded at my door, and I cracked it open to see Laurence in his banyan. "Are you all right?" he asked.

I opened the door wider so he could come in, but he stayed on the other side of the doorway. I leaned against the doorjamb. "I think so," I said.

"You were brilliant. Do you know that?"

"With Parks? It did feel good to say all of that at last. I'm sorry he was so awful to you. Not the rats part. All of the insults. He's dreadful."

"Oh, angel," he said, reaching up to cup my face and stroke my cheek with his thumb. "I'm sorry you were stuck with that horrid fellow as a friend for years."

I shrugged. "It's my own fault."

"It's not your fault he's so horrid. I am curious about how you became such close friends."

I winced.

"Perhaps you'll tell me about it some time," he said gently. "Did Mr. Hartford say when he wants to see you again?"

"Day after tomorrow"

"Did he say anything on your drive here?"

"He said we both handled ourselves well. He was sitting in the card room before dinner and heard... well...everything."

"That's good, isn't it?"

"I suppose. I was shocked to see him."

"I know. You went very pale at the sight, poor thing."

I scrubbed a hand over my face. "He said it wasn't a good time to talk about my future. But he did say he was glad I'm friends with you now and not Parks. He said you seem very respectable."

Laurence smiled.

I leaned forward and kissed him, trying not to pour my agitation into the action, but likely failing. Well, definitely failing, if Laurence's fingers on my jaw were anything to go by. I broke off the kiss. "I'm sorry."

"For what, my love?"

"I keep kissing you in a way that—" I sighed, unsure of how to put it.

"You kiss beautifully, Sebastian. Although you always kiss with urgency, as if you're pressed for time, or as if you're afraid I'll disappear." He smiled, still stroking my cheek. "I only seek to remind you there's no need for that. Get some rest," he said, swiping a thumb over my cheekbone. He kissed me again and then left.

My hand is tired, but I don't quite have the nerve to ask the dukex's staff for tincture ingredients.

22 September 1817

DEAR BARTLEBY,

Breakfast was a solemn affair. Mr. Voss and Laurence were subdued by the prospect of their audiences at the palace. Bertie had left early to go and pick up Mrs. Fossett so she could travel to the palace with us. The dukex gave me a warm smile when I sat down and asked me how I slept and if my father was well and said how nice it was to have dined with him. They spoke as if they hadn't seen me after I came home the night before. Laurence joined the conversation, and they both had a great many nice things to say about Father. Mr. Voss even added a compliment or two, which was, frankly, surprising. I suppose Father is intimidating enough to impress even him.

When Bertie returned with Mrs. Fossett, he pulled me aside before we left.

"I'm very pleased that you will be joining us, m'dear," he said. "I've compiled all of your excellent notes and put together my thoughts on each contestant, as well as a formal recommendation." He handed me a neat stack of papers as well as a pencil. "There are some blank pages at the bottom of the stack, in case more notes need to be taken. Any questions?"

I considered. "Is there anything I shouldn't talk about?"

He laughed. "No, darling. You will do just fine. I annoyed Prinny by rejecting the position, so he might be in a *mood*. But the Royal Spellcaster is a very kind and intelligent man.

I'm sure he will like you. If they ask you about the contestants, you are welcome to give your honest opinion. If either of them asks for my notes, go right ahead and hand them over. My aim is to encourage some informal conversation first so they can form their own opinions about each person. Then I should like to give my personal recommendation to the Prince Regent and the Royal Spellcaster in private. After that, I imagine they will want interviews with each. Understand?"

I nodded.

"Very good. And don't worry. You'll do just fine."

He led us all outside. It was a bit of a tight squeeze, with the five of us, but Bertie has a very nice carriage, so it wasn't as bad as it might have been. The palace was, naturally, very impressive. I was quite awe-struck at the sight. I fancy Mr. Voss and Mrs. Fossett were too, but she merely paled a little, and he did his best to hide his nerves. I glanced at Laurence to see if he was nervous, but he merely winked at me. If he does get the position, it is nice to see that he will still be able to function in the face of such grandeur. Bertie seemed very at ease, but he is clearly accustomed to this sort of thing.

We were led into a large sitting room. I was relieved it was not a throne room. Granted, it was the fanciest sitting room I'd ever been in, and the Prince Regent's chair was almost fine enough to be a throne. He was an older man, a little younger than the dukex. He was tall and round with a handsome face. His clothes were beautiful and he sat toying with his cuffs in a way that managed to be both elegant and exude an air of boredom. There was an older couple on a settee beside him. The gentleman was short and thin with dark brown skin and wrinkles around his eyes, while the lady was pale skinned and rosy cheeked with a stocky build and a little taller than the gentleman. The couple rose when we walked in; the prince did not.

The Prince Regent smiled at Bertie and said, "Well,

Finlington. It seems you managed it after all. Although I still can't see why you don't take the position yourself."

Bertie returned the smile and gave a neat little bow. "I hope you will indulge my eccentricity, Your Royal Highness. But I do believe I've found some promising prospects for you." He pivoted a little and said, "May I introduce Mrs. Lydia Fossett, Mr. David Voss, and Mr. Laurence Ayles? They are my recommendations for the post."

They all bowed or curtsied as they were introduced.

"Making me do your work for you, eh?" the Prince Regent said.

"I'm happy to make the decision for you, sir. But I suspected you would like to have a voice in the matter."

The Prince Regent snorted. "Damn right I do. I'd still like you, old fellow. Still can't convince you to take the post?"

"I am quite set in my decision."

The Prince Regent heaved a sigh. "Oh, all right. You know Sir James Badgeley, don't you? Current Royal Spellcaster to the Crown? And of course Lady St. John, Sir James's assistant. And you haven't introduced me to the little fellow behind you."

"I do beg your pardon. This is my assistant, Mr. Sebastian Harford."

I bowed, feeling awkward. I could feel the Prince Regent's eyes on me which made me feel very self-conscious.

The Royal Spellcaster drew the three contestants into a conversation. Lady St. John offered me a seat beside her, which I took, mostly to get out of the way. Once I was seated, Bertie was engaging in the conversation with Sir James and the three contestants, but he seemed careful to not participate too much.

"So, Mr. Hartford," Lady St. John said. "How long have you been working for Lord Finlington?"

"Since July, my lady."

"Do you like it?"

"Yes, my lady. Bertie—that is, Lord Finlington—is wonderful."

The Prince Regent chuckled. "In love with him, are you? Well, you wouldn't be the first. I reckon he has several dozen pining for him here in London."

I startled a bit because I hadn't realized he was listening. "N-no, sir. I'm actually engaged."

"That does not exclude the possibility of you being in love with someone else, does it? But no matter. Who is it then? Anyone I know?"

"Er..." I glanced at Laurence, unsure if I should admit it was him. What if the Prince Regent took it the same way Mr. Voss did? Laurence noticed me looking and gave me a brief smile.

They both followed my line of sight.

"That Ayles fellow?" the Prince Regent said.

"Why don't you tell us about him?" Lady St. John said. She spoke in a way that was both warm and crisp.

I decided it was a good opportunity to talk him up. "He's very intelligent. And he has wonderful ideas about magic. He's brilliant with it, you know. And he's very kind and he's —he's one of the best people I know, really."

"Besotted," the Prince Regent remarked. "It's a shame, really. I might have sponsored your coming out, if only to steal you away from Finlington."

"Are you—" I stopped, realizing I had been about to question the Prince Regent.

He raised an eyebrow. "Go on."

I swallowed. "Are you angry with him for turning down the position, Your Royal Highness?"

He shrugged. "Not angry so much as annoyed that he really seems to be staying in the country for the foreseeable future. London has been a dead bore since he quit it. What is that you're clutching?"

"Bertie's notes," I said. "He compiled everything we wrote

about each contestant and put together a formal recommendation."

He held out his hand. I separated the notes from the blank pages Bertie had given me and handed them over. He began reading through them, our conversation clearly at an end.

Lady St. John gave me a small smile and asked if this was my first time in London. I told her that it was. "And how are you liking it?"

"I'm afraid I haven't seen much of it yet, my lady. We went to Nesbit's last night and then came here this morning." I hesitated and then said, "Is there anything you'd recommend I see while I'm in town?"

Then she launched into a description about the tower, Somerset House, Hyde Park, the opera, Almack's, Astley's Amphitheater, Peerless Pond, and Vauxhall Gardens. I felt winded by the time she was done and I hadn't even been the one talking.

After some time, the three contestants filed out of the room. I looked up in surprise.

Bertie smiled at my confusion. "Sir James and I thought it might be best for the contestants to leave while we discuss them. You're welcome to join them if you'd like, m'dear."

I was not overly fond of the idea of being left alone with so many grand people, so I hurried out as well. The other three were milling about the hall. Mr. Voss was pacing. Mrs. Fossett was sitting in a small chair, her leg pumping a little. Laurence was studying a painting of a bouquet. He looked over as the door was closed behind me and held out his hand. I immediately walked over and took it. He gave me a small peck on the cheek.

"All right?"

I nodded. "The Prince Regent is very intimidating."

"I can imagine. I expected the Royal Spellcaster to be as well, but he wasn't, which was nice."

"What was he like?"

"He's a friendly fellow. He's been in the position a long time and is ready to pass the responsibilities to someone else. He seemed very down-to-earth. I quite liked him."

"The Prince Regent knows I'm engaged to you," I said in a low voice. "I hope I didn't ruin your chances or anything."

He stroked my cheek with the back of his fingers. "Angel, if they don't like that we're engaged, then clearly this isn't the position for me. I wouldn't worry about it."

A quarter of an hour later, Bertie walked out and informed Mr. Voss that they were ready for him. To my surprise, he said that I was wanted for notetaking. "Prinny was impressed with the notes you gave him," he explained. "Thought it would be best to keep the style consistent throughout the process."

Laurence gave my hand an encouraging squeeze. I was dreadfully nervous, but I knew better than to object. I straightened the blank papers I was holding and walked in after Mr. Voss. Bertie stayed behind with the other contestants.

They were all waiting for me, so I hurried in.

"Thank you for indulging us, Mr. Hartford," Sir James said.

I muttered that I was honored. And without further ado, the interview began.

Sir James asked most of the questions, although the Prince Regent chimed in a fair amount, and Lady St. John had a few questions too. I wrote down everything as quickly as I could, relieved that I'd had so much practice with Bertie. My hands were shaking at the beginning, but I noticed the Prince Regent referring to the stack of notes on his lap a few times, which made me feel better about the whole thing, and I started to calm down.

I could tell Mr. Voss was nervous from the way he spoke a little too loudly and too quickly. Both Sir James and Lady St. John gave him encouraging nods or smiled at some of his answers. I think they were trying to make him feel more comfortable. He got animated when asked about his goals for the position.

Then he left and Mrs. Fossett was sent in. I was a little worried about her because she's so quiet, but she raised her chin and straightened her back. Her voice shook a little, but she spoke less hurriedly than Mr. Voss. I was proud of her, even though I really wanted Laurence to get the position. Like Mr. Voss, she seemed most impassioned when asked about her goals. Lady St. John seemed to like her, I fancy, although it really was hard to tell.

Finally, Laurence was brought in. He seemed the calmest out of the three of them, and even answered some of the questions with more technical detail than the other two. At one point, he and Sir James got into a full discussion about how Wolfe's *Essay on English Magic* was outdated and overly conservative in its approach. It was all a bit over my head, but I wrote everything down, feeling pleased that Laurence was so intelligent. When he was sent back out, the Prince Regent held out his hand for my notes.

I expected to be sent out as well but, to my surprise, Sir James turned to me and said, "And what are your thoughts on the matter, Mr. Hartford?"

"Me, my lord?"

"Yes, you've been part of the process from the beginning. Finlington said that you've proven to be a valuable assistant. I'd like to hear your opinions on the three applicants."

I let out a long breath, trying to get my thoughts in order. Part of me wanted to speak at length about Laurence, but I had a feeling that would make me seem too biased and my opinion less helpful. So I said, "All three of them would be marvelous for the position. They all have very good ideas about what they hope to accomplish. To my mind, they'd improve the country in terms of magic no matter who you picked."

"What have you observed of each of them?" he asked.

I thought back to the conversation we'd had when Laurence came over to dinner. "Mr. Voss is very clever. He might have been the cleverest of the bunch, really. But...but I think he can be overconfident in his spellcasting and he sometimes makes mistakes because of it. Mrs. Fossett is very instinctual. She doesn't even have to think about what she's doing sometimes, she's that good. But I've noticed she's bolder with spells she already knows because she's relying on instinct so much. With newer spells, she's less confident. And with Lau—that is, Mr. Ayles—he's very steady. He was never the fastest spellcaster of the group, but he wasn't the slowest either. And he isn't easily flustered by distractions. When he got his spells wrong—and, you see, they all got spells wrong occasionally—he was the least upset about it and he seemed to recover more quickly and move forward."

"I'm impressed," the Prince Regent said. "I expected a far more biased opinion from you."

I felt myself flush. "I'm sure you know who I'd like you to choose," I said. "Even before I was engaged to Laurence—Mr. Ayles—I hoped he or Mrs. Fossett would be selected because they've always been the nicest ones. There were a few contestants who I wouldn't have liked you to pick, but they're not here anymore. So I can honestly say that you'd be making a fine choice with whoever you decided on."

The Prince Regent gave me a long, unreadable look. Then he told me I could leave. "You may come in with the others when we've reached a decision."

When I stepped out into the hall, all four of them looked up at me expectantly. "They said they'll call us in when they've reached a decision."

"How did it go, m'dear?" Bertie said.

"I think it went all right. They were asking me for my opinions, which was strange. I didn't expect that."

"I did," Bertie said with a grin.

"I daresay you spoke only of your fiancé's charms," Mr. Voss said testily.

I felt my face get hot. "As a matter of fact, the Prince Regent said he was impressed by how unbiased I was."

He snorted and resumed his pacing.

"He liked your notes a great deal," Bertie said. "You really do have excellent penmanship. I wouldn't be at all surprised if he offers you a position before we leave."

"What?" I said, alarmed.

"Something secretarial in nature."

"Oh. I'm not sure I'd like that," I said quietly. "I like working for you, but that's because you teach me things and…and you're pleasant to be around."

Bertie's smile broadened. "How kind of you to say, darling! Well, I wouldn't worry about it. I know from personal experience that he can be testy when his offers are rejected, but he does get over it. And it is no bad thing to have attracted the Prince Regent's attention, especially for good reasons."

I swallowed, uncomfortable with the whole notion. Laurence seemed to notice my discomfort for he came over and pulled my arm through his and led me in a slow stroll as he continued to study the paintings in the hallway. I tried to relax, listening to him comment on the way the Merlin's ivy was painted, or how comfortable a particular chair looked, or how pretty one of the subjects was.

Finally, we were all summoned back in. I took up position at the back of the group, next to Bertie.

The Prince Regent stood when we all walked in. "You are all three highly qualified," he said. "And I'm pleased to say that this was not an easy decision to make. But after due consideration, we are in agreement that I shall be appointing Mr. Laurence Ayles to be the next Royal Spellcaster to the Crown."

I wanted to cheer at the announcement. I also wanted to

pull Laurence into a kiss, but that seemed inappropriate. As it was, Laurence was busy shaking everyone's hand and being solemnly congratulated. The whole thing was very quiet and polite. Laurence got drawn into a conversation with Sir James and the Prince Regent beckoned me forward.

He sat in his seat and leaned back, looking me up and down. "How would you like a position as secretary, Hartford? Now that your young man has been selected, you can come work in London too."

When he phrased it like that, I really had to consider. "I thought the position was eventually going to be a correspondent type of thing," I said slowly.

He frowned a little. "Yes, it can be. Sir James lives in London, so that hasn't been an issue. And if you're both working here, there's no reason for you both not to settle in the city as well."

I thought about Laurence's plans for the garden and the unfinished treehouse. I thought about Gavin and Charles and how I wouldn't be able to stay with them anymore. I wouldn't work for Bertie. I wouldn't get to practice my assignments with Pip and Gerry. I took a deep breath and said, "I can't tell you how honored I am, sir."

His mouth twisted into a smirk. "Ah. But you will regretfully have to decline?"

I nodded. "I don't wish to leave Tutting-on-Cress."

"What is it about that confounded place that has so many people wanting to live there?" he muttered. He sighed. "Ah well. I'm not surprised. When your betrothed does start to work via correspondence, he might want to consider employing you in some fashion. Be sure to tell him so."

"Er...I will. Thank you, sir."

He picked up a glass of brandy and waved me off.

Laurence was told to return the following day to sign a contract and then we were dismissed. When we were finally outside the palace, I pulled Laurence into a hug and kissed him. "I'm so proud of you," I said softly.

"I still say this," Mr. Voss said, gesturing at us, "is the reason you were picked, Ayles."

Laurence rolled his eyes. "I doubt the Prince Regent picked me because of my relationship with Sebastian."

"And what did he say when he was alone with them, hm?" Mr. Voss said, stepping closer. "I'm sure he said all sorts of things about all of us. What did you say to them, you little—"

To my surprise, Laurence stepped in front of me, tucking me behind his back. "There's no reason to bring Sebastian into this, Voss. You know perfectly well he was here as his lordship's assistant, not my fiancé."

"He was here as both!" Voss said, his voice louder. "I'd like to know what was said."

"I said you were probably the cleverest person in the group," I said, getting angry. "Although I daresay I regret that now."

He rocked back, clearly surprised. "What?"

"I said you were clever, that Mrs. Fossett was one of the most instinctual spellcasters, and that Laurence was steady."

I felt Laurence squeeze my hip where he was holding me behind him.

"It might interest you to know," Bertie said in a calm voice, "that my opinions were taken into account as well."

"My lord, I didn't mean—"

Bertie held up his hand. "Sebastian's presence *has* had an impact on my recommendation, but not for the reasons you think. I'm quite aware of your dislike for him. You've treated him with disdain since you first entered my home. I almost didn't call you back after your interview, you know. But you were so talented, I decided to give you another chance. Do you recall Sir James giving us that anecdote about how he got an idea from his scullery maid?" He waited until Mr. Voss nodded. "This position is an impressive one, but I wanted to be sure that whoever was appointed was someone who did not consider themselves above others. Would you have the humility to notice a spell your servant was casting? If Sebastian had made a comment that inspired a spell, would you have been paying enough attention to hear it? Your ideas for this position are good ones, Voss. You are a brilliant, strong, and talented spellcaster. This process does not signal the end of your career, but rather the beginning of it. What you make of it is up to you, and I encourage you to learn the right lessons from this experience."

Mr. Voss let out a long breath. "My apologies, my lord. And…and my apologies, Mr. Hartford." The apology was stilted and did not sound entirely genuine, but I nodded anyway. "Congratulations, Ayles. You do deserve it, disappointed though I may be. However, with all due respect, I shall take my leave of the dukex's house."

He turned to leave, but Laurence stayed him with a hand on his arm. "The deal is still on, Voss. As we all agreed. Your goals are mine."

I didn't know what he was talking about but Mr. Voss must have for he pressed his lips together and gave a curt nod. "Thank you, Ayles." Then he pushed past us and strode away.

Mrs. Fossett watched him go and then she gave Laurence a hug. "You *do* deserve it," she said. "I'm so proud of you. I know you'll do grand things." To my surprise, she gave me a peck on the cheek before she too left, telling Bertie she could take a hansom to her cousin's place.

Laurence looked sad at her departure. I cupped his cheek and he put a hand over my wrist. "I'm so glad I got it, Sebastian," he said. "But I wish the other two could have gotten it as well."

I frowned. "But it's just the one position, isn't it?"

"Unfortunately."

Bertie's carriage was brought around and we all got in.

"I'm sorry the good news is mixed with such reactions, m'dear," Bertie said.

Laurence gave a small smile. "Thank you, my lord. I can understand his disappointment. I would have preferred it if he'd taken it out on me rather than Sebastian."

"Or on me," Bertie said. He looked at me. "Are you all right, my sweet?"

"Yes, thank you," I said. "You were right, by the way. His Highness did offer me a job."

"Did he really?" Laurence said.

"I turned him down," I said quickly. "I didn't think living in London would make either of us happy. I...I hope that was all right."

He gave me a soft kiss. "Of course it was, angel. You have very good instincts."

"He's right, m'dear," Bertie said. "I imagine the two of you will accomplish great things."

I wasn't sure I agreed with that. After all, Laurence is the one destined for greatness, isn't he? But I thought about how the Prince Regent wanted to hire me and had even advised me to work for Laurence eventually. Why is that when I finally feel as if I know what my future holds, everyone starts offering different options? There are too many decisions to make and I'm not sure I like it.

I leaned my head on Laurence's head. "I already have a job," I murmured. "That's enough for me."

Laurence squeezed my knee. "Well, there's plenty of time for us to figure it all out."

When we arrived at the dukex's home, they led us to a sitting room toward the back of the house and rang for tea. "Mr. Voss is packing his things to leave," they explained. "There's no need for us to make him uncomfortable during his departure." Then they congratulated Laurence and told him he'd do a fine job. "When do you start?"

"In a fortnight. Sir James is giving me time to go home and pack. Then I'm to come back here for a few months."

"You're welcome to stay here for that time, if you'd like, child. As you can see, I have plenty of room, and I'd love to have you."

"Thank you, Your Grace."

"Of course, if you'd like your own place, I can understand that as well." The dukex, Bertie, and Laurence discussed possibilities for neighborhoods he might look into for renting when he returned to London.

A footman walked in and gave the dukex a nod.

"It would seem our third guest has taken his leave."

"Thank you," Laurence said. "I'd better go upstairs and write to my parents."

Bertie left as well, with the promise to return for dinner.

"How are you doing, poppet?" the duke said.

"Exhausted," I said. "It was a rather exciting morning. I didn't expect to…to be such an active part of it."

I told them all about meeting the Prince Regent and the Royal Spellcaster, and how I'd been offered a position and turned it down.

"That was probably for the best," they said. "I do not think you'd have been happy in that position. And if there are ever disagreements between the crown and the Royal Spellcaster, you would have been put in the middle of the debate, which would not have been comfortable for you."

"I didn't even think of that," I said.

"I'll wager the Prince Regent did, and that was likely part of the reason he wanted you," they said. "He's no fool, much as the papers like to describe him as such. Yes, he's vain and a spendthrift. But he's cannier than most realize."

I considered this, feeling relieved that the dukex supported my decision. I'd been afraid they would tell me it was foolish or irresponsible.

"You look tired, child," they said after a long moment. "Why don't you go upstairs and rest until dinner?"

I did as they suggested. Several hours later, I found Laurence in the same room where I'd found him the evening before, playing the piano softly. I sat down next to him.

"I've been trying to wrap my head around it all afternoon, but I can still scarcely believe I got the position," he said.

"I can," I said. "You're brilliant."

He kissed my cheek. "Thank you, my love."

I leaned my head on his and he wrapped his arm around my back.

"I'm glad I shall have better means to support you," he said. "I shall be pleased to report that to your father."

"And you can get your piano and your father's books and your papa's clothes."

"I love that you remember things. What shall I buy you?"

"Me?"

"Well, if I'm going to spoil my whole family with gifts, you can be sure you're included in that."

I considered. "I don't recall seeing a bench in your garden. I should like a nice bench for us to sit on at night and watch your butterflies."

"Oh, Sebastian," he whispered.

I sat up to see Laurence crying. "Good heavens!" I said. "What did I say? What's wrong?"

He smiled at me through his tears. "Nothing, angel. You're perfect."

I reached up and returned the favor he so very often gave me, wiping his tears away with my fingertips. "Far from perfect."

"Perfect for me," he said, cupping my cheek and kissing me.

I leaned my head back on his and he played a song softly on the piano.

We all had dinner at the dukex's house, rather than going

back to Nesbit's. I was glad of that, as I had rather lost my taste for the place. We spent most of dinner talking about all of the grand things Laurence would get to do in his new position. Bertie was very curious about Laurence's plans for his garden. It was enjoyable to watch him get so enthusiastic, now that he knew it would be a reality.

Bertie informed me that he had requested for some things to be sent up to my room. When I went upstairs, I found all of the ingredients for the hand-soaking tincture. I was very relieved. After all, I did write an awful lot at the palace and tonight. It made me think of how Bertie had noticed the way Voss treated me, even though he hadn't said anything. Bertie really does pay attention more than he lets on.

23 September 1817

DEAR BARTLEBY,

Visited with Father today. Laurence, Bertie, and the dukex attempted to encourage me throughout breakfast. I did try to act like it was working but I don't think I was very successful. After breakfast, Bertie escorted Laurence back to the palace to sign the contract. Laurence gave me a deep but gentle kiss, and wished me luck.

I watched them go and, after a brief hesitation, I ran upstairs to fetch my journal. The dukex was waiting for me when I got back downstairs.

"The carriage has been sent for," they explained.

"Thank you," I said. "That's very generous of you."

They smiled and said, "I won't keep you long as I know you're quite anxious to leave, but while we're waiting for the carriage, I hoped I might talk to you about *my* offer." They smiled. "I expect your answer remains the same, considering your refusal of the Prince Regent's offer. After your interaction the other night, I would have been surprised if London held quite the same temptation for you."

"You're right," I said. "I certainly don't want to run into Parks again. Although it's a shame because I do want to see more of the city some time."

They cupped my chin. "While my initial offer was one made from concern for you and your future, I must admit I'm pleased to see you're doing just fine without my help. I want you to know that my house is always open to you, should you wish to come again." They gave another smile. "And of course Mr. Ayles is included in that invitation. A fine young man, I must say. You both are."

I let out a long breath. "Thank you, Your Grace."

They winked at me. "Off you go now. Good luck."

I put on my coat, hat, and gloves and then left in the dukex's carriage. I felt as though my heart was in my mouth when I finally knocked on the door to the townhouse.

I was shown into a cozy drawing room with a small fire burning. Father was sitting in the room, reading a paper. He stood to greet me and directed me to sit on the sofa opposite his armchair. I realized it was closer to the fire and that he had purposely left the better seat for me, which made me feel odd. It was very unexpected.

He leaned back in his chair. "So," he said. "How have you been getting on?"

I launched into a report of my work with Bertie, my lessons, the schedule Charles had designed for me. I concluded with the assurance that I had been diligently keeping up with my journaling, then offered it to him as evidence. I felt a little winded by the end.

He took the journal with a small smile. He set it on his lap and said, "That is all very well, Sebastian. I'm glad you have been so disciplined. But how are you getting on?"

I looked at him blankly.

He sighed a little. "How are you?"

"Oh," I said. "I'm well, I think."

He waited.

"I like Tutting-on-Cress," I ventured. "I like living with Gavin and Charles. I've learned so much from them. They give good advice when I ask, although I wish I didn't have to ask quite so much. Gerry does too, actually. Give good advice, I mean. She's very busy with the shop, you know, so I don't see her as often as I'd like. But I do like being able to see her. Mr. Standish, you know, who lives with them—" He nodded. "He's very nice. We've gotten to be friends. He's a good deal kinder than any friends I've had before. I like working with Bertie and I adore my magic lessons. And—"

I took a deep breath. "I like being walking distance to Laurence's house. We want to make it a long engagement, you see; I want to get to know him better before we get married. Get to know myself better too," I added. "I rather hated it all when I first arrived. It was so quiet and so small, but I-I like that about it now. I'm quite happy there. Do you… do you think I might be permitted to stay?"

"I admit that I would like you to come home for a little while," he said. "But, yes, after that, you may stay."

"Thank you," I said, trying not to sound too relieved. "And about Laurence…"

He looked at me, waiting.

"I really love him, Father. He's so good and kind and clever. He makes me want to be the best possible person."

He gave a small smile again. "I'm looking forward to getting to know him better."

"You mean you haven't made up your mind yet?"

"I have not."

I clasped my hands together. "Were you waiting until he heard back about the appointment? He got the position, you know."

He frowned a little. "Well, I didn't want to distract him from that, of course. I received messages from you both yesterday with the news. But the results of his appointment are, frankly, immaterial to me. They tell me little of the young man's character."

"So you're not…worried about his financial situation?"

He tilted his head in consideration. "I would feel better if you had a bit more money. But your dowry will add to that somewhat. He can provide you with the necessities, which is what really matters. Besides," he went on, "I shall be at peace with the arrangement, knowing you are close enough to Charles and Gavin should you have any serious need. How is the journaling going?"

I was a little taken aback by the abrupt change of subject. "Er…well, I think? I'm doing it every day."

He flipped through the pages, going too fast to really read any of it. "Gavin mentioned in an earlier letter that he noticed you have been addressing the entries to someone. Would you care to explain who you are writing these for?"

I felt myself blush. "Oh, it's nothing, Father."

He sighed. "Sebastian, I won't be angry."

"No," I said. "I explained it all to Gavin. It really is nothing. I felt…foolish writing just to myself. I invented someone to write the entries to so I wouldn't feel so…pathetic."

He ran a hand over his face. "What did I do wrong with you, Sebastian?"

"What?" I said, alarmed.

"You were always so bright and cheerful as a child. Then you went away to school and got mixed up with terrible people. Despite all of our best efforts, you got so silly and foolish. When I finally pulled you out of school, you lapsed into what I can only describe as complete loneliness," he said, waving the journal. "What happened?"

I looked down at my hands, still clasped together. I wished that Laurence were there to cover them with his own hand. "I've always been lonely, Father."

He stood and moved to sit beside me on the sofa. "Tell me."

"It wasn't anyone's fault," I said. "It's just—Gerry and Gavin have always got along so well. Not that they didn't invite me along, of course," I added hastily. "But it was never the same. I was always the baby brother tagging along. I hoped it would all change when I went to Oxford. But no one talked to me for weeks. Until Parks—"

I broke off and glanced at him. He was sitting silently, waiting, so I continued. "Parks dared me to liven things up. The headmaster's address was very boring, you see. So I turned the lectern invisible. I learned that was the best way to keep in his good graces. Parks, I mean. Not the headmaster. I rather think he hated me."

"Why did you never tell me, Sebastian?"

I shrugged, unwilling to be honest.

"Son, look at me."

I dragged my eyes up to meet his.

"I'm sorry I never recognized your unhappiness. I certainly should have. But I wish you'd have told me."

I looked back down at my hands. "Gavin suggested once that I might be better coming home and learning from a tutor. But I was worried you'd be even more disappointed in me."

Then Father did the most surprising thing. He pulled me forward and held me to his chest, wrapping his arms around my back. I was so shocked, I didn't know what to do for several moments. "I have never been disappointed in you," he said. "Disappointed in some of your choices, yes, but never you."

I buried my face in his coat. I started crying and I was a little worried he'd be irritated with me ruining his clothes, but then it occurred to me that he has never been upset with a person for crying. He held me close for a long, silent period. Then he kissed the top of my head and let me go.

I sat up, feeling wobbly and pulled out my kerchief. "I thought you didn't like me very much."

"My word," he said, taking the kerchief out of my hands

and wiping my face with it. "How could I dislike my own child?"

I shrugged.

"I should have tried to get to know you better, son. Can you ever forgive me?"

I was feeling weepy again and he pulled me back toward him.

"You've done marvelously well living with Gavin," he said. "I am relieved my instincts were right on that account."

"They were," I agreed. "I really love living with them."

He pulled me away to look at me. "I should very much like for you to come home for a little while, perhaps after this trip from London is concluded." He held up a hand when I started to protest. "Not as punishment." He sighed. "I'd been putting you on the same path as your siblings, thinking you would do as well as they did. University seemed to suit them just fine. But the truth is, I barely know you now." He wiped a thumb under my eye to catch a tear that was falling. "I can never forgive myself for that neglect. But if you will allow me to make it up to you before you go off and get married, then I would be very grateful."

"Of course, Father. Although," I added, frowning. "I can't be gone very long. Bertie quite depends on me as his assistant, you know."

He chuckled. "I believe he'll indulge me for a little while. I am sure he will be happy to have you back when you return."

I latched on to something he had said earlier. "Do you mean you do approve after all? Of me and Laurence?"

"I still want to have a better acquaintance with the young man," he said. "But I am pleased with your decision to make it a long engagement. It worked very well for Gavin. I confess I wish John had had such practicality."

"You'll like him," I said. "He's wonderful."

"He makes you happy?"

"Very."

He kissed my forehead. "Then I'm sure you shall have my blessing before you leave London."

Then I did something I hadn't done since I was very, very little: I gave Father a hug.

He called for tea to be brought in. He flipped open the journal again, glancing at the empty pages in the back. "We shall have to get you a new one," he said. "You've almost filled the pages."

"I'd like that," I said.

He smiled. "Good. Perhaps we can go shopping tomorrow morning. Charles has kept you well stocked with clothes, which I appreciate, but I would hate to have you come all the way to London without taking you out for some new things."

I stared at him in shock. "Really?"

He chuckled and tousled my hair. "Yes, really."

The hair tousle was even more surprising—does my entire family enjoy treating me like a child? It would appear that they do. Even Father. He chuckled again at my stunned expression.

I stayed with him until after lunch. I told him all about my magic lessons, how the application process had gone, what the visit to the palace had been like, the Prince Regent's offer of employment, my walks home with Laurence, the ball, Laurence's garden and treehouse, Pip, Laurence's parents, Gerry's shop (even though he had already seen it). I gave him loads of details about my life in Tutting-on-Cress.

"Charles wants to put me on another learning regimen when I get back from London," I said, "To learn all about how to take care of a house and whatnot. I daresay I won't mind missing that if I go home and visit you right off."

He looked thoughtful. "You may not have to miss it. It would be good for you to see how multiple households run. I shall talk to your mother about it. I'm sure we both have a great deal we would like to teach you."

I groaned. "Damn ruddy mouth."

He laughed. "Well, I won't keep you. I'll take you shopping tomorrow morning. And then tomorrow night, you, Finlington, Ayles, and the dukex will be coming here to dine with me."

"We will?"

"I've already written to Finlington on the subject. I invited all of you but the other fellow—Voss, I think his name is—won't be joining us."

"Not sad about that," I said. "He's very unpleasant."

Father's lip twitched much like Gavin's does. "Off you go then."

I grabbed my journal and put on my things and left. The dukex, Bertie, and Laurence were waiting for me. Laurence wrapped an arm around my waist.

"How did it go, m'dear?" Bertie said.

"Well," I said. "My father does not dislike me, as it turns out. That was rather nice. And...er...he is almost ready to give his approval."

"I daresay he will give it with enthusiasm after dinner," Bertie said.

"Oh, yes," I said to Laurence. "And we're going to his house for dinner. Our house. My family's house. Tomorrow night." Laurence kissed my cheek. "And he's taking me shopping tomorrow morning."

"Good," Laurence said, taking my hand and leading me to the settee. "You'll be busy then. I'm going back to the palace tomorrow. I have a contract to sign and everything."

"I thought you were doing that today."

He glanced at Bertie as we sat down. "Well, I did go to the palace today. But...well, there's been a change in plans."

I felt a small chill of panic. "Don't tell me you aren't taking the position after all."

He laughed and cupped my cheek. "No, nothing like that." He took a deep breath. "I asked if I might form a council of spellcasters. It means less money. It's still a very good wage, of course, but a little less than we'd expected. I'm signing on Mr. Voss and Mrs. Fossett to be part of it."

I was shocked. "Why?"

He smiled and took my hands in his. "It shouldn't all be one person, making decisions about magic for the country. Now we can cast votes between us. I'll be head of council, so my vote shall be the deciding one, and my opinion will be the one given to the crown. But their ideas are so important. It only felt right to make sure they were a part of it too."

"But Voss is so unpleasant," I said. "Why would you want to work with him?"

"I am hopeful that he will improve upon further acquaintance. I have not entirely forgiven him for the things he said or the way he's treated you, but I wish to give him a chance to redeem himself. And he and Mrs. Fossett will get a stipend for their input. It means I may be in London a little bit longer in the first place, to establish things, but it also means if I need to take time away—for illness or emergency or anything like that—then I have people in place to keep the work going. If we should go to war or anything, only one of us need go. I'm sure Voss would be excellent at that—he's strategic, but not as militaristic as Wilburforce was."

"So you didn't sign the contract after all?"

"Not yet. They're drawing up a new one, and contracts for the other two as well. I'm sorry about taking the lower pay without asking you first."

I was taken aback. "Why should you be?"

"Well, it affects you too. You don't mind then?"

"Will you still have enough for your piano and your garden expansion and everything?"

He smiled broadly. "Yes, plenty for all of that. And your bench. Enough for us to live comfortably, just not as lavishly as I would have liked."

"Then that's all that matters," I said.

He pulled me into a kiss. After a moment, the dukex cleared their throat quietly and we pulled apart.

Then we talked more about what the council meant for Laurence and how he envisioned the future of the position. Bertie asked me to pick up some things for his magical experiments during the shopping trip. We discussed different shops and I wrote down a list of items he needed. He gave me a purse full of money for the venture as well.

Laurence patted my leg. "I might have a lie-down" he said, and stood.

"Do you mind if I tell my family about the news?" I asked him. "I haven't even told them about you getting the position, but I'm sure they'd like to know."

He stood behind me and ran his hand through my hair. "Not at all. Send them my love, will you? I've already written to my parents about my appointment, so you needn't worry about that."

After he left, I went up to my room and wrote letters to Gavin, Gerry, Charles, and Pip. Each letter was slightly different, but each one contained the news that Laurence had been appointed the next Royal Spellcaster to the Crown, and most of them detailed, to some extent, what Father and I discussed. I felt a little embarrassed to be wrong, yet again, about something that my siblings had been trying to convince me of for ages. But learning I was not a disappointment was a much more pleasant thing to be wrong about than the discovery that my friends had all been rotters.

To my surprise, Mrs. Fossett and Mr. Voss joined us for dinner, having received their offers for a position in the council. So we had another celebratory meal, this time congratulating them as well. I noticed Mr. Voss made a particular effort to be nicer to me. He was very awkward about it, but it was much more pleasant than our previous conversations.

When I got back to my room after dinner, I realized I

never told Laurence that Father wanted me to come home. So I went and knocked on his door.

He opened it, dressed in his banyan again. "Sebastian," he said, beaming at me.

"I forgot to tell you earlier," I said. "My father wants me to come back home for a little while after London."

"Oh," he said, leaning against the doorjamb. It struck me that we were having a somewhat parallel discussion from our first evening in London. "Do you mind it?" he asked.

"I don't know," I said. "I…I don't actually know him very well. That was one of the things we discussed today. He said he'd like to get to know me better."

"That's nice," Laurence said, smiling.

"I don't know how long I'll be gone, though."

"I'll be in London for a few months anyway, so it might work out rather perfectly."

"I'd almost forgotten that." I noticed suddenly that he was holding the door somewhat close. "I'm not bothering you, am I?"

"Hm? Oh," he said, glancing at the door. "Not at all. I just —" He gave me a considering look. "Here." He pushed the door open a bit more and angled back so I could see into the room.

There was a long strip of muslin, about the width of my hand, laid out on the floor. I could see Laurence had been in the midst of casting a spell on it, for a sprig of rosemary had been set on top of it and a sigil had been chalked in front of it. A circle was partially drawn around it, unfinished, from when Laurence had answered the door.

"What's it for?" I asked.

"Well, the fabric is what I use to wrap my chest, you see. The spell makes it less noticeable, keeps people from looking. I do it the night before because I always put a little too much power in it, and letting it sit out for a night helps the magic to mellow a bit."

"The spell lasts you all day?" I said in wonder. "It must be very powerful."

"Usually," he said, with a little smile. "When I first started doing it, I always overloaded the spell because I was so anxious to make it strong enough. I'm not anxious anymore, but I haven't bothered to correct the habit. I'm getting better. Sometimes I have to step into a room and refresh it a little. Bertie has always been terribly kind about having rosemary on hand for me if I need it. I don't wear it to bed, of course. Not particularly comfortable, you see. Although," he added, "when we get married, I might wear a shirt...for a little bit...until I get accustomed to sharing my bed, you understand."

He seemed a little uncomfortable with the conversation. I remembered what Charles had said about the possibility of him having less experience, as well as what he had said about respect and listening, and how Laurence has always managed to calm my own fears so easily. So I tried to think of what he would do in my place. I reached up and stroked his cheek. He leaned into the touch.

"We haven't talked about it much," he said. "I haven't been sure if you've entirely understood...that aspect of who I am."

"I don't entirely understand," I admitted. "But I think I'm beginning to. I know I want to. And I love all of the aspects of who you are."

He smiled. "Even the dancing?"

"Even that."

His smile widened a little at my response. "When I first... told my parents I was a boy, we discussed the possibility of... well, you see, there are operations one can...including ones regarding this..." He tapered off and shrugged. "At any rate, it's very expensive. I had no desire for my parents to go into debt for it or anything, although they offered. And even with magic to make it safer, it can be quite risky."

"So you never wanted it? You'll have more money now with the position."

"I've considered it, of course. The new position does mean I could probably afford it, but...well, I can't very well be laid up for months when I'm working a new position. Besides, I've lived this way for years. I'm quite satisfied with how I look. And although I would never suffer a spouse who didn't agree, it is gratifying to observe that you seem quite satisfied as well."

I raised an eyebrow. "'Quite satisfied' is putting it rather lightly. I've been taken with you since I saw you audition for Bertie months ago. Before that, even. I've been taken with you since I saw you go into Gerry's shop. It's that smile of yours, you know. It's very effective."

"Well then," he said, sliding his arm around my waist. "In that case I daresay I can make do with using the extra funds to buy myself a piano, and expand the garden, and purchase your bench and..."

I pivoted so I could press him a little against the doorjamb. "Make sure it's a nice piano," I said, and then I kissed him as slowly, carefully, and tenderly as I knew how.

Laurence broke off the kiss and smiled at me. "We'd better get some rest. I must say I quite like being able to say goodnight to you like this."

"So do I."

He gave me a brief kiss on the cheek. "Well, I don't want to keep you or the dukex up. Goodnight, angel."

He closed the door, and I turned to see the dukex sitting in a small chair on the other end of the hallway. "Goodnight, poppet," they said amiably.

Embarrassed, I wished them goodnight and hurried off to bed.

24 September 1817

DEAR BARTLEBY,

Breakfast was much cheerier this morning. There wasn't the cloud of Laurence's audience or my meeting with Father hanging over us. Bertie arrived after breakfast to escort Laurence back to the palace. He informed us we would leave London the following morning, if all went well. It is so strange to go to London for such a short time.

I was rather glad to have gone shopping with Father for I actually got to see London. He helped me find the items for Bertie and bought me a whole bundle of new clothes, which was very nice. I bought a few gifts as well: a book on magical plants for Laurence, some fashion plates for Gerry, a book of poetry for Gavin, and cravat pins for Charles. I also found a lovely fountain pen for Bertie and a set of fancy kerchiefs for Pip. I've never been one to give gifts, really, so I was relieved when he didn't comment on the expense.

He bought me a beautiful new journal. I quite like it. And he got me a nice pen to go with it. It took much longer to go shopping than I'd anticipated. We had lunch at a posh restaurant, and didn't get back to the family townhouse until it was nearly dinnertime. I was so busy all day, and had found myself relaxing so much in his company, that I forgot to be nervous about dinner.

Once we arrived, however, and sat waiting for everyone, I remembered to be nervous. Fortunately, we didn't have to wait long. They arrived just in time to be called in to dinner.

Father congratulated Laurence on his appointment as we sat down at the table.

"Thank you, sir," he said. He hesitated. "Although, I'm afraid, the position will be slightly different from what I originally explained in my letter."

"Indeed?" Father said.

Laurence explained about the council and how they'd all gone to sign their contracts this morning.

"Very sound plan, Mr. Ayles," Father said.

"Thank you, sir," Laurence said. "I realize it means a little less money than what I'd described in my letter to you. It will be plenty to live on and support Sebastian. Of course, I don't mean to presume. This is all assuming we get your blessing."

Father chuckled. "We shall talk after dinner, Mr. Ayles. But I think you can rest easily on that point."

Laurence and I both breathed a sigh of relief.

After dinner, I bid Father goodbye. I'm to go back home in a fortnight—almost exactly when Laurence goes back to London. Father told me it would give me time to pack and see everyone before leaving for a few months.

Father took Laurence into his study and the dukex and Bertie took me back to the dukex's townhouse, along with all of my purchases. The dukex called for a pot of chocolate as soon as we arrived and had me tell them all about my shopping trip. I believe they were doing it just to distract me, because as soon as Laurence returned and walked into the room, the dukex gave me a wink and advised us not to stay up too late talking.

Laurence didn't say anything as he took my hand and walked me back to the ballroom. We sat down together on the piano bench. It was dark in the room, but I could see the light from the hallway on his face.

"Did he give his blessing?" I asked.

He smiled and cupped my face with both hands. "Your father is quite remarkable," he said.

"I'm beginning to come to that conclusion myself," I said.

"He gave his blessing and what's more, he's invited me to come to your house in the country when I'm finished up in London."

"Oh, good," I said. "And then we get to go back home? To Tutting-on-Cress?"

He grinned. "And then we go back home."

He kissed me and I reveled in the realization that this was

just the beginning. I would get to enjoy being cherished and loved by Laurence Ayles for the rest of my life.

After we broke off the kiss, he pulled a box of matches out of his pocket, lit one and whispered his incantation while making a swift and complicated movement. This time, only two butterflies split off the light of the flame. I leaned my head on his and watched them dance and flutter over our heads and over the piano, the little illusions reflecting against the dark wood.

My good friend Pip once told me a little quiet can be very restful. So I relaxed into it, allowing myself to enjoy the silence, Laurence's hands over mine, and the prospect of many such quiet evenings together.

The End

NOTE FROM THE AUTHOR

DEAR READER,

I hope you enjoyed reading Seb's story as much as I enjoyed writing it. Seb was a character I impulsively decided to give a voice when I writing Letters to Half Moon Street. As soon as his letters were added, I knew he needed his own book.

A little fun fact for those who like them: if I were to live in this world, I would absolutely want to learn magic the way Seb does.

Affectionately,

Sarah Wallace

ACKNOWLEDGMENTS

As ever, this book came to life thanks to my own found family. To Ashley, who helped me to avoid repeating myself in the earliest drafts of this project and helped me to avoid repeating myself in the final draft of this project, thank you. To Alexis, thank you for reading this story so many times. To my beta readers, Kayla, Katie, Anna, Lauren, Karen, and Allison, thank you for all of your valuable feedback! To my editor, thank you for giving me that extra push to include the Buckingham Palace scene, because I can't imagine the story without it now.

And to my incredible readers, thank you for continuing to read my stories. This book marks the halfway point of this series and I'm so delighted that my stories have found their audience.

Editor: Mackenzie Walton
Proofreader: Ashley Scout
Sensitivity Reader: Salt & Sage Books
Historical Consultant: Alexis Howard
Front cover photo by Tim Cooper via Unsplash
Back cover photo by Aleksandra Boguslawska via Unsplash
Author photos by Toni Tillman

ABOUT THE AUTHOR

 Sarah Wallace lives in Florida with their cat, more books than she has time to read, a large collection of classic movies, and an apartment full of plants that are surviving against all odds. They only read books that end happily.

ALSO BY SARAH WALLACE

Letters to Half Moon Street

**Start from the beginning with the first book in the Meddle &
Mend: Regency Fantasy series!**

*I must have been drunker than I realized because all I remember is
how well he tied his cravat and how perfectly his coat fit him...*

London, 1815: where magic can be purchased at convenience, and
the fashionable and wealthy descend for the start of the social
Season. But 25-year-old Gavin Hartford finds the city intimidating
when he arrives, alone, to his family's townhouse. The only company
he seeks is in his beloved books and weekly letters to his sister,
Gerry.

Then dashing man-about-town Charles Kentworthy gallantly rescues
Gavin from a foolish drunken mishap and turns his life upside-
down. With Mr. Kentworthy, Gavin finds himself discussing poetry
and magic, confessing his fears about marriage, expanding his social
circle to shocking proportions — and far outside his comfort zone.

When family responsibility comes knocking, Gavin's future looms
over him, filled with uncertainty. As he grapples with growing
feelings for his new friend, Gavin will need to be honest with Mr.
Kentworthy — but he'll need the courage to be honest with himself
first.

This epistolary Regency romance is the first in a historical fantasy series, Meddle & Mend.

One Good Turn - Book 2 in *Meddle & Mend*

The Education of Pip - Book 3 in *Meddle & Mend*

The Glamour Spell of Rose Talbot - *Meddle & Mend* Prequel

Free to all newsletter subscribers!

SIGN UP FOR MY NEWSLETTER!

ARE you signed up for my newsletter? Join now at sarahwallacewriter.com to be in the know!

NEWSLETTER SUBSCRIBERS ARE THE FIRST TO SEE BOOK COVERS, receive the first chapter of new releases a month before release date, get sneak peeks at preorder campaign art, and a free novelette! I've also been known to send deleted scenes or scenes in alternate POV and I plan to do more of that!